THE BLOOD OF KINGS

OTHER BOOKS BY JOHN MICHAEL CURLOVICH

(as Michael Paine):

Steel Ghosts

The Colors of Hell

Owl Light

Cities of the Dead

The Blood
of Kings

John Michael Curlovich

alyson books
los angeles

MANUFACTURED IN THE UNITED STATES OF AMERICA.

THIS TRADE PAPERBACK ORIGINAL IS PUBLISHED BY ALYSON PUBLICATIONS,
P.O. BOX 4371, LOS ANGELES, CALIFORNIA 90078-4371.
DISTRIBUTION IN THE UNITED KINGDOM BY TURNAROUND PUBLISHER SERVICES LTD.,
UNIT 3, OLYMPIA TRADING ESTATE, COBURG ROAD, WOOD GREEN,
LONDON N22 6TZ ENGLAND.

FIRST EDITION: JANUARY 2005

05 06 07 08 09 **a** 10 9 8 7 6 5 4 3 2 1

ISBN 1-55583-885-5

CREDITS
COVER PHOTOGRAPHY OF PYRAMIDS BY KENNETH GARRETT/NATIONAL GEOGRAPHIC
    COLLECTION/GETTY IMAGES, MAN BY ANTONIO MO/PHOTODISC/GETTY IMAGES.
COVER DESIGN BY MATT SAMS.

for

Jerry Priori

PROLOGUE

Danilo.
The love of my life.
And the even greater love of my death. Or my life-in-death.
Gone now. And yet still with me, there in my blood.

It seems death has always been with me—death and sadness. And fear. But they have hardly been with me in the way they are now.

My father died when I was four years old and my mother a year later. The relatives who raised me told me she died of grief at his loss, which I think was supposed to make her sound noble or tragic or something. But all it told me was she valued him and her love for him, and not me. When I was still a boy I was able to see through sentimental rot like *I Remember Mama*. A hard lesson to learn when you're that young, but that's the way it was.

I was raised on a farm outside Ebensburg by a cousin of my mother named Millie. She and her husband took me in more out of obligation than anything else, but at least they did it. Their "Christian obligation," I should say. I still remember them reading the Bible at me, and even the apocrypha, though I was never much interested and didn't try to hide it.

There was a small trust fund out of my parents' insurance, administered by a law firm in Pittsburgh, so all their expenses were covered, with a bit more to reward them for their trouble. They made sure I was fed and clothed properly, and there were Christmas and birthday presents. But they had their own kids. I don't remember anything warmer than indifference from them most of the time.

From junior high on, I swam. First time I went in the water I took to it. Breast stroke, butterfly; I was never much good at the backstroke, but I was good enough overall to be one of the stars of the school team. Not that it counted for much. Central Pennsylvania is football country; the rest of the school athletes barely got noticed unless they won especially big. Which we did, now and then, but nobody paid much attention anyway once football season started.

In high school I met Tim—Tim Johanssen. He was my first love. Two years older than me, captain of the swim team in his junior year. Tall, blue-eyed, black-haired, pale-skinned. He had what everyone calls a swimmer's build, of course, since that's what he was. Lean smooth body as beautiful as anything I had ever seen.

Not long after I made the team we were in the locker room alone one day, showering. He smiled at me. "You're good."

"Thanks." He was a senior and the team captain; I was a tenth-grade rookie. I didn't know what to make of his attention.

"You need to work on your backstroke, though."

"I know. I've never been any good."

"You'll get better. Why don't you let me work with you? The backstroke's my event."

And so we worked. There was so much physical contact between us, in and out of the water. Coach Harrison watched us quite approvingly. At night in my room I made imaginary love to Tim. He had a girlfriend. Every time I saw him I went numb with love and fear.

Love and fear. It was the first time I had felt either. Now they are constants.

My other passion was the piano. I honestly don't remember how or why I first put my fingers on the keys, but I know it felt right to me instantly. At first I played very badly, of course. All I could do was try and imitate what I heard on the radio, bits of Chopin, Mozart, the simpler Beethoven.

But as I said, it felt right, and I couldn't *not* play. After trying for months and knowing how bad I was, I finally got up the nerve to start taking lessons. I persuaded Paul Kowalski, my trust fund administrator, to let me buy a battered old spinet so I could practice. It wasn't an easy step. The other kids listened to hip-hop, house, techno, metal, anything but Chopin, and I was different enough already. Millie made me put the spinet in the basement.

When I got good enough to play even a bit well, when my fingers and my mind were limber enough, I can't tell you what a thrill it was. For the first time in my life I was free to express myself.

It was Chopin I loved most. Not the lighter stuff, the "Minute Waltz" and such. It was the dark, agitated Chopin, the nocturnes, that I loved. It seemed to be the music I had been hearing all my life without knowing it. And then there I was, playing it myself. When I played I thought of Tim.

One winter day we practiced late, just the two of us in the pool. Somewhere, I'll never know where, I found the courage to kiss him. I was terrified of what he'd do. But he kissed back. Should I take the next step? I couldn't stop myself.

"Tim, I think I'm in love with you."

He said nothing. It seemed to me he was actually shaking. Then he kissed me again. "Jamie."

I read the life of Chopin. Then I went on to read his letters. There among them were the ones he wrote to his friend, his lover, Tytus Woyciechowski. He always ended them, "I send you big wet kisses on the mouth." Somehow I had always known. At my next piano lesson I told my teacher, Mrs. Crevanti, what I had discovered.

"Nonsense. Chopin was not like that. He couldn't have been."

One afternoon late in the school year Coach Harrison caught Tim and me. We were making love in the shower. Our passion must have been obvious to see. For a moment he just stood and watched, and we froze when we realized he was there.

"Dunn! Johanssen! What are you two doing?"

We were too scared to answer. Finally Tim stuttered, "N-nothing."

He took a few steps toward us and pushed us apart. Then he rounded on Tim. "Johanssen, you just won a scholarship. You want to lose it?"

Tim was terrified. His family was poor. Without an athletic scholarship he'd never be able to go to college. "No, sir."

"Then don't do any more of this shit. Hear me?"

"Yes, sir."

"And you, Dunn. What are you, a fucking girl?"

"No, sir."

"Maybe you ought to quit the team and stick to your dainty little piano."

"Please, sir, no."

"Both of you get your clothes on and don't let me catch you like this again, you hear me? I catch you even staring at each other and you're off the team."

Silently we got dressed. Tim avoided looking at me. He was still trembling. Outside I tried to talk to him but he turned his back and walked away. I wanted to cry, but of course it was not something I could do then and there. Later, in my room...

That night I sat at the piano and played through the Chopin nocturnes and forced myself not to let what I was feeling show, except in the music.

Tim barely talked to me again for the remainder of the school year. He made a big show of keeping company with his girlfriend. Then school ended, we didn't see each other at all, and he finally left for college.

When I was a senior I outgrew Mrs. Crevanti and started commuting to Johnstown for more advanced lessons. That spring I gave my first recital. Some Chopin, one of the Bach English Suites, a few Prokofiev waltzes. I went online and found Tim's address at the University of Western Pennsylvania in Pittsburgh and mailed him an invitation, with a handwritten note that said, "I'll be playing the Chopin for you." He never came.

One day I saw Coach Harrison having sex with one of the new kids on the team. He realized I was there, watching, and he glared at me. There was a threat implicit in it, and I understood what it meant. I never told anyone.

There were a few news stories about some mysterious murders on the West Penn campus. Young men had been found stripped naked and mutilated. Others had gone missing. I remember vaguely hoping Tim would be okay there. Then I promptly forgot about them. It certainly never occurred to me that one day I would become involved with them in the way I did.

There were two scholarships for me, both partial, one athletic and one for piano, so I could go to school without draining my trust fund. I decided West Penn was the right school for me. Tim was there, and I tried to tell myself that wasn't the reason I chose it, and I had no reason to think we could be lovers again, but...

I was not one for illusions, not one to dream or imagine things. Reality had forced itself on me early and never left. And yet I knew what I wanted, and I knew love was a part of it.

I hardly understood what to make of myself or my feelings or my talent till I met Danilo, and he showed me so much that was thrilling, so much that was dark, and so much that was very, very frightening. He took me on a journey of discovery, not just a physical one to France and Germany and Egypt—to the secret chambers of the Louvre, and to ancient, hidden tombs—but an interior journey too.

Love and fear again, but both of a different kind from what I'd known before. Life without death. And, oddly among them, hope. Those were Danilo's gifts to me.

And I will not go back.

CHAPTER 1

First day on campus, Freshman Day, and of course it was nothing but confusion for me. The campus was huge, the streets bewildering. Like all eastern cities Pittsburgh doesn't actually have streets, just paved-over cow paths. I didn't think I'd ever remember where everything was. After living in Ebensburg, Pennsylvania, the real world came as a shock.

My dorm room was miles too small. They had me in with another jock, a guy named Norm Pulaski, who played baseball. The first thing he said to me when I found the room was, "Boy, you sure have a lot of books."

"Silly me. They told me this was a college."

"It is." My sarcasm was lost on him. I made up my mind then and there to get my own place as soon as I could. Freshmen were required to live in the dorms; after that…sophomore year couldn't come soon enough to suit me.

"You a swimmer?"

"Yeah, I am."

"You a fag?"

I did a double-take. "What did you say?"

"Nothing, I guess. Just don't try no fag stuff in here."

I put on a big phony smile. "Well, okay, but you'll have to promise not to read any of my books."

He gaped at me. I got my keyboard out of its case, set it on its stand and plugged it in. It sounded fine.

"You gonna play that here?"

"This is my room too, Norm. I have to practice."

"I don't like listening to concertos and stuff." He pronounced it "con-sert-os."

I decided to ignore his rudeness and try to be helpful; he needed it. "We're supposed to go to orientation."

"I'm not gonna bother with that shit."

"Oh."

He made another stab at jock camaraderie. "There's a game Saturday night. You goin'?"

"No, I'm not gonna bother with that shit."

"Fag."

I laughed at him. He seemed not to know what to make of me, which struck me as a good thing.

"The chick I'm takin' has a girlfriend. You want me to set you up?"

"Thanks, Norm, but I'm not gonna bother with that shit either."

He didn't know what to say. He picked up one of my paperbacks and thumbed through it, puzzled, like it was an alien object.

I finished unpacking and got out of the room.

Orientation was mostly what I expected. Dull speeches, dull rules and instructions. There was a long code of student ethics; I wondered what Norm would make of it.

It was a gorgeous late summer day, which made being indoors that much worse. Then they divided us into groups of twenty so student volunteers could show us around campus. Like Norm, I was going to skip it. I had made a point of visiting the campus twice during my last year of high school, so I knew where the main buildings were, at least a bit. But the guide for our group introduced himself as Justin Hollis, a member of the diving team. I shook his hand and introduced myself.

"Good to meet you, Jamie. Why don't I make the sports facilities the first stop on our tour?"

"I've already seen them."

"Even so, it's the only place on campus I really feel at home." He had a sweet smile.

So we saw the Olympic-size pool, the diving platforms, the gymnastics equipment, basketball court, and on and on, even the bowling alley. Most of the students in the group were girls; they seemed happy for the chance to check out the male athletes. When we took a break it became obvious to me why Justin wanted to stop there first. He spent more than a little time with one of the gymnasts, a red-haired guy.

When we left, one of the girls in the group asked him something about a murder, or a series of them.

"We're not supposed to talk about that."

"Oh."

Naturally this made me curious. I sidled up beside her and asked her what she was asking about.

"There have been some murders on and around campus. Guys. Most of them jocks, I think, and some of them in the arts."

I'd forgotten about those news stories. My curiosity was up.

"I didn't think it would be anything to worry about, anyway, you know, but if our guides were told not to talk about it, then there must not be anything to worry about. If there was any danger, they'd warn us." She shrugged and walked over to one of her friends. They whispered something about me and giggled.

Then came the rest of the campus. One academic building after another, science labs, the fine arts building, the library, the Academic Tower, "the tallest scholastic building in the world—wait till you see it lit up at night." There was the Z, the campus sandwich shop and general hangout. "Short for the Zone," Justin told us. The university owned an observatory, he said, but it was off north of the city; there would be bus rides for people who want to see it. It was all pretty exhausting, and there was no way to remember it all; not that I needed to. Besides, I wanted to find Tim. But at least the weather was nice, and I did manage to find where most of my classes were.

Last of all, and with fairly obvious distaste, or maybe just disinterest, Justin took us to the university museum. An old Gothic Revival building, the oldest on campus, he said. It looked like something out of a Hitchcock movie.

On the first two floors there were rooms full of Greek and Roman statues, medieval tapestries, Renaissance manuscripts, dinosaur skeletons, collections of butterflies on pins. We breezed through them all quickly. He told us there were classrooms on the upper floors.

In the last room we visited was a huge collection of Egyptian things. They caught my attention for some reason. Justin made sure we all knew how to find our way back to our dorms and said the tour was over. I found myself lingering, checking out the statues.

Justin came over to me, smiling. "You interested in this stuff?"

"I don't know. I like it, but I really don't know anything about it."

"I hope my tour wasn't too boring for you."

"No, it was fine."

"Thanks." I don't think he quite believed me. "Listen, you want to get together later on? Some of us from the team are heading to the Z for burgers."

"What time?"

"Around 7."

"Well, maybe I'll see you there, okay?"

He left. I found myself alone in an enormous room filled with strange things, statues of men with the heads of birds, pieces of fantastic jewelry, ancient scrolls covered with hieroglyphics, even mummified cats and birds. A framed papyrus depicted a beautiful woman with her arms outstretched; they were wings. The caption identified her as Maat, the Goddess of Truth.

There wasn't much light, and I couldn't see a switch for the overheads, so I checked it all out in the half-light. Somehow it seemed appropriate. The room was cool, almost chilly. I wanted to be out looking for Tim, but something held me there—I didn't know what.

There was a mummy on display in a glass case. I inspected it, got as close as I could. The eyes were closed, the lips drawn back exposing the teeth, which were rotten. The bandages were dirty and frayed. There was a layer of dust on the glass and I brushed it off with my hand. The card said his name was Sekhem-wa-Set.

"He died 3,200 years ago. He was your age."

The voice startled me and I jumped. A man was standing in the shadows a few feet behind me. He stepped closer. I could see he was quite striking, tall, handsome, in almost a movie-star kind of way. His eyes were the deepest green I had ever seen. They showed brightly even in the dim light, and his hair was jet black. His lips were startlingly full and sensual. Pale skin, high cheekbones; he might almost have been an older relative of Tim. He was wearing jeans, sneakers, and a plaid shirt.

"I thought you heard me come in. Sorry to have startled you." He smiled.

"I'm okay."

"I'm Professor Semenkaru. I curate the collection here." He spoke with a slight accent; I wasn't sure what kind. He took a step toward me, and he was lean and graceful, almost catlike, when he moved. Even through his loose clothes I could tell how muscular his body was. I decided he must have been an athlete when he was younger, maybe a gymnast. Maybe he still was. He was about forty or so, I thought.

"I'm Jamie Dunn."

"Freshman?" He smiled and opened a panel in the wall to turn the lights on. Soft atmospheric lighting bathed everything, including us. He was even more handsome than I had first thought.

I was a bit abashed. "Yes." I had never felt an attraction to an older man before; I had never thought it was quite right, but…

"I don't suppose you're actually interested in Egyptology? The department needs students."

"I'm a music major. Piano."

"I'd like to hear you play sometime." I didn't want to let myself be flattered; it was only polite conversation.

"I'm not really good enough to play in public yet. I mean, student recitals, sure, but…"

"You will be." He smiled again. "Do you know anything at all about ancient Egypt?"

"Only what I've seen in *The Ten Commandments*." I fluttered my eyelashes and did my best Anne Baxter impression. "'Oh, Moses, you stubborn, splendid, adorable fool!'"

Semenkaru laughed. "My colleagues would be scandalized to hear me say it, but I've always loved that film. Have you ever noticed how the Egyptian villains stay young and beautiful while the heroes all age pretty horribly?"

It had never occurred to me, but he was right.

"Why don't you let me show you around for a few minutes? If you have the time, I mean."

His eyes were so green, his skin so pale, lips so full. I could eat anytime; Justin and our teammates could do without me. "I'd like that, yes."

And so I got a private tour. Sekhem-wa-Set, he told me, had been eighteen or nineteen when he died, "the same age as Tutankhamen. He had crippling arthritis and walked with a limp." Then he taught me a bit about hieroglyphs, a bit about the ways the Egyptians carved their statues out of the hardest rock known, and a bit more about a lot of other things. Somewhat to my surprise I found it fascinating.

We stopped in front of the most impressive statue in the place, nearly twice life size. Like most of the others it was of a man, dressed only in a kilt, standing with his left foot forward. He was holding a spear or a scepter of some kind. And he had the head of a bird, a falcon. The stone was black, polished. Despite myself I found myself studying the lines of the body. It was beautiful, lean, muscular, perfect. *Like the professor's,* I thought.

"This is the great god Horus. The divine embodiment of the pharaoh. His spirit flowed in the king's veins. It's carved from quartzite, one of the hardest stones known. But look at it. See the way they made the unyielding stone almost alive, almost sensual."

It was beautiful. I said so.

"Everyone always says the art of the Egyptians was so stiff and formal, but look at what they've accomplished here. There's real passion in this work. Look at the muscles in his legs. See the contours of his chest—you can almost see it rise and fall. You can almost feel the beating of his heart."

He took my hand, quite gently so I did not resist, and placed it flat on the statue's chest, just where the heart would be in a living man. It was warm. The stone should have been cool, like the air in the room, but it was warmer than my hand. There might almost have been blood flowing in it.

I looked at Semenkaru and saw him watching me, gazing at me as if he'd been looking for me for a long time and didn't know what to make of me now that he'd found me. I let him hold my hand for a long moment before I pulled away.

"How is that possible?"

"I don't know what you mean, Jamie."

"That warmth. The stone should be cool, room temperature or cooler."

"I don't know how to account for it." He shrugged then smiled again. "Some things are warm, some aren't."

I found myself feeling suddenly uncomfortable. "I have to be going, professor."

"My students call me Danilo."

"Danilo, then. Thank you for the tour."

"Perhaps when you play your first recital you'll invite me."

"I will."

"My guess is, you play with the deepest passion."

I turned to go.

"You hear the music, Jamie." I turned back and he was watching me quite pointedly. "The music all around us, that most people never know. You hear it and understand it."

When I left he was smiling. There was not much doubt in my mind what he had been trying to tell me. And I wanted him too. But it seemed so...so...I didn't want to think about it.

There was a reception at the music department at 7:30. I decided I'd eat there. I met several other students and several teachers. One of the boys, maybe a year or two older than me, was wearing a rainbow pin. I stayed carefully away from him. Ebensburg High had taught me better than to be that open. Roland McTavish, who was to be my private piano instructor, wasn't there. I had met him before, anyway. Three string players approached me and asked if I'd like to form a piano quartet with them. I had never played in an ensemble and didn't much like the idea. The food wasn't much more than heavy snacks, but I ate enough to fill me up.

Then I headed to the library and sifted through back issues of the local newspapers. I wanted to know more about the murders. It took a while to find the stories. Young men, found naked and cut open from throat to abdomen. Their eyes were gone, and they had been mutilated sexually. A number of other men were missing, quite a few more than had been found. Just the news I needed on my first day.

It was after 9 when I got back to the dorm; Norm was out someplace. Chasing "chicks"? I felt sorry for whichever one he had in his sights.

Feeling restless, I decided to head for the sports building. What with packing, moving, and bracing myself for a new life, I hadn't worked out for a couple of weeks. I stuffed some gear and a Speedo into a gym bag and went out again.

It was after sunset, and the air was getting cool. The streets were brightly lit and crowded with students. It was easy to tell which were the freshmen; I hoped I wasn't that obvious, but I knew I probably was. Traffic was heavy, stores were lit up. Gosh, Toto, I don't think we're in Ebensburg anymore.

The sports building was ablaze with light. Everyone seemed to want to start getting in shape as soon as possible. The weight room was full, the indoor running track crowded, the basketball court a blur of action, the gymnastics equipment all in use. Everyone was there except the one I wanted to see.

Justin Hollis was there. I watched him practice a few dives. He was good.

"Jamie! You didn't meet us for dinner."

"Sorry. I got tied up with something. And I had to go to a reception at the music department."

"You're a musician?"

"Yep. Piano."

He smiled. "An intellectual. Most of us major in sports medicine and stuff. It's easier to stay on the team if your coach is the one giving you your grades."

"But doesn't that mean they have more control over you?" This seemed to be a new thought for him. "Anyway, playing's a compulsion for me, like swimming."

"I know what you mean. I want to get back up on that platform, okay? But let's get together, though. For sure. I want you to meet Grant."

Grant had to be the gymnast he had been with that afternoon, the redhead. "We will."

He smiled again and headed up the ladder. I decided I liked him. He seemed to know me better than I would have liked, better than I felt quite comfortable with. I tried so hard to be neutral with people, but...wanting me to meet his boyfriend. I watched him. He was beautiful, so graceful in the air. Lucky Grant. But then I was making assumptions, or so I told myself. The might have been friends. Or brothers, for that matter.

I watched the divers for another minute or two. And for the first time I had doubts about college. This was so unlike the atmosphere I was used to. It would take me a while to learn to decipher all the signals. Rather than think about it, I decided to change and get wet.

And then...

There in the locker room I saw him. He was toweling off after a shower. I didn't even have to see his face; I knew his shoulders, I knew the line of his legs. Nervous, terrified, I approached him.

"Tim."

He turned slowly. He had recognized me from my voice, before he even saw me. I could tell by his body language. For the life of me I couldn't read the expression on his face. "Jamie."

I was Jell-O. "Hi, Tim."

He paused for a moment, as if he was trying to decide how to react. Then he smiled. There were fireworks in it, or in me. "Jamie! It's great to see you!"

Ebensburg was past. "I was hoping I'd find you."

"Well, you did, and I'm glad." He toweled his hair.

Awkward silence. I groped for words. "How have you been?"

"I've been great, I guess. I just came back from the Olympic trials."

"Did you make it?"

He laughed. "Hell, no. I was more than three seconds off. But I gave a decent enough showing, I guess."

"I wish you had."

"I can live without the pressure. It's bad enough around here. Have you met Coach Zielinski yet?"

"On one of my campus visits. Is he rough?"

"Worse than Harrison. Is he dead yet?"

Despite myself I laughed. I had never found anything funny about him before. "No, people like that never seem to die."

"You said it."

Tim was naked. It took all my will power not to look him up and down. For all I knew he had a boyfriend. Or worse yet another girlfriend. It was an awful thought. I made myself smile. "Well, I'm going to change and get a few laps in."

"You sure? Why don't we get a burger and catch up?"

"Oh, I ate at the—" I caught myself. But I didn't want to seem too eager. "I really need to limber up."

"Do it tomorrow."

"Tomorrow morning I have to go to the orientation for new jocks. Then Coach Zielinski's going to meet with the new swimmers."

"Talk. They all like to talk so much. Come on."

"Well…okay, I guess. I'll meet you outside."

It wouldn't take him long to get dressed. I hung around just outside the locker room. Idling the time I noticed a flyer on the wall.

There was a photo of a young man with the name Josh Mariatta underneath. He was a diver and he was missing. Anyone who knew anything about him was to call the campus police.

Tim came out. I pointed at the flyer. "Do you know him?"

"I've seen him around."

"What could have happened to him?"

"Who knows?"

Ten minutes later we were at the Z, eating greasy burgers and greasier fries. I'd have to do extra laps to work them off. Music blared, students shouted, the staff shouted even louder. Everyone seemed to be having fun. As for me…I was with Tim again. I was nervous as hell, terrified. We hadn't touched, not even to shake hands.

"You want some mustard, Jamie?" I'd forgotten how he liked to soak his food in it.

"No, I'm cool."

"I hate this place."

"Then why'd you bring me here?"

"Rite of passage for a freshman." Was he laughing at me? "There's a nice quiet sandwich shop a few blocks away from my place. That's where I usually eat."

"You're not in the dorms?"

"Be serious. I've got an apartment in Shadyside. Two bedroom—I share it with one of the seniors on the team. Scott Trask. Have you met him?"

I shook my head. Just roommates? I was terrified to ask.

He guessed what I was thinking. "Just roommates." He said it firmly. "Friends, but nothing more. A lot of the guys on the team…" He left the thought unfinished, but of course I knew what he meant. "But not me."

I had to ask. "A lot of them?"

"Well, some. More than you'd think."

A guy carrying a tray of beer stumbled and spilled it; it missed us by inches.

Tim looked faintly disgusted. "Let's eat up and get out of here."

As we were leaving a blond girl came over and kissed Tim on the cheek. He introduced us. Her name was Rachel. "Jamie's an old friend from home. He's on the team here now."

She nodded at me, but she seemed to have no time for small talk. "Have you heard anything about Josh?"

He shook his head. "Nobody's seen or heard a thing."

"Let me know, okay? I'm so scared."

They kissed again and she rejoined her other friends.

"She and Josh were seeing each other."

"Oh."

"I don't know how serious it was. Like I said, I didn't know him that well. I saw him at a few parties, but—" He spread his hands in a "What can I do?" gesture.

The night was getting cooler still; I wished I had worn a sweatshirt. The sky was a deep transparent blue and a nearly full moon shone down over the campus buildings. It was perfect for urban romance. Part of me wished I had been able to stop loving Tim. He was being so careful with me.

I decided to take the plunge. "You never came to my recital."

"Oh." He was embarrassed. Good. "I got, you know, hung up with so many things. Finals. You know how hard I have to study for tests."

"I was hurt."

"I'm sorry, Jamie."

"I was playing for you."

"You shouldn't have. We were miles apart then. And things between us had…" He sounded a bit helpless.

Every fourth or fifth telephone pole we passed had another of those flyers about Josh Mariatta. Some were about other missing guys. They seemed to be everywhere, and I was surprised I hadn't noticed them before. But there had been so much else to take in. "What's this all about? Does anybody know what's happening to them, Tim?"

"Here, let's walk this way. There's a park across that bridge. We can talk better there."

We crossed the bridge. There was nothing but darkness underneath; the ravine it spanned could have been a mile deep.

"It's called Panther Hollow."

I didn't much care. "About Josh…?"

We reached the park. There was grass, there were flowers and trees, all ghostly in the moonlight. Across the road from us there was an elaborate old Victorian greenhouse. The stars were brilliant. We sat down on the grass.

"Over the last year seven guys have been found mutilated. Five jocks, a cellist in the school orchestra, and some guy from fine arts. They were all cut open. Some of their organs were gone, their eyes, their cocks. The others, the ones who disappeared...." He let the sentence go unfinished.

"Did you know any of them?"

"Not really, not very well. Just to see, you know. But the thing is, only the ones that have been found have been reported on. The ones who are missing.... I'm not sure anyone knows how many more there might be. I mean, you hear rumors, but...some of the ones who disappeared turned up months later, cut like the other ones. The university doesn't want it talked about, so nobody really knows how many are gone. And I guess nobody really knows if the missing ones aren't just...missing."

"What's your guess? What's happening here?"

He looked right at me and said, "I think there's some kind of sick psycho faggot loose here. It's what everybody thinks, but nobody's saying it."

I wasn't sure how to react. This wasn't what I wanted to hear.

"When I saw you just now, the first thing I thought was, *God no, Jamie shouldn't have come here.* Because of all this, I mean."

I looked at him, wondering what, precisely, he meant. He was staring up at the moon. "Well, I guess you're stuck with me, Tim."

"Good. What I meant to say was, that was only my first thought. Now that we're back together—"

"Are we back together?"

He touched my hand. I felt it all through my body.

"So when I give my first student recital...?"

"I'll be there. Nothing could keep me away."

"And if I announce that I'm dedicating the C-minor nocturne to you...?"

He laughed. "Hell, I don't even know what a C-minor nocturne is."

"Well, you'll just have to learn, that's all." I took his hand and squeezed it.

"I want you to be careful, Jamie."

I looked around.

"No, I mean when you're out alone around campus. These killings. You're not the biggest guy, and…"

"Don't worry, I can take care of myself."

"Josh had a brown belt."

"Oh." As I had once before, I decided to be bold. "You'll just have to protect me then."

I leaned over to kiss him.

"Not here! Someone might see us." He got to his feet and brushed off his pants.

"Tim."

"Come on, let's get back."

"You just said we were back together."

"We are. I mean, we are. But not here. Jamie, we'd both lose our scholarships."

"This isn't Ebensburg. There are laws." I had checked.

"The hell with the laws. If they decide they want to cut us, they'll do it. Come on. Besides, now with all these disappearances and killings…. Jamie, we have to be careful, that's all. People are a lot more tense than you realize."

We walked back to my dorm. There was small talk, nothing too heavy. I brought him up to date on some of our friends back home. He saw me to the front door. I looked into his eyes, wanting like anything to kiss him. He shook my hand. "I'll see you tomorrow."

So much for my reunion with my old love.

✳

A week before Thanksgiving. I had taken to school, loved everything about it. Under Roland McTavish's instruction I was improving my pianism. Under Coach Zielinski I was improving my swimming. I nearly set a school record for the butterfly. Tim cheered me on, which I honestly think was the only thing that gave me the energy to do it.

There were more disappearances. A promising new quarterback, a goalie on the hockey team, and a voice major I had met briefly, a baritone. Only the quarterback had been found, inexplicably mutilated like the others. For a while the school authorities wanted people to think the missing men were simply, well, missing. But each time a body turned up it was harder to maintain the pretense. People talked, rumors spread. There was something terribly wrong on campus and it was spreading, like a disease, a plague.

The first student musical program was set for just before Christmas break. I told Roland I wanted to play the Chopin second sonata, the one with the funeral march in it. I said that with the atmosphere, a funeral march seemed appropriate.

"I haven't played this before, Roland. I'm not sure I'll be good enough by the recital."

"You're not ready for that. It's a complete bear. There are only a handful of pianists in the world who can really play it well. Argerich, Pollini, Ashkenazy, maybe one or two others."

"I still want to try."

"If you're prepared to be embarrassed in front of the department, fine, go ahead. I'll work with you. But don't say I didn't warn you."

I felt a bit smug. "Thanks."

"You're asking for it."

"Everybody does, one way or another, Roland."

"If you want to play something by a gay composer, how about some Schubert?"

"It's not just that. Chopin is special to me." I hesitated. "What about Schubert? I didn't know."

"He lived in a house with a group of 'bachelors.' He was never involved with a woman. And he died of syphilis."

"How cheery." I really hadn't known. And I had never explored his music, really. I made a note to start. Again I hesitated, not certain whether to ask. "Did you know the singer who disappeared, Roland?"

He frowned; I don't think he wanted to talk about it. "No, not really. The voice teachers all say he was good."

Roland was a large man, a bit shaggy around the edges, not what you'd expect in a music professor. He had a lover and was quite open about it. That made him unusual on the faculty; most of them were much more circumspect. He was my advisor too. We had become friends over the months, and had talked about a lot of personal things together. He knew about Tim and me. What little there was to know.

"Roland, I don't know what to do. I still love him, but…"

"You should find someone in the music department."

"The department's not much more open than the swim team. Too much pressure to conform."

"Be yourself. You have to be, to be a good musician. Have you listened to Thibaudet's recordings?"

I knew what he meant. The great pianist was quite open about himself and had made a fine career. "But, Roland, he's the only one."

"Then make it two."

It was too upsetting to think about. I knew I could trust Roland, but how could I trust anyone else?

Justin Hollis and I became friendly. I think it was because he was so completely clueless about music. I always felt one up on him. When he dove from the high platform he was quite graceful, quite beautiful really. It seemed Grant and he were only friends after all, or else they were being more than usually cautious. Most of the jocks had girlfriends; most actually wanted them. The ones who used their girls only for cover…well, that was okay with everyone as long as they maintained the pretense.

One afternoon Justin and I went and watched the gymnasts work out. Grant's event was the rings. Hanging there, suspended by his own strength, every muscle in his body taut, he was a bit like a god. When he moved he was even more so. I watched Justin. He was a bit in love. Not Grant. Unrequited. Grant seemed oblivious to everything Justin was feeling. Maybe that was what drew me to Justin.

Afterward we headed to the Z for sandwiches. I hated the place, but everyone else seemed to go there without thinking about it.

Tim was there. He was sitting with a girl, a blond in a cheer-leader's outfit. They were giggling together. He saw me and waved, and I dutifully smiled and waved back.

Her name was Glinda, which caused a lot of joking around the locker room. "So are you Dorothy, then, Johanssen?" That kind of thing. I always laughed extra loud, so he'd hear me. I was never certain how he felt about her, whether he was using her the way some of the other guys used their girls, for cover. He never looked at her the way he looked at me.

Since that first night we had been friendly but not very much so. Tim's old caution came back. He kept a discreet distance from me without ever becoming too open. My feelings for him were…tangled. At times I still wanted him, very badly. At other times…. I decided to say hi to them; I crossed to their table with a big artificial smile.

"Hi, Glinda, Tim."

The both said hi. Glinda had a milk shake, with only one straw. I fixated on details like that, as if they might tell me something.

We chatted. She said she was going home to Iowa for the holidays. Not having any family I really cared about, I had decided to stay on campus and work on the sonata. Tim wasn't sure yet. He looked really uncomfortable, which pleased me. I made my excuses and rejoined Justin and Grant.

When we were finished, just outside the Z, Tim caught up with me. Grant and Justin went on ahead.

"Jamie, I need to talk to someone."

"What's up?"

"Not here. Someplace where we can be alone. Just a second." He dashed back to Glinda, said something to her, and kissed her.

We headed to the library and found a secluded corner. He was upset about something.

"My parents are getting a divorce."

"Oh." It wasn't what I had expected. "Well, I never had the impression they got along very well."

"They never did. I guess this has been coming for years. But it's still…" He had a habit of not finishing his sentences, especially when they dealt with feelings.

"So, are you going home, then?"

"I don't know, probably not. The last thing they need is me there.

But I'm really bummed out about it. I'm going to need company."

He was asking. For three months I had waited for it. Now I wasn't sure how I felt.

He touched my hand again, as he had that first night. "Can I…you're staying too, you said?"

I nodded.

"Can we hang out together?"

"I have a really rough sonata to learn." I didn't want to make it easy for him.

"Jamie, please."

I paused for dramatic effect. "Well, listen. Norm's going home too. Why don't you stay in my room for the weekend?"

It was bolder than he expected, I could tell. Hell, it was bolder than even I expected. He looked around to make sure we were alone. I thought he was going to kiss me. But instead he only said how much he'd like to spend the holiday with me.

For better or worse we had a long weekend's date.

A week later there was another disappearance. A history major, a captain in the campus ROTC. The police were completely baffled. People tried to carry on with school as usual, but it was harder and harder to keep up the pretense.

And then the holiday break came. Norm left on Wednesday morning. Tim brought his things over that afternoon. He needed me; knowing it felt so good. He hardly stopped smiling. "Should I go home and get my TV?"

"What on earth for?"

"So we can watch Macy's parade."

"Somehow, Timothy, I think we'll find other things to fill our time."

"Well, okay, if you don't have any culture…"

We both had a good laugh, cuddled for a while, then went out for a sandwich at the Z. For once it was nearly empty and nearly quiet. The weather had turned cold; there were snow flurries predicted. Tim looked sexy as hell in jeans and a red sweater.

That night we made love five times. And it was wonderful holding him, feeling him hold me. Even the sound of his breathing seemed sweet. I was still a kid, I guess.

After the fifth time, even he was too tired for more. We lay side by side in the dark room. I would never have thought that crummy little dorm room could seem so wonderful. Moonlight poured in, the only illumination. Neither of us seemed ready for sleep.

I kissed him for the hundredth time. "You've been practicing."

"Well…" He was embarrassed by it, I could tell. "It has been two years, Jamie."

"Two years very well spent, if you ask me."

"You shouldn't talk about it like that."

Not sure what he meant, I got up and switched on my keyboard. And played what I knew of the Chopin sonata. For a time he sat and listened. Then I felt him standing behind he. He kissed the back of my neck, very gently. "You can't really be thinking of me when you play that."

"I can and I do."

For a moment he was silent again. "I don't feel like that."

"No, but you make me feel that way."

He kissed me again, long and deep, and before I knew what was happening we made love again.

The whole weekend passed like that, just the two of us, being young men in love, ignoring the rest of the world. It seemed so perfect.

The world, the campus, the mysterious deaths and disappearances all around us, none of it seemed to matter.

Tim and I saw a lot of each other in the next weeks. I practiced the sonata till I had it down perfect and understood every bit of feeling Chopin had poured into it. He was separated from his lover so many times, for so long. Everything he felt I felt too when Tim wasn't around.

Neither of us was going home for Christmas either. I had nowhere much to go; his house was a battleground, or so his sister's letters said. I couldn't wait for more of him.

Over lunch at his favorite sandwich shop he asked me to move in with him at the end of the spring semester. "Scott's graduating. You can have his bedroom."

All I could do was grin.

It was three days before the end of the term: the day of my recital. Backstage I was nervous as hell, and not just because I'd be playing before a demanding audience for the first time. I had my little speech of dedication rehearsed. A quartet played some Haydn; a tenor sang some Schubert; then I was on.

I adjusted my tie and stepped onto the stage. Tim had promised to be in the front row. He wasn't. I scanned the audience, and there was no sign of him.

I went numb. I wanted to cry but of course it was impossible. Wanting to be any place in the world but on that stage, I sat down and began playing.

I seemed to go into a trance; my fingers played without my mind being conscious of it. I had practiced so hard, and I knew the music so well. But when I came to the second movement, the scherzo, I found it suddenly too much for me. I missed several fingerings, I blew a chord. I covered well enough, and I didn't think most of the audience noticed. But I saw Roland from the corner of my eye. He knew.

Then came the third movement, the funeral march, and I found myself again. I poured everything I was feeling into it, the pain, the grief, the awful disappointment.

The audience was hushed. Somehow I knew I was playing it as Chopin had wanted it played. I kept glancing sideways, hoping Tim would show up. Tears came to my eyes. I tried to tear through the brief final movement, the presto, sending my agitated soul into it. But it was too much for me. This time I was sure the entire audience picked up on my mistakes.

The audience applauded. Game try, Jamie. I tried to avoid looking at Roland.

Then I saw someone else in the audience. In the fifth row, just off the aisle, was Danilo. He seemed enraptured; he was not moving, not clapping, just watching me. I hadn't seen him since my first day on campus, but I remembered what he had said to me then.

People crowded around me. Nothing much they said registered. I wanted to get back to my room and be alone.

Just as I was finally about to leave the stage Danilo moved through the crowd to me.

"Congratulations, Jamie. You must be very happy."

"No." I didn't want to look at him. "I'm not, really."

"Oh. I'm sorry."

"My teacher told me I wasn't up to it, and he was right."

"But you played with such deep feeling. Everyone was moved. I could tell."

There were too many people; the crush was terrible. "I don't mean to be rude, Professor Senk- Semenk-"

"Danilo. Please."

"I really don't like to be rude, but I'm not feeling at all well. Thank you very much for coming."

"It was my pleasure, believe me."

I asked Roland to make my excuses and slipped into the wings. My overcoat and scarf had been moved from where I left them; it took me a moment to find them. Then I headed for the rear exit.

It was cold, much colder than when I'd gone in. Night had fallen and a gentle snow was coming down. I hadn't used the rear exit before; it opened into an alley, which led into several more. There were utility lights at the back of several buildings or I would have been in complete darkness. It took me a few seconds to get my bearings.

Or so I thought. Every alley I tried was a dead end. There had to be a way out. It was so confusing I almost forgot how much Tim had hurt me.

The snow began to fall more heavily. I found my way to a larger alley. There was a streetlight; snowflakes filled the cone of light.

And then I saw the body, lying alongside a dumpster. Young man. Naked. Bright red hair. Cut open, throat to crotch, exactly as the news stories had described. Eyes torn out. Genitals cut off. Worse than that was the agonized expression on his face. And I recognized him; it was Grant. A large rat was chewing busily on his insides.

He lay perfectly still; a layer of snow was beginning to cover him.

"Grant!" I chased the rat away and shook him, foolishly, as if there was a chance he could answer me. "Grant!"

I looked around helplessly. What could have happened to him? Was whoever did this still there?

The snow let up a bit and I could see the end of the alley and a street beyond it. I covered him with my coat. Then I ran and found the nearest emergency post, and pushed the signal button.

A voice came though the speaker, almost obscured by static. "What's your emergency?"

"I found a dead body. A boy. Like the others, I think."

"Where are you?"

I told them.

"We'll be right there."

I stood there waiting, looking around, not knowing what to do or what to expect.

Poor Grant. I hadn't known him all that well; I didn't even know his last name. Justin would be shattered. I went back and stood over his body, staring at it, absurdly, as if it might tell me something. He looked…I don't know, not peaceful the way the dead are supposed to look, but frightened, in pain. I touched him: cold, literally, as ice. If only Tim was there with me, I found myself thinking, he'd somehow know what to do, somehow he'd make it better. Laughable thought.

The campus police arrived, followed a moment later by the city police and an ambulance from the morgue. A dozen or more of them combed for evidence, took photos of Grant's body, knocked on nearby doors. A detective questioned me and I told him what little I knew. "His name was Grant."

"First or last name?"

"First. I don't know his surname. I didn't really know him very well. Friend of a friend…"

After a few minutes they let me go. I'd have to get back to my room and call Justin. I was dreading it.

I passed near the museum, and unexpectedly there were lights on in the Egyptian Galleries, not bright ones, soft spotlights highlighting various exhibits. I couldn't see anyone inside. One shaft of light fell directly on the statue of Horus. Stupidly I stood in the snow staring at it, I don't know for how long, as if it might have some resolution to the horrible things that had happened. Bizarre thing, for a moment I thought I saw it move. Then the lights dimmed. There had been no one there to dim them, but that hardly made an impression.

Finally, cold and shivering, trying not to cry, I made it back to the dorm. Tim would be there, I told myself. He had been sick, too ill to come to the recital. He had twisted his ankle, or…

I was being foolish. The room was empty.

I should have called Justin right away, I knew that. But the night had been so awful. Talking to him, telling him about Grant…it would have been too much. I crawled into bed and cried for a while and fell asleep.

That night I had a dream, one I was to have again and again. All the swimmers I knew were corpses, pale and mutilated; they stared unseeing into a night sky lit by a full moon. All the other athletes lay ringed around them, equally cold, equally dead. I sat in the center of it all, playing mournful Chopin nocturnes on a concert grand piano. And there with me was Danilo. Not visibly so; I couldn't see him. But I could feel his presence, the way you sometimes can in dreams.

CHAPTER 2

Late in the night, so late the sky was already beginning to lighten, Tim came back to my room. He switched on the light and stood looking at me. I stared at him groggily. "Go back to your own place."

"I…I can't. Scott has his girlfriend with him. He asked me to…" He was drunk. Very.

"I don't care. Go anyway. I don't want you here."

"Jamie, I'm sorry."

"Will you please go?"

He moved to the side of my bed and got down on one knee. "I'm sorry. I couldn't let you…I couldn't let you do what you wanted to do to me, announce my name like that."

"So it's you that this was done to?"

"I don't mean it like that. But I can't have people knowing about us. I can't."

"Then go home."

He grabbed me rather violently and kissed me. I resisted, but he kissed me again and again. "I'm so sorry, Jamie, I really am so sorry. I'll never do it again."

"You won't have the chance."

"Jamie, please." He pressed his face into my chest and started to cry.

I pulled away from him. "Grant's dead."

He looked up, not seeming to understand.

"The gymnast. Justin's…" I almost choked on the word. "…friend."

"No."

"I found him. Like the others. Dead, naked, cut lengthwise, nearly in half."

"God. It must have been…"

"It was."

For a moment we both went quiet. Tim paced a few steps. "What a mess I've made of us, Jamie. I never wanted that. I only want…"

"What?"

"I want you. I want us, together."

The night had been so long and so awful. That dream had left me shaken. I needed someone to hold me. Even Tim. I stretched out a hand to him and he got into bed beside me and we cuddled till the next morning. I slept on and off; he did too. But we never let go of each other.

Next morning he left to do some laps at the pool. I told him I'd join him later. Somewhat to my surprise, after our intimacy, I didn't mind having him go. It was a relief.

Justin had gone home for the holidays. Knowing how he'd react, dreading it, I called him. He was of course surprised to hear my voice. When I gave him the news he cried, not loudly, but I could tell.

"Jamie, no."

"It was him. I saw him."

"No."

I couldn't say anything.

"He was supposed to come home with me for Christmas to meet my parents, Jamie."

"Then you really were—"

"I told them he was my best friend."

"Oh."

We talked for a few more minutes, but of course nothing I said helped him. It was absurd to expect otherwise. I told him he could call me if he needed to talk, and we said goodbye. Feeling more lost and alone than I ever had, I got undressed and crawled into bed again. I needed sleep. The room was cold, or I was; I took an extra blanket off Norm's bed.

I heard more rumors. Two guys from the political science department had run off together. The student who was expected to be valedictorian in International Affairs was gone. And more. The campus was so big that no one knew everyone, there was no way to, so we all listened for rumors and wondered if they were right. And wondered what was behind them. It was impossible to know what to believe.

For the next months things between Tim and me continued the way they had been. I love you, stay away from me. I need you so deeply, keep your distance. Your love matters to me more than anything else, but I could never tell anyone about it.

I was so torn. Part of me still loved him, still remembered all the reasons I had fallen in love with him in the first place. Part of me wanted him gone. I kept telling myself it wasn't his fault, there were too many pressures on him. But in the last analysis he was the one in charge of our relationship, and that was what he wanted.

It was doing horrible things to me. My playing suffered. Roland asked me about it. "You were so promising at the recital. Now your heart just isn't in it."

"My heart isn't in much of anything these days."

"Do you want to talk about it?"

"I can't."

And my swimming was off too. I was still competing passably but nowhere near the level I was capable of. Coach Zielinski called me on it. I told him a story about family problems. "It'll pass," he said. I don't think he believed me, but there wasn't much he could do.

When I saw Tim, when he touched me…we felt so perfect together. His body was so beautiful, he tasted so delicious, he made me feel so full. The ancient Greeks and Egyptians, I knew, believed that physical love was what gives us the spark of the divine. With Tim, I could almost believe it. I tried half a dozen times to end it, knowing what it was doing to me. When he told me how deeply he loved me I relented.

A month before the end of the semester we were having lunch at the sandwich shop Tim liked. It was a bright early spring day, there was actually some green in the world, and we were both in good spirits. Things had been going well between us lately. I had convinced myself that if I only loved him enough, he'd love me in return, and that was the way things had gone. We made small talk about finals and the coming end of the semester.

"I'm not looking forward to moving, Tim. I hate it. I have so much junk."

He bit into his sandwich. "You're getting a place?"

I went slightly numb. Nervously I reminded him he had invited me to move in with him.

"Oh. Jamie, I'm sorry. You can't do that."

"Why not?"

"I'm...I didn't want to tell you this way. Someone else is moving in. I'm..." He looked away from me. "I'm marrying Glinda."

Of course I was hurt. Of course I was not surprised. "You didn't want to tell me this way. So, how did you want to tell me?"

"I don't know."

"No, of course not."

"The wedding's going to be back in Ebensburg. My family loves her."

Ebensburg. "You're not going to have the bad taste to invite me, are you?" Before he could say another word I got up and walked away. The bright sun outside hurt my eyes.

He ran after me and caught my arm. "Jamie."

I pulled free of him.

"Jamie, you have to understand. I can't live like that. I can't have people know. This isn't a good time to be..."

"No, of course not. It never is. Goodbye."

"Jamie, please!"

"Leave me alone."

"Jamie, you have to understand. If people knew...the school, the coaches, my family..."

"I don't care about them."

"I do."

"Then be happy with them." I kept walking.

"Stop, goddamn it!"

I walked.

There was no way I could avoid seeing him, of course. We were on the same team. I'd be seeing his body in the locker room, in the shower, in the pool, and I knew I still wanted it. But I couldn't let him do to me anymore what he had done so many times.

Justin had a hard time recovering from the way Grant had died. We spent a lot of time together, crying on each other's shoulders, not always metaphorically. I had gone with him to Grant's memorial service. It was mostly jocks—dull speakers saying the obvious things. Justin wasn't asked to speak and didn't make an issue of it.

Over pizza I told him about Tim and Glinda.

"Are you surprised, Jamie?"

"No, I guess not. Something like it was bound to happen, sooner or later."

"Do you think he really loves her?"

"I don't know or care. He's her problem now. I'd like to think she deserves him."

He laughed. "That's an awful thing to say about anybody."

"Probably." I laughed too. "What women put up with."

"And the things they never know."

He mentioned he didn't want to live in the dorms anymore; two years was enough for him. We decided to get a place together.

"If you don't mind my practicing, that is. How do you like Chopin?"

"Is he that center on the hockey team?"

"God, you sound like Norm."

"Bitch."

"You staying in town for the summer?" I asked him.

"Yeah. I have to take a geology course over."

Next day, after a long night of avoiding Norm's obtuse prying—"Chick trouble, huh?"—I met Justin and we visited the campus housing office. With unusual good luck we found a good-size two-bedroom place right away, in Shadyside, the same neighborhood as Tim. I didn't know the area all that well; I hoped my place wasn't too close to his. His and his wife's.

It was a huge apartment, two enormous bedrooms, a dining

room, and a living room—all on the second floor of an older woman's house. She lived alone on the first floor. I thought she might have been a widow, but of course I didn't ask.

The semester ended. I did okay on my finals; Roland's review said I was one of the most promising students he'd ever had. And I finally managed to tie that school butterfly record I'd been chasing. So my scholarships were intact.

Tim tried to congratulate me. I didn't want to talk to him.

"Please, Jamie. Can't we be friends?"

"Good gosh, no. Somebody might find out."

"You're being a shit."

"I learned from a master."

He tried a few more times but finally got the message and left me alone. We were civil but distant, and that was the way I wanted it.

It was a bright, glorious spring day when Justin and I moved our things into the apartment; first his, then mine. The landlady, Mrs. Kolarik, fussed and tried to help arrange things. We were fairly exhausted by mid afternoon.

But I made Justin get up and take a quick shower. "There's one more thing we have to do."

He looked around. "What?"

We got into fresh clothes and I led him a few blocks to the neighborhood animal shelter. We stopped outside the front door. "Here. We need a cat. It'll make the apartment into a home."

He grinned at me. "That's a great idea, Jamie."

There was a whole wall of them to choose from, in little cages that must have been uncomfortable for them. One singled us out and started clamoring for our attention. A little longhaired black-and-white thing, a female. We stood back and watched for a while, and she ignored everyone else. But when she saw either one of us she went frantic trying to get our attention.

"That, Justin, is the cat for us."

We got her home, set up a box for her, and let her explore the place. She seemed to like it.

"We need a name for her, Jamie."

"Let's wait. When we find the right one, she'll let us know."

Justin and I had a brief affair. Desultory sex, words of love neither of us meant and neither of us believed, strictly a rebound thing for both of us. We actually cried in each other's arms once or twice. But it never went anywhere serious, because I think neither of us really wanted it to. Mutual sympathy, not much more. He was a nice man, but…at least it cemented our friendship.

There had been a letter from my cousin Millie asking if I could come home and help with the farm. They'd had a rough year and could use another hand. But there was no way I could face that. Ebensburg seemed a thousand years behind me.

I needed to stay on campus to bury myself in work, in music, in anything to occupy my mind. It was technically too late to register for the summer term, but there had to be a few courses still open. Roland would be on campus that summer, and he promised to give me as much of his time as he could.

"Here. I want you to work on this."

It was the Schubert D-major sonata. I had never heard it; I barely knew Schubert's music at all. "Why this?"

"I think you might find something good in it, that's all."

I looked through it. There were some difficult passages, and there were some deceptively simple ones. "I'll start on it tonight."

Every morning I swam like a fiend, like a madman, trying to work off all the horrible feelings I had had. It worked, a bit. Coach Zielinski was happy with me. And the sonata helped. Under its easy surface it was dark, turbulent, full of passion, almost like Chopin.

But I needed more. The registrar's office gave me a list of summer courses that were still open. One listing jumped out at me:

ANCIENT EGYPTIAN CIV. MSM 401 M–F 1:00–2:00 SEMENKARU

I don't know how I knew, but it was what I needed. I registered, paid the late fee, went to the bookstore, and bought the required texts. It was Friday; the course would start the following Monday. I couldn't wait. It would be different enough from anything I knew to engage me; it would be challenging enough to occupy my mind a bit—or at least I hoped so.

Browsing through my textbook I happened across the name of the ancient Egyptian cat goddess: Bubastis. Not thinking, I said it aloud, and our kitten purred happily. I had found her name.

That night I had that dream again: me, playing passionate music in the midst of a field of dead men, and Danilo somehow there beside me.

This time I did not find the dream disturbing.

The weekend seemed to take forever. Justin and I were getting used to each other, and getting to know each other in ways we hadn't before. He was from a small town called Zelienople, north of the city. It sounded a lot like Ebensburg.

We compared notes about our backgrounds, our families, our hopes. He asked me about Ebensburg. "What's the big attraction there?"

I had to think for a moment. "Um…we have a Motel Six."

Bubastis was always clamoring for our attention. When I sat down to browse my new textbook she curled up in my lap and purred herself to sleep. I took it as a good sign. At night I dreamed of Egypt and Danilo. The dreams were sexual. We made love in the shadow of the pyramids. When I woke, I felt a bit embarrassed. A crush on my teacher. How juvenile.

Then Monday came. First, practice at the fine arts building. Then a few laps. Tim was just arriving when I left. I smiled at him, an exaggerated, artificial smile, knowing it would bother him.

Our class was in the museum, on the fourth floor. For a time I stood outside. I could see Danilo in the Egyptian gallery; I couldn't really tell what he was doing. He noticed me, smiled, and waved.

He was even better looking than I'd remembered. But this was the first time I had seen him in daytime. He seemed in his mid thirties; I had taken him for older. I waved back.

"Jamie! Hello!" He pushed a window open.

I returned his greeting.

"It's good to see you. Come on in."

I did. He was arranging a new display, some ancient jewelry.

"I saw your name on the class list." His accent had a lilt that was almost musical.

I shrugged. "I guess that tour you gave me stuck."

"Good. We need some bright, young blood around here. Most of the people in these departments breed dust."

There was an awkward moment of silence. I felt attracted to him again, instantly. In daylight his eyes were such a deep green. It was every bit as strong as what I always felt for Tim.

I groped for something to say. "Thanks again for coming to my recital."

"It was my pleasure. Hearing Chopin played that way…it was the way he meant it."

Odd comment. "Having someone I knew in the audience was nice." I quickly added, "Not that I know you all that well, but you know what I mean."

"A familiar face."

"Right."

"What about your family?"

"Oh, they never had much interest in my music." Without even realizing it, I began telling him about my parents' deaths, about Millie, about Ebensburg. Talking to him that way, opening myself up to him, seemed perfectly natural, like something I ought to be doing as a matter of course.

"And what about Tim?" He asked the question pointedly.

It startled me. I didn't remember ever mentioning Tim to him. Suddenly, for the first time, I felt self-conscious. "Tim?"

"Your friend." The way he said it made it clear he meant more.

I must have mentioned him—us—without remembering it. "We're not as close as we were."

"Oh. That's too bad." He looked at his watch. "We should be getting upstairs. It's almost time to start."

How could he have known? I felt vaguely uncomfortable, not with him but with myself. "I'll be right up."

"I'll see you in class, then." He smiled at me and looked directly into my eyes. "I'm glad you'll be with me for the summer. I think there's a great deal for you to learn." He headed up the stairs.

Again, it seemed an odd thing to say. But I put it out of my mind.

I was alone in the room. There was something I had to do. Looking around to make sure no one was there, I crossed to the far end of the gallery, to the statue of the falcon-headed god Horus. Shining stone, twice life-size, gazing into eternity with that time-less expression the ancient sculptors did so well.

A bit afraid, or at least uncertain what to expect, I reached out and placed my hand on its chest, as I had that first time with Danilo. It was cold.

I ran my fingers along the line of its chest. No warmth. It felt colder than the air in the room.

When I had touched it that first time, with Danilo beside me, it had been warm as a living thing.

It was class time. I climbed the steps and found the classroom. Not wanting my infatuation with Danilo to be too obvious, I sat at the back of the room. There were a dozen or so other students, a mix of guys and girls. They were chatting among themselves light-ly, asking all the usual questions, are you in the dorms, what's your major, do you know so-and-so. Danilo had his back to us; he was writing something on the blackboard.

Everything about him—the way he moved, everything—was so sensual. Yes, I thought, he had a great deal to teach me. But I forced the thought out of my mind. A crush on my teacher. If any-one had known, I would have been so embarrassed.

I watched him make some symbols on the blackboard, hiero-glyphics. Then he glanced at his watch and turned to face us.

He introduced himself, said he was pleased to see so many fresh faces in that dusty old building, all the usual kinds of things professors say on the first day of class. He asked a few general questions, trying to get a feel for how much we knew about ancient Egypt. Most of it came from silly TV shows like *In Search Of…* and sillier movies like *The Ten Commandments.* The course would fall into two parts, first a history of the ancient civilization, then an overview of its culture. Religion, mummies, hieroglyphics, the pyramids, King Tut's tomb, all of them would get discussed, and a lot more besides.

The time passed quickly. I found nearly everything he told us intriguing, and it sparked my interest to learn more. Finally he pointed to the symbols on the board. It was a rudimentary alphabet in hieroglyphics. Only a beginning, he emphasized; the way the Egyptians actually used the symbols was much more complex than mere transliteration. But he thought writing our own names out in hieroglyphs might be a good way to end our first session.

Someone asked about cartouches, those oval frames you sometimes see around names.

"No, you don't need to worry about them. They're strictly for the names of kings and queens."

Laboriously I copied out my name:

It took a moment, but when I got it done I found myself smiling. Danilo didn't bother to check what we'd done; it wasn't much more than a fun little exercise. He thanked us all for our attention and dismissed the class.

Almost at once he came to my desk. "Do you mind if I see what you did with your name, Jamie?"

"Of course not."

He looked. "Good work. But there's something it needs." He took the pen out of my shirt pocket and drew a cartouche around it.

"But you said those frames—"

"Cartouches."

"You said they were for the names of kings."

He looked straight into my eyes. "Exactly."

Not for the first time, he left me wondering exactly what he meant.

"I have to go down to the catacombs. I'm looking for a piece of New Kingdom jewelry that's listed in the catalog but that no one can seem to find. I was wondering if you might like to come along. See a bit more of the place. Not many students get to go down there."

I didn't hesitate. "Of course. I'd love to."

I didn't know what I expected or why the invitation excited me. Maybe it was just that he was paying attention to me. Or that he was taking me to a hidden place—after all I'd been through, I needed that.

I followed him down to the ground floor, then to another staircase nearby. We went down flight after flight of stairs. "How far down does this go?"

"There are four basements, or subbasements. I've never actually explored them all myself." He looked back over his shoulder at me. "This building was part of the Underground Railroad. There are all sorts of alcoves and covered recesses and hidey-holes." The slangy word sounded odd with his accent. "I'm not sure anyone has even found them all."

At the first sublevel he stopped. There was an impressive steel vault. He spun the combination and pulled open the heavy door. There was the glint of gold and silver; there were jewels. "This is where we keep our most valuable things. The missing tiara should be here, but it isn't." He smiled and pushed the door shut.

We continued down to the second subbasement. "All museums are like this. They need space for storage. At any given time, only a fraction of what they own is on display." The stairs continued downward, into complete blackness, but we stopped there; I was a bit grateful we weren't going any deeper. He threw a light switch just inside a doorway and led me along a corridor. There wasn't much light—just bare, clear light bulbs, not bright ones, strung every twenty feet or so.

The wiring that linked them was exposed; it must have been nearly as old as the building itself. The walls were bare masonry. Here and there doors opened to one side or the other. Some of them were marked—ANIMAL MUMMIES, CANOPIC JARS, MIDDLE KINGDOM MAGICAL PAPYRI—but most weren't. Anything might have been inside. Despite myself and despite Danilo's presence I found I was a bit nervous.

He chatted. "I've only been here two years, and the department has been accumulating things for more than a century. It could take a lifetime to learn where everything is down here. Or what everything is."

"Shouldn't it all be catalogued?"

"There are only four of us in the department, and two part-time teaching assistants. No one in America cares about the past. We're all so loaded down with teaching duties, none of us has time to sort through all the collections. We've talked about hiring a research assistant to do it, or at least part of it, as much as one person could do. But we never seem to get around to it."

"I could use a job." I'm not sure what made me say it. Of Egyptology I knew nearly nothing. But I had been thinking a job might help take my mind off things, and I did find this interesting. And I found Danilo even more so.

"I'm being a poor guide, Jamie. Let me show you what we have behind some of these doors." He pushed one of them open; it seemed to be stuck. The sign stenciled on it read LATE PERIOD MUMMIES. Danilo laughed. "Who knows when someone was last in here. We're explorers."

The door made a scraping sound as he forced it open. We stepped into a dusty, very dark room. Danilo groped for the light switch and finally found it, up above the door lintel.

The room was perfectly silent, almost unnaturally so, I thought. All around the walls mummy cases were propped against the walls. More were stacked in corners and against walls. Even through the layers of dust on them I could see they were wooden and elaborately painted in bright vibrant colors, even some gold; human faces, their eyes seeing nothing but death.

"They made them this way? I thought they were made of stone."

"Only in earlier times. These people lived almost when the Romans conquered the country. Here, let me show you."

He took one of the coffins from against the wall and laid it on the floor. Then he got down on one knee and very slowly, very carefully began to open it.

"Should you do that?" I had seen enough movies to be nervous.

He smiled. "How else could we see who's inside?"

He lifted the lid. Inside lay the mummy, completely wrapped, the bandages crisscrossing in intricate geometrical designs. Even in the dim light I could see it was beautiful.

"This was a young man named Ahmose the Merchant. It says so here." He pointed to a line of characters on the case. "He died when he was not much older than you."

I got down beside him. "How do you know that?"

"Because he's been unwrapped then wrapped again, of course. His body is of a young man in late adolescence." I think he sensed my reaction to that because he quickly added, "Or early adulthood."

"When they preserved them…"

"Yes?"

I wasn't quite sure what I wanted to ask. "What does a mummy feel like?

He stood up and said softly, "Touch it and see."

I hesitated.

"Go ahead, Jamie. Touch it."

I looked from him to the mummy. Very carefully I touched it. It felt like dry cloth, nothing more. Again I looked at Danilo. "I feel a bit foolish."

"Don't. It's natural curiosity. Let's put the lid back."

I helped him lower it into place.

"I'm not sure why, Danilo, but a lot of this feels really familiar to me."

"Because you're a movie buff?" I wondered how he knew. He smiled in the half-light. "I'm sure there's a reason. Now come on, I still have to find that necklace."

He switched off the light in the room and we stepped back into the corridor. Something ahead of us moved: a pair of rats. When they saw us they froze, then bolted quickly into a crack in the lower part of the wall. Startled, I put my hand on Danilo's arm.

He put his hand on top of mine. "It's all right."

I relaxed. "Sorry."

"I mean it, it's all right. You can find all kinds of unexpected things prowling loose in a place like this. One of my colleagues found a garter snake once. No one could imagine how it got in here."

The electric lights flickered. For a moment I was afraid they'd go out and leave us in complete darkness. But they came back on again right away. Danilo walked on ahead of me and stopped at the entrance to another room. "Here. There's something in here that will help satisfy your curiosity."

I followed him into the room, not at all sure what to expect. He didn't turn on the light; the only illumination came from the hall, and there wasn't much. I groped around for the switch, but this room, it seemed, wasn't wired. Another coffin sat in the center of the room, a heavy rectangular one in black stone, much larger and more ornate that the first one. The lid was off, leaning against it on the floor. Danilo rested a hand on the edge of it.

"Basalt. One of the hardest stones known. Look at what they've accomplished with it."

In the dim light I could make out gods and demons carved into the stone, and rows of hieroglyphs. Very elegant, very beautiful. At the center of the lid was a magnificent falcon flying toward the sun. "It's wonderful, Danilo."

"He was a nephew of Ramses the Great."

I ran my fingers along the outside of the coffin. Cold smooth stone, beautiful carvings. I don't know why, but I felt I had to touch them or they wouldn't be real.

Then I realized the mummy was still in his sarcophagus. And that he was unwrapped. The dead face gaped in the shadowed room. Eyeless sockets looked upward into near darkness. Cold hands grasped nothing at all.

Impulsively I looked down at his groin. In the dark sarcophagus I could just make out pubic hair and genitals; he was that well preserved.

Very quietly Danilo said, "His name was Neferu-Ra." It was almost a whisper, but in that room it seemed to echo.

I looked at him. Why was he showing me these things?

"Go ahead, Jamie."

I didn't know what he meant.

"Go ahead. Touch him."

"I…isn't it fragile?"

"He can withstand your touch."

"But I—"

"Don't be afraid. You wanted to know what a mummy feels like. Touch him, Jamie."

Slowly, carefully, I did. Touched the tip of my finger to his cheek. It was like old, dry, brittle leather. Again I looked at Danilo.

He stepped to my side and put an arm around my waist. "If you want to work here, you'll have to get used to the dead. They're our constant company."

His touch felt so good to me. In that cold, shadowed place it felt unimaginably warm and alive. Quite deliberately I leaned against him, pressed the weight of my body against his.

And he stepped away. Not far. He reached up and touched my hair, then brushed it with his fingers. "There's so much dust down here. I should really get you back upstairs."

"What about that tiara you were looking for?"

"It will keep. No, I think perhaps you've seen enough of this unpleasant little world for now."

I hesitated. My eye followed the line of hieroglyphs. Men, women, gods and goddesses, birds, snakes, abstract symbols. There was an animal I didn't recognize. It looked like a giraffe with a short neck and enormously long ears. I pointed at it and looked at Danilo. "What is this character?"

He inspected it. "No one knows, really. It was sacred to the god Set. In early times he was one of the greatest Egyptian gods. Later he was demonized—literally made into a demon. Linguists think 'Set' may be the original root of 'Satan.' Since no one has ever identified his animal, we simply call it the Set animal."

"It's an odd-looking thing."

"Like no animal known to science. There's a lot of reason to think the cult of Set lasted for thousands of years, cultivated privately by kings and their priests. Here is Set's symbol on the coffin of a king's nephew. In the Middle Ages the sacred fools were symbolized by a kind of donkey that may have its origins in this little symbol."

"You mean Satan worship?"

"Not exactly. But it's as good a name for it as any. But it's time for us to go back upstairs, don't you think?" He put a hand on my shoulder and we left the room. Something in the way he had talked about it made me think it meant something to him personally, not just academically.

In the corridor I helped him pull the door shut. And we went back the way we had come. Something else scuttled away from us at one point, I couldn't see what. After a few moments we were back at the ground floor. Afternoon light dazzled my eyes.

For a moment we stood awkwardly looking at each other. I tried to think of something to say that wouldn't make me sound like a gosh-wow kid.

"Are you serious about wanting to work here?"

The question caught me a bit off guard. I had thought we were just making idle conversation before. "I think I would, yes. I do want to get a job, and I find all this really interesting. These last few months haven't been easy for me. Something to help me take my mind off it all would…"

"I read about you finding that boy. It must have been terrible."

"Terrible doesn't begin to describe it, Danilo."

We walked toward the front entrance. "Had you known him?"

"Only slightly. His friend was a friend of mine. In fact we're sharing an apartment now."

"Finding him that way…and on the night of your recital." He smiled so I'd know he wasn't being ironic.

"It was one of the most horrible nights of my life. I don't even remember much of it anymore."

We had reached the door. Again Danilo smiled. "That's really too bad, Jamie. To hear Chopin played like that. With that much feeling. I still cherish the memory."

"Thank you." I looked away from him.

"I had friends there too that night. They all had the same reaction."

I felt flattered and a bit embarrassed at the same time. I was an eighteen-year-old kid who'd played a college recital. I knew I wasn't that good. "I just put what I was feeling into the music, that's all."

"Perhaps that's enough."

I wanted to feel his arm around me again. Instead he took a few steps away from me. "Let me see what I can do about getting you a job here, all right?"

"I'd really appreciate it." I wanted him to make love to me. I wanted that. "I'll see you at class on Wednesday. Thanks for spending so much time with me."

"It was my pleasure." He started to go back inside. Then he stopped and added, almost like an afterthought, "Chopin was one of us, you know."

It couldn't have been more unexpected. And I wasn't at all sure what he meant. I didn't think he was simply talking about the composer's friend Tytus. He meant something more than that. What, exactly, was lost on me. "Thank you again. I'll see you on Wednesday."

When I got home there were police. Mrs. Kolarik was with them in her place, in a bit of a dither. "These gentlemen have been waiting for you, Jamie."

One of them was Detective Wellman. He had questioned me back when I found Grant, and had been in touch two more times, asking follow-up questions. I said hello and invited him upstairs to our place. Bubastis sniffed curiously at his shoes, and he rubbed her back. He explained he just had a few more questions, things I might have noticed that night but that had slipped my mind. He tried to jog my memory about some things, but it was no good. I had told him everything I knew back then; maybe if my mind had been clearer when I found Grant, it would have been different. But that night was so…I felt useless.

"Do you have any leads, detective?"

"Nothing really, Jamie. We're questioning everyone who might have seen or heard anything again. But as for leads—" He spread his hands apart to express how little they had to go on. "The reason we're here is that another body has been found only a few yards from where you found that other one. One of the students who disappeared last autumn. We were hoping you might have remembered noticing someone or something you hadn't before."

Justin came in. He was working at the library for the summer. He and Detective Wellman recognized each other from the investigation. There was a bit of hope in his voice as he asked, "Have you found anything?"

"No, I'm afraid not." He told Justin what he had told me about the latest body being found, and asked if he had perhaps remembered anything about Grant that might have provided a clue. But he was no more help than I was.

"Oh, I…I…I just have to go to my room." He left us. It had brought up all the memories, I could tell.

After a few more minutes the detectives left. I switched on my keyboard and began playing idly, a bit of Schubert, thinking through the day's happenings. To work with Danilo…I was afraid I'd have dreams that night, disturbing ones about being trapped in a maze of underground corridors, chased by rats.

Mrs. Kolarik knocked timidly at the door. "Are they gone?"

"Yes. It was nothing, really."

"Do you know something about these deaths?"

I told her about finding Grant that night. She made the expected comments about how awful it must have been, and I assured her it was.

"Do you…do you have any idea what might have happened?" She avoided looking me in the eyes. "Or who might have done it? Or why?"

"Not really, no."

"My son Steven was...I shouldn't bother you with this."

I had no idea what she might have on her mind. I made the polite comment: It was no bother.

"Steven was one of the first young men to disappear. Almost two years ago."

"Oh, Mrs. Kolarik, I'm sorry. I didn't have any idea that—"

"Well, no, of course not. How could you?"

I was lost for what to say to her.

"He was a senior in political science. I still remember how proud I was when one of his professors called him a rising star in the department. Then he was gone. This is his apartment you're living in."

Oh. Not knowing how to react, I made a neutral comment, sympathy: "It must have been so hard for you."

She seemed suddenly embarrassed by our conversation. "I shouldn't trouble you with this."

"It's no trouble, believe me."

"You have your own problems. I shouldn't be so selfish. But having someone to talk about it..."

We talked for a few more minutes, nothing substantial, mutual expressions of condolence. She said goodbye and I went back to my playing.

It was no good. A wave of restlessness had come over me. I tried to nap for a while but it was no good either. I went to the pool and did some laps. Justin was there too; I hadn't heard him go out. He was working on his springboard dives, and afterward we went out for pizza.

CHAPTER 3

Yes, there were dreams that night.

I looked into Danilo's eyes and seemed to lose myself there. Large, sad, dark eyes, with the whole world contained in them.

I was at Danilo's side, and he had his arm around me. I let him pull me inside himself.

The pyramids loomed over us under a brilliant moon, and we made love more passionately than I had ever known.

Always we were in darkness, or near darkness, and having him beside me was the only thing that made it bearable. The lightest touch, even the scent of his breath made me ecstatic.

And then I woke and felt so foolish.

Justin got up at about the same time I did. We sat at the kitchen table eating cereal. I poured a small dish of milk for Bubastis, and she purred happily and lapped it up.

My mood must have been obvious to him. "You look like you haven't been sleeping well."

"I've been having the strangest dreams." I knew as soon as I said it he'd assume I was dreaming about the night I'd found Grant. But I didn't want to tell him the truth. A crush on my teacher. How…undergraduate. I liked to think of myself as more sophisticated than that.

He drank some juice. "I'm haunted by it too." He made himself smile. "I wish I wasn't."

"You'll get over it." I felt self-conscious at mouthing such a cliché, but I really couldn't think of anything else to say.

"I don't want to, Jamie."

"You'll meet someone else."

He fell silent. I knew what he was thinking: "You're not over it, so how can you expect me to be?" And it was true, I wasn't over it. The thought of that night still made me go numb, or sick to my stomach, or both. I needed Danilo, if only for that.

I tried to change the subject. "How's your geology class?"

He shrugged. "I'm not cut out for science. But this one's being taught by a grad assistant. I'll do better. How's Egyptology?"

"Actually, I find it pretty intriguing. I'm not sure why." I poured myself a glass of milk.

"Probably because it makes you feel like you're in one of those silly old movies you love. What's the professor like?"

"Danilo Semenkaru. Um…he's gorgeous. Damn close to irresistible."

"That's why."

I laughed. "No, it isn't just that. There's something about it all—the style, the design, what little I know about their culture so far—that all seems…I don't know…right to me."

"How mysterious."

"I feel like Zita Johann in *The Mummy*."

"There, you see what I mean? Besides, I never saw it."

"You should. It's a terrific movie."

"Maybe I will some day." He didn't mean a word of it. "What happens to her?"

"Well…she goes through a lot of hell before she gets her happy ending."

"So do smart-ass boys who flirt with their professors. I don't know why you bother with those old movies. They're in black and white." He wrinkled his nose to show his distaste.

Why did I think I'd ever fit in among jocks? If I didn't love swimming so much… "Danilo says he might be able to get me a part-time job in the department."

"Danilo? So we're on a first-name basis already, are we? You move mighty fast."

Again I laughed. "Or he does."

"He has a really odd name."

"It's not odd, Justin, just foreign."

"Where's he from, then?"

"I don't know. Someplace in Eastern Europe, I think."

"Aha! Transylvania!"

"Don't be silly. Besides, Bela Lugosi never sounded so sexy."

"Boy, you've got it bad, haven't you?"

I did. And I knew it. We fell into another of those awkward silences.

"Jamie, I don't mean to keep dwelling on it, but…the whole thing with Grant dying the way he did…I…"

"Hmm?"

"I'm thinking of transferring to another school."

"Oh." It was unexpected. "I'll miss you if you do."

"You're a good friend. I'd miss you too. But every time they find another body—every time I hear another rumor about someone who's missing, even—I remember Grant. Even just seeing one of the other gymnasts work out makes me feel so…I don't know if I can stand being here anymore."

Bubastis jumped onto my lap and started purring. I rubbed her ears. "It doesn't make any sense to me, Justin, but living here with you, even for this short time—this feels more like a home to me than anything I've ever known."

"Little lost Jamie."

"Don't make fun of me."

"I wasn't. I can't transfer till the January semester at the earliest. I'll see how things go till then." He looked away and added, "I kind of feel that same way, though. I really would miss you."

"Thanks."

"You really want to work with mummies?"

"I don't know. I need a job to help occupy my mind."

He made his voice sweetly ironic. "A job with Danilo."

"Don't be dumb, Justin. He's my teacher. It would violate all kinds of policies."

"They've been violated before this."

"My own ethics haven't."

"Lord, lord, lord, an athlete with a sense of personal ethics. What won't they think of next?"

"How about an athlete with a bitchy streak a mile wide?"

Bubastis jumped onto the table and tried to get at the milk in my bowl. I let her drink.

"You're going to spoil her, Jamie."

"Good." I put on a smug grin. "No one's ever spoiled me. So I have to do double work to make up for it."

She slapped at a floating bran flake with her paw and got milk all over the tabletop. I picked her up, nuzzled her, and put her on the floor. She jumped up again. Justin and I both laughed at her persistence.

"You deserve to be spoiled, Jamie. You're a good guy."

"If only someone would chase me as single-mindedly as Bubastis goes after her milk."

"Someone will."

Feeling restless, I did extra laps in the pool that morning. Tim stood at the side and watched me. His wedding had been the week before. Even at a distance I could see the ring on his left hand. Afterward he tried to talk to me. I was short with him. His eyes were so green, like Danilo's. It was a bit unsettling.

"Hi, Jamie."

"Tim."

"How's it goin'?"

"Okay, I guess." I was as abrupt with him as I could manage.

"Good. You deserve it."

"I deserve a bit of peace, don't you think?" I toweled off and tried to ignore him.

"What are you doing these days?"

"Fingering dead bodies." I walked away from him, into the locker room to get dressed. He called after me, but I kept going.

Then I headed to the fine arts building. Roland was nowhere around; it wasn't like him to be late for a lesson. I sat down at the piano and thumbed through some music. There were some pieces by Poulenc I had never played. I started the three *Mouvements Perpétuels*—dark, restless, agitated music. It felt good under my fingers.

After a few minutes Roland came in, without my noticing.

When I had played through them the third time he finally coughed to let me know he was listening.

"Roland. 'Morning."

"Maybe you ought to think about specializing in twentieth-century music, Jamie." He crossed the room to me and thumbed through the sheets. "This is difficult stuff, and you're playing it wonderfully. Have you been practicing them without mentioning it?"

"No, I just found them here."

"Do you want to explore this repertoire more?" He sat on the bench beside me.

"As long as I don't have to give up my Chopin."

"Absolutely not. With this stuff, you're good. With Chopin, you're almost brilliant."

That "almost" stung a bit, but I knew I had a long way to go, despite what Danilo said. I started playing through them again.

"The first one," Roland said, "was used in Hitchcock's *Rope*. He was a bigot but he had a sense of irony, I guess. A hateful little movie."

"I know. I've seen it."

He sat and listened. Every now and then he'd interrupt me with suggestions for fingering or technique. Sometimes he'd put his hands on top of mine to show me the correct way to approach a passage. It wasn't the same as when Danilo touched me. But the time passed quickly.

Then it was time for Egyptology class. Determined not to let my crush on Danilo get the better of me, I decided to focus on the artifacts in the museum. There was so much in the Egyptian rooms: jewelry, small sculptures, ancient things from ancient tombs. Without realizing it I found myself staring into the face of Neferu-Set again. Set: the devil-god. Danilo had said there was a cult devoted to him among the kings, and here was this nephew of a pharaoh with the god's name part of his own.

A few other students came in, groups of two and three, and began looking around. One of the guys, who I recognized as a basketball player, started making fairly obvious jokes about it all, lame puns on "mummy" and "mother." I didn't much want to talk to them.

I was curious what else might be stored in the subbasements. Not actually expecting to go down, I ambled to the head of the descending staircase. It was closed off with a velvet rope; the brass fittings at either end were turning green. From it hung a notice: NO ADMITTANCE. I was tempted to step over it and go down, even though I was sure I'd become lost down there if I did.

There were still twenty minutes till class. I looked around. There was no one in sight. Carefully, and I hoped unobtrusively, I stepped across it and began to go downstairs. Guiltily I kept looking back over my shoulder.

And so I didn't see the man who was coming up. Rather elderly, gray hair, gray skin. Thick eyeglasses, bad suit. "This area is off-limits to students. Can't you read?"

I stuttered, "Are you an Egyptologist?"

"I'm a Romanist, not that that makes any difference. What are you doing here?"

"I'm...er...I'm looking for Professor Semenkaru. I'm one of his students."

He stared at me, not buying it. "Really."

"He showed me some of the storage rooms down there yesterday. In the second subbasement."

"Indeed."

"I thought he might be down there."

"This stairwell is clearly posted as off-limits to students. If you want Professor Semenkaru, you can find him in his office. Or leave a message for him there."

"Yes, sir."

From below we heard the sound of footsteps. A moment later Danilo came up into sight. He looked from one of us to the other. "Jamie. Feld. Is there some problem?"

"I found this student sneaking downstairs."

Danilo smiled. "Not sneaking, surely. Professor James Feld, this is Jamie Dunn. I'm planning to hire Jamie as my research assistant."

Feld looked doubtful. "You should have introduced him to everyone."

"Well, it just developed yesterday. Nothing's finalized yet. You know how long it can take to get all the paperwork through. Really, Feld, there's no cause for alarm."

Feld muttered a few more words of disapproval and left us. Danilo laughed a bit as he watched him go, then turned to me. "You shouldn't go down there till everything's official. There are a lot of valuable things in storage, more than most people realize. Besides, it's quite a maze. You could easily get lost and join the mummies without ever intending to."

"I just thought I might find you, that's all."

"It's no problem." He smiled to show me that it was a problem, at least a bit of one. "Wait until we have the chance to get you orientated down there, all right?"

"Absolutely." I felt an inch tall.

"And Jamie?"

"Yes?"

"Whatever you do, don't go below the second subbasement. There are several levels below it. You're not to go there. I'll show them to you when the time is right."

Still another odd statement. "Yes, Danilo."

"I'm perfectly serious. I don't want you below the second sublevel. Not now, perhaps not ever. Am I being clear?"

It was the first time he had talked to me as an authority figure. A bit to my surprise, it only made him more attractive to me.

"Believe me, it won't happen again."

Suddenly he smiled at me, a genuine smile this time. He reached up and brushed his fingers through my hair, as he had done the previous day. "Now, come on. We're both going to be late for class."

We climbed the stairs together. I was a bit shaken from the little conflict. "This must be the only building on campus with no elevators."

"There's one at the back of the building for freight. Some of the exhibits are so heavy. But most people never go above the second floor. The money is better spent elsewhere."

"I was only saying, not complaining."

"You mustn't let Feld intimidate you. He'll try."

"I know the type."

"He's the senior member of the antiquities department. He's practically old enough to be one himself."

"Do you have trouble telling him from the mummies?"

He laughed. "To be honest, no. Take a good look at him. Who would waste the money to embalm him?"

I had been meaning to ask him about his status at the university. "Does 'visiting professor' mean you'll be gone next year?" I made the question sound casual; but I was terrified he'd say yes.

"Technically. But seasoned Egyptologists aren't exactly thick on the ground."

"So you'll be here for a while?"

He brushed his fingers through my hair again and smiled at me. "I think so, yes."

God, how I wanted to kiss him. Each of us wanted the other. It was so clear. Neither of us could do anything about it.

"Besides, I find I rather like Pittsburgh."

"So, do I, Danilo. But I'm from a farm. After Europe, this place must seem…"

"Uneventful?" He was wry.

"I guess that's one way of putting it."

"There's a lot here that interests me. And I like this campus. It's the largest I've ever worked on. All these people, all this activity. All these athletes." He reached for my hair again; obviously he liked it.

I backed a step away from him. "We shouldn't. We're student and teacher. Soon to be professor and assistant, I hope. There are standards, ethics."

"Do they matter to you so much?"

"It's not a question of them mattering to me, or you. They matter. People would disapprove. Your position here—and mine, for that matter."

"They couldn't find someone else with my qualifications for what they're paying me."

"Even so. They might—"

"They won't." He said it so emphatically it startled me. His supreme confidence was...well, it turned me on. At the same time, I knew how impractical it was even if he didn't. Coach Harrison's lesson was still not lost on me. Before I could say so he went on. "Surely the man who finds all that meaning beneath the surface of Chopin must have some idea what I am about too."

He kept saying things that didn't quite make sense, as if there was something there in front of me I couldn't see but that he expected me to. "I—I don't want you to leave West Penn, that's all."

"I won't, Jamie." He lowered his voice to a smooth, silky whisper. "Not without you."

"I mean it."

"Jamie, so do I. Not unless I have no choice. And even then I'll make provision for you."

He touched my cheek. There was electricity in it. Or energy. Or...I didn't know what. But the touch of his fingertip thrilled me.

"You and I, Jamie, are bound by ties much stronger than anything the university could understand."

I looked into his eyes. And I believed him.

We heard some other students coming up the steps, and we stepped apart. They were talking and giggling among themselves and barely seemed to notice us. They went into the classroom and we followed.

"Good afternoon, everyone." He checked the class roll. Everyone present. I overheard two of the girls whispering. They both had crushes on him. I can't tell you how smug it made me feel.

The lecture that day was on the earliest beginnings of Egyptian civilization. We learned how the country had been fragmented, a patchwork quilt of little fiefdoms, till it was united by the great warrior-king Narmer around 3100 BCE. We traced the reigns of his first descendants and saw slides of their tombs and monuments, those of them that still survived from that far-off time.

The earliest kings, he told us, had not written their names in cartouches like the more familiar later pharaohs. Instead they put their names in rectangular frames called *serekhs*, which represent-ed the facade of the royal palace. You could always tell when a *serekh* had a pharaoh's name inscribed in it: It was mounted by a falcon, emblem of the god Horus.

But as the slides were projected I noticed some of the early kings also had the Set animal atop their *serekhs*, side by side with the falcon. And one of them had only the Set animal. So the cult of the demon-god went back to the beginning of history.

I waited for Danilo to explain the cult and the strange animal, but he only said that the two figures represented religious unifica-tion. As he explained it he winked at me. Apparently the truth about the Egyptian kings and their private devotion to Set—Satan?—was for me alone.

He expected us to do research papers. We could choose any aspect of Egyptian history or society that interested us. After class he was surrounded by students wanting to field ideas for them. I left without talking to him again.

My coaches had always told me what coaches everywhere tell their athletes, I think: When you're upset or preoccupied, work out till it passes. Make yourself too tired to think about whatev-er's on your mind. Even if you're simply falling in love, or in lust. I went to the gym and swam. It didn't work. I knew I was falling in love with Danilo.

It was not an at-first-sight thing as it had been with Tim. With Danilo, the more I knew him the more I wanted to. I don't know how much a boy of eighteen can know about love, real love, but it seemed to me I was learning.

That night, in the darkness of my room, Danilo came to me.

It was a warm night; all my windows were open. There was a summer breeze. Outside, as I was nodding off, I could see the quarter moon rising, white and enormous.

Then I was deep asleep. Bubastis was on my pillow, purring softly. I didn't know if I was dreaming, and I didn't care. There he was, sitting on the edge of the bed. Bubastis got up and crossed to him; he picked her up and cuddled her, and she licked his cheek.

I sat up. "How did you get here? How did you know where I live?" The breeze stirred the curtains.

Instead of answering he kissed me. A long, deep, passionate kiss. It sounds corny, but it thrilled me; I felt like I had never really been alive before. I kissed back, hard as I could. He stroked my cheek.

A sudden stiff gust rattled the windows. I opened my eyes. And was alone.

Very early the next morning, before the sun was up, I showered, dressed, and went out. First I took a long walk. It was unusual for me; I had never been much for aimless strolls. Shadyside is an old section of the city, filled with wonderful Victorian houses. Sunrise made it all beautiful in a way I hadn't noticed before.

Then to the gym, much earlier than was usual for me. I swam for more than an hour, hoping to…I didn't know what. To tire myself beyond my romantic fixation on Danilo, I suppose. I hadn't had a calm night's sleep for days. I was beginning to feel the strain. Still, Coach Zielinski said I was performing better and better.

While I was in the shower Tim came in. He stood under the showerhead next to me and posed, obviously wanting to attract my attention. "Morning, Jamie."

"Tim." I turned to face away from him.

"Let me wash your back."

I couldn't believe I was hearing it. My voice dripping with sarcasm, I asked him what would happen if someone saw us.

"It's too early for anyone else to be here."

"Still," I mimicked his best paranoid style, "someone might come in." I pretended to have a terrible realization. "Maybe your mother!"

"Jamie, stop it."

I turned into Ingrid Bergman and made a big, melodramatic gesture. "Oh Tim, I'd simply die if anyone knew."

Tim caught me by the shoulders and shook me. "Will you stop it, for Christ's sake?"

I pushed him away. "You're the one who needs to stop it. How many times do I have to say it?"

"I want you."

"You had me. You ended it. Whose problem is that?"

Pleading was getting him no place. He switched to a different tack. His voice turned slightly menacing. "Jamie, I'm bigger than you."

It caught me a bit off guard. "Are you threatening me with rape?"

"Don't put it like that."

"But that's what this is, isn't it? 'Make love to me or I'll force you.'" I rinsed off and started to walk away. He caught me by my shoulders again. I pushed him hard. He slammed into the wall and I kept going.

"Stop!"

I kept walking.

"Jamie, stop!"

I turned and looked at him.

"Don't make me do it, Jamie."

"The only thing I want to make you do is leave me alone. How many times do I have to repeat that?"

"Jamie, will you think? We have the perfect cover now." He held up his hand to show me his wedding ring, as if I might not have noticed it before. "No one will suspect. You should find a nice girl too. Then we'd be free to—"

"*Nice*? Is that really the adjective you mean?"

"I want you. I'm going to have you."

I walked back to him and got in his face. "Now, listen to me, Tim. If you ever touch me again—so much as touch me—I'll shout rape so loud they'll hear me on the other end of the campus. See how long that ring stays on your finger then."

The threat shook him. "You—you wouldn't. It would ruin your career here too."

"I'd be the unwilling victim, remember?"

"You wouldn't do that."

"Push me just a bit further and see."

I could see half a dozen emotions in his face, none of them pleasant. He seemed not to know how to react. I had no idea if I'd really do what I threatened, but the mere threat was enough to stop him. I started to go again.

"Jamie."

I paused and looked back over my shoulder.

"Jamie, I love you."

"Jamie," I mimicked him, "I love you and I'm going to brutalize you. What an empty human being you are." We stared at each other without speaking for a few moments, then I turned and kept walking.

Behind me he whimpered something, I couldn't hear what. And I didn't care. I got dressed, got my things and left.

A few minutes later I was at the fine arts building. I needed Chopin. Not the quiet music, I played the wild, agitated Chopin, the études, the polonaises.

Roland came in and I stopped. "You're early today, Roland. Everyone seems to be."

He shrugged. "Sleepless night. I shudder to think what I must look like."

"I just saw Tim."

"You're on the same team. You can't really avoid him, can you?" He was looking for something in his briefcase.

"He threatened to rape me if I don't go back to him."

Roland froze. It took him a moment to react. "Would he do it?"

I played a few notes. "I don't know. He's four inches taller than I am. He's probably stronger, if it comes to that."

"Do you want me to do anything?"

"No, I just need to talk."

"If someone calls him on it—"

"That's what I told him. I told him if he ever even touches me again I'll tell everyone on campus."

He sat down on the bench beside me. "That's usually enough to silence that type. 'Oh, good gosh, I could never have anyone know!'"

"I know it. I think he's scared. He got married last week."

Roland laughed. "They always think they're being so subtle."

I fingered a key. "I'm scared too."

"Never mind that he's bigger than you—would he actually do anything to hurt you?"

"I don't know. He has a pretty big ego. Even when we were in high school."

"Swimmers do."

I looked at him.

"Not you, Jamie. Whatever you are, you're not a typical jock."

It was something I needed to hear, just then. "Thanks. But you're right. He doesn't seem to be able to deal well with rejection."

"Why don't you let me have a word with him? Discreetly. I think I can scare him so he'll never bother you again."

I stood up, nervous, then sat down again. "Can you do that? If he knows I told someone about this—"

"Then he'll know he'd be the first one suspected if anything happens to you."

I think I was actually shaking. He put an arm around my shoulder.

"Please, Roland. Just make him go away."

"I'm a piano teacher, not Houdini. But I'll do what I can."

I hugged, him, thanked him and started to gather up my things. It was almost time for class.

My mind wasn't really on Egyptology that day. Danilo lectured on the Old Kingdom, the early period when the pyramids were built. I followed what he said, but in a distracted kind of way. When I was a kid sometimes some of the other kids would threaten me with beatings or worse. To have someone who said he loved me threaten me that way...I had no idea how to sort through all the unpleasant emotions.

When it came time for questions the other students all had the same thing on their minds: slaves. Danilo had said once there was no force involved in building the great monuments. The workers did what they did to keep busy during the infertile times in the Nile Valley. And out of love for the king. When he said that last bit, he looked straight at me.

But the class didn't believe him. Everyone "knows" slaves built the pyramids. The little dispute went on and on; I was bored with it and with my classmates. Danilo finally ended it by suggesting the more insistent among them do their research papers on the subject.

After class I lagged behind everyone else, I guess because of my mood. Danilo came over to my desk and asked me what was wrong.

There was hardly any way I could tell him. I made a vague comment about personal problems and hoped he'd let it go at that.

"Is there anything I can do to help, Jamie?"

"I don't think so, but thanks."

"I can be a good listener."

"No, really. Thanks, Danilo, but there wouldn't be any point."

He put a hand on my shoulder. "Will you let me take you to dinner later?"

"Thanks, but I don't think so." Being near him wouldn't have helped, not after what happened with Tim. "I really appreciate it but…but I think I need to be alone for a while."

His grip on my shoulder tightened a bit. "You're not alone, Jamie. Not anymore."

I knew he meant this in a positive way, but it wasn't really what I needed to hear. So many times he had seemed to be telling me something I couldn't know or understand by myself. I stood up. "A rain check, okay?"

He smiled. "I'll tell you what. I'll be in my office most of the afternoon. Downstairs, Room 353. Stop by later, if you feel like it, and we'll have dinner, all right?"

"I'm not sure I feel like it. I don't mean to blow you off, but—"

"No, no, it's quite all right. You know what you need."

I thanked him again, gathered up my things, and left.

Back at the apartment I switched on the keyboard and tried to play, but nothing felt right. I thought for a moment about going to back to the gym and doing some more laps, but there was no way I could do that. I kicked off my sneakers and stretched out on the couch.

Bubastis had been sleeping under my bed. She came out, yawned, and stretched, then came right to me. Purring happily, she jumped onto my chest and curled up. A few moments later I fell asleep.

I woke up late in the afternoon. There had been dreams again, not about Danilo this time but about Tim, forcing himself on me. The dream had aroused me. When I realized it I felt a bit sick.

Justin was home. He looked into my room. "I was wondering how long you'd sleep."

I sat up and yawned. "Long, lousy day."

"Why? What happened?"

He wasn't really the one to talk about it with. I told him I hadn't slept well and felt out of sorts all day, and hoped he'd leave it at that. Thankfully he did.

"I was thinking I'd bake a homemade pizza for dinner. Should I make it for two?"

"Oh, thanks, Jus, but I'm not really hungry. I think I need to take a walk or I'll never sleep tonight."

"I know what you mean. I hate being like that."

I pulled my shoes on and got up. Justin disappeared back into the kitchen. Bubastis was off somewhere, doing something only another cat could understand. I went out.

The sun was already low in the sky. It would be a warm evening. I walked around the neighborhood, lost in my thoughts, ignoring all the beautiful houses. I nearly walked past a voice student I knew. She planted herself in front of me. I made some embarrassed small talk, gave her an excuse, and got away from her. All day long I' d been telling people I'd had a bad day; I was sick of it.

I couldn't swim. I didn't want to go anywhere near the gym.

There was a practice meet that weekend in Philadelphia. Being on the bus with Tim for the trip would be unbearable.

There was the museum. There was Danilo. I wasn't at all sure being with him that evening was what I needed. But I honestly had no idea what else to do with myself.

Room 353. The door was slightly open. I pushed it a bit. It was empty. I stepped inside. It was larger than the other faculty offices I'd seen. Compared to Roland's it was like a pavilion.

On the walls hung framed papyri, images of gods and pharaohs, pages from *The Book of the Dead*, some things I couldn't recognize offhand. There was a long golden knife on the desk, covered with engraved hieroglyphs; I wondered why it wasn't down in the vault. And there were some beautiful old engravings, Victorian I thought, of places in Egypt. The pyramids, the colossi of Ramses the Great at Abu Simbel, temples and tombs, even a study of crocodiles on the bank of the Nile. Danilo's world. Strange, beautiful, unlike anything I knew.

On his desk an oversize book sat open, more old engravings. When I realized what it was open to I froze, astonished. It was a line drawing, intricate, elaborately detailed. Two pharaohs stood facing each other in a field of reeds and flowers. Each wore the royal crown; I didn't understand how that could be. One was slightly larger than the other, or maybe slightly older. A man and a boy. Each extended a hand to touch the other one's shoulder. And they were kissing.

I told myself I couldn't be seeing that, couldn't be interpreting it properly. If the kings of Egypt had been—

Then I noticed the label at the bottom of the engraving: THE KISSING KINGS. 18TH DYNASTY. AMARNA.

The Kissing Kings. It was impossible to mistake their embrace, the affection. Even in the formal style of Egyptian art it was possible to see they were in love. And all I could think was that of all the million Egyptian images Danilo could have been studying, this was the one he chose.

It was one thing too many to think about that night. I

walked for hours, around the campus, around my neighbor-hood. There were stars. There was a late moon. Academic Tower was floodlit, as always after dark. I couldn't see them at all; all I could see was Danilo.

It suddenly dawned on me that the next day was my birthday. Nineteen. Why did I still feel like a kid?

Next morning a card came in the mail. Plain white, with just a written greeting on it, "For your special day, because everything about you is special. D." I wondered how he knew the day. And how he knew I wouldn't want to be fussed over. I had never wanted that. Not that there had ever been a chance of it before.

CHAPTER 4

For the next month things continued pretty much that same way. Swimming; work with Roland on Chopin, Poulenc, and Schubert; ancient Egypt. Danilo and I talked often after class. Once he took me down to the catacombs again to show me a few things he had discussed in his lecture.

Except for the fact there were no classes, weekends weren't much different. I practiced on my keyboard instead of the grands at the fine arts building; I read about Egypt instead of hearing Danilo's lectures.

And most nights I dreamed; most nights it was about Danilo. Well, Danilo and me.

There were times I felt like I didn't have a life independent of all that. I complained about it to Justin once.

"That's your, life, Jamie. It's the one you chose."

I hadn't realized it, but he was right. "It's going to seem really strange when the fall semester starts and I have to take other classes."

"Poor Jamie, his life is turning ordinary."

"Poor Justin, he got the crap kicked out of him by his room-mate for being a smart-ass."

The student union at West Penn is a reconverted hotel from the belle epoque, a huge, ornate building I loved. Afternoons when class was over and weekends after swim practice I used to sit and relax there in one of the large rooms that were filled with sofas and plush chairs. Now and then I'd nap.

Late one Friday as I was nodding off there I heard Danilo's voice.

"Men always look sweeter asleep."

I opened my eyes and gaped at him, a bit surprised. I hadn't seen him anywhere but the museum. "Danilo. Hi." Without quite realizing it I yawned.

He smiled. "Maybe it's the innocence. Or the illusion of it."

He was in shorts, a tight tank top, and sneakers. I had never seen him dressed so casually before. His body was lean, smooth, and muscular, even better than I'd imagined. His legs were just perfect. I couldn't help thinking he had the body of a king from one of the old Egyptian carvings. But in the light there he looked older than he had before; if I hadn't known better I'd have taken him for a man in his fifties.

I started to tell him he had seen me asleep before. But I caught myself; that had only been in my dreams. I yawned and sat up. "I'm sorry you're seeing me this way."

"It's all right, Jamie. As I said, you look—" He broke off, made a vague gesture with his right hand, and smiled. "I wanted to give you the news right away. The paperwork came through. You are my assistant."

It took a moment to register. It seemed like I'd been waiting forever. "That's great. I can finally see those subbasements." I tried to make it sound like a joke, but I was genuinely curious.

"Not yet. You're not to go lower than I've taken you." His voice was stern. "Do you understand that?"

"I was only making a joke, Danilo."

"It is not amusing."

"Sorry."

"You're to go to the student employment office and sign something or other. You begin Monday."

"Sure. I'll go right now."

He sat down next to me. "No, let it wait for a while. Have you eaten?"

"No."

"Then let me buy you lunch to celebrate."

Ten minutes later we were at a local eatery, waiting for take-out. Then we walked across the Panther Hollow Bridge to that same park where Tim and I had gone that first night.

It was a brilliant summer day, floods of sunlight, a few wispy white clouds. The park was in full flower, a riot of color. There were sunbathers and people running. Danilo looked at the near-naked guys and smiled a lot. "Do you run, Jamie?"

I told him no.

"I do. It's the best exercise for me. I find I can think more clearly when I'm running."

"Like the pharaohs." He had told us the ancient kings always celebrated their jubilees by running the perimeter of a symbolic course that represented their realm.

He seemed pleased that I remembered. "You're learning."

I knew the park was popular with a lot of students and faculty, but I hadn't been there since that night with Tim. The memories weren't pleasant. But that day, with Danilo...

We sat on the grass and ate. He asked me about my life before college.

"There's not a lot to tell. It was always boring."

"Bore me, then."

I laughed. "Ebensburg, Pennsylvania. Half dried-up farmland, half played-out coal mines. Lots of rusting machinery everywhere, tractors, mining equipment—not the kind of place where things like Chopin count for much."

"Chopin," he said with mock sternness, "counts everywhere."

I laughed. "I think I was a really naive kid. Or maybe inexperienced would be the word. Or callow, or trusting."

"Was that unusual there?"

"Not exactly unusual. But not really something you'd want to be. There were kids like me, and there were predators."

"There always are."

I shrugged. "I was different. In a lot of ways. Too many, I guess. I was a target."

"Frederick the Great used to say that if he hadn't been the son of a king, he would have been tormented to death by the other boys."

"Frederick and I would understand each other, then."

"More than you think. He was one of us too."

I looked at him, not sure what to say.

"And he always added that surviving that was what made him a good ruler."

He had used that turn of phrase about "one of us" before.

The first time I thought I knew what he meant. Now I wasn't so certain. "You're an Egyptologist. What do you know about Frederick the Great?"

"I know a lot of history. A lot." It might have been my romantic imagination, but I thought he sounded terribly sad when he said that.

"I used to spend time in the Ebensburg Public Library. As often as not, I was the only one there. It didn't help my image."

"Did they have the kind of book you wanted to read?"

I shook my head. "Once I got online I started finding things."

"There's more for you to discover, Jamie."

"I know it, believe me." Still again I wasn't quite sure what he meant. "There are things I'm anxious to learn about."

"Such as?"

I lowered my voice and looked away from him. It was time to be bold with him, I decided. I had made the first move with Tim, way back when. But with Danilo it was different. I actually found myself stammering. "The...the K-kissing Kings."

Danilo looked straight into my eyes. For a moment I couldn't read his expression. Then he smiled. "I think you already know about that. Something about it, at least."

"Not nearly as much as I want to."

We had finished eating. He stood up. "It's getting late. I have a department meeting at 4." It was the last thing I wanted him to say. Not then. Not after what I'd—

"Why don't you walk me to my office?"

I must have broken out in the largest grin. "Yes, boss."

The day was so gorgeous there were people everywhere, jogging, playing volleyball, basking in the sun. There were pairs of lovers holding hands. I swear the only one I saw was Danilo. We crossed the bridge back to the campus. Friends, acquaintances, said hello to one or the other of us. Us. It was the first time I thought of Danilo and had the word *us* come into my mind. *Us.*

At his office he invited me in and closed the door. "We don't want Feld interrupting us."

"Not now, no."

"There's an empty office down the hall. It'll be yours. It's small, but—"

"I don't need much room."

"I'll have to get you the keys."

There was an awkward silence. This wasn't what we wanted to be talking about, not either of us.

"What do you know about the Kissing Kings, Jamie?"

I told him I had seen the engraving in a book on his desk. I told him what I thought it meant.

"There is more to it than just that."

"What could there be?"

"You couldn't read their names."

"No. I'm not good with hieroglyphs yet, but I—"

"Suppose I told you the two men in the engraving are father and son?"

I didn't know how to react. "I—they—"

"Are you shocked?"

"No. Not at all. I mean, I've never had a father. I've never known how I'd…I don't know."

"And they are pharaohs, co-regents."

"I would have guessed that."

"And they knew secret things. Not just their love for each other, but deeper secrets."

I couldn't think of anything to say.

"The secrets are there for you, Jamie, if you want them." He touched my hair the way he always did.

"I want them. You know I want them."

He put his arms around me and we kissed.

And I had never been kissed before, not like that. I swear I felt all his energy rush into me, and it exhilarated me; I'd almost say it made me high.

For the longest time we sat there in each other's arms, kissing, fondling. I could have stayed forever.

There was a knock on the door. We pulled apart and arranged

our hair and clothes. It was one of the girls in my class, one of the ones who had a crush on him.

"Come in."

The door opened. "Excuse me, professor. I didn't know you had someone in here." She smiled at him, ignored me.

"It's all right, Jane. What can I do for you?"

"Well…" She had not stopped smiling at him. "I wanted to discuss my research paper with you. I have a topic I like, and—"

"After class on Monday, all right? I'm afraid Jamie here has a prior claim to my time this afternoon."

She looked at me dismissively. That geeky boy from the music department. "Oh. Well, I've found some interesting things about the Sphinx, and I—"

"Monday, Jane." He smiled at her and made his voice firm. "Please."

Suddenly her smile was gone. Her moment with the dreamy prof would have to wait. "Well, I'm not sure I can make it Monday."

"Some other time, then."

"But I—"

"I'm sorry, Jane. But Jamie was here first."

She finally gave up and left, looking more than slightly unhappy.

For a moment we stared at each other without talking. Then we broke out laughing.

"We really have to be careful, Danilo. She could spread a lot of scandal."

"She won't."

"You'll have to charm her next week."

"I will. I don't have many gifts, but that one I do know how to use. My wife used to tell me—"

"Wife?" It hit me like a sucker punch.

He realized how it had affected me, and he spoke slowly, deliberately. "Wife, yes. My family expected it. She's been dead for a long time."

"Oh." I was still reeling from the revelation. "I'm sorry."

"Don't be. It was an arranged thing. You know the Old World."

I laughed again. "I know Ebensburg. The same kind of thing

goes on there, pretty much. Only nobody ever acknowledges it. They just let you know what's expected of you, keeping up appearances and—" I shrugged.

I wanted, more than anything else in the world at that moment, to ask him if he had loved her. But of course there was no way I could.

Still, he knew what I was thinking. Very softly he said, "No, Jamie, you don't have to ask. I didn't."

I played dumb. "Didn't what?"

"I didn't love her." He shifted his weight and looked out the window. "I told you it was strictly a family thing, all arranged for me. I would never have—" He glanced at me and smiled a shy smile, then looked quickly away. "When I…when I made myself unavailable to her, she married my brother. Then she… It was all a long time ago."

"I'm sorry, Danilo, I didn't mean to pry."

"Yes, you did. And it's all right." With that gesture that had become so familiar by now, he touched my hair, ran his fingers through it. "You are such a beautiful man."

Right then I was so happy I could have cried. Instead I forced myself to say, "Danilo, we can't be doing this. You know how the university feels about faculty-student affairs."

Instantly he was himself again, confident and in control. "They won't do anything to us, Jamie. Not even if they find out about us, which I doubt they will." He looked directly at me. "I promise you that."

I gestured vaguely at the office door. "Jane…"

"She saw what she wanted to see, a rival student, nothing more."

"She's not dumb. And she's not the only one."

"Believe me, Jamie, they'll never understand what's happening between us. There's no way they could."

The smart-ass in me wanted to ask him, all right then, what is happening between us? But I kept my mouth shut for once. I touched his hand. "I hope you're right."

"I am."

"Thinking about it makes me a bit afraid."

"Don't be. You—we—are more important than you can imagine yet. And more powerful."

"Try telling that to the dean."

He took me by the front of my shirt and pulled me to him. And we kissed again.

Nothing else mattered, not my academic standing, not Tim, nothing. I actually found myself shaking. "Danilo, make love to me."

He stood up and took a step away from me. "Not yet, Jamie. Not till the time is right."

I wanted him so badly. "I'd do anything to have you here and now. I'd kill to feel you inside me."

Again he pulled me to himself and kissed me. I felt his hands exploring my body. I touched his. My palm pressed his naked thigh.

Then it was over. The time was getting late. "I have that department meeting. It started five minutes ago. I should get to it." He picked up his briefcase. "I'll see you in class Monday. All right?"

"Can't I see you tonight?"

"I have plans, I'm afraid. Soon, soon enough, we'll have all the time in the world together." He kissed me, lightly this time. "Believe me." And he was gone.

There in his office, once he left, I felt more alone than I think I ever had. I started collecting my things, started to go. Then I decided I had to see it again. The Kissing Kings. I sorted through a few books on his desk looking for that one.

It didn't take me long. They were exactly as I remembered them. Lean bodies, muscular legs, full lips; I tried to convince myself they looked like Danilo and me, but that was absurd.

I needed to get over to the fine arts building. There was a passage in one of the Chopin polonaises I wanted to work on, an exuberant piece of music that caught my mood at that moment. I had always focused on the darker Chopin. Now—there had to be music he wrote when he was in love. I'd find it, and I'd know it when I found it.

Another book on the desk caught my eye. Thick, heavy, over-sized, obviously an old book and I thought probably a rare one. Gilt-edged pages. Embossed gold letters on the leather binding. It was *The Book of the Dead*. I knew nothing about it except that it was a collection of spells for the dead, for the afterlife. But it was such a beautiful volume I found myself opening it and thumbing through it.

It was a bilingual edition. On the left pages were the hiero-glyphs, on the right an English translation. The title page said the translation was by a man called Flinders Petrie and carried the date 1878. It had to be worth a fortune. Danilo had told me there were valuable things in the department, but an antique book like this…I didn't expect it.

A purple silk bookmark hung out of the bottom of the vol-ume. I carefully turned to the page. Hieroglyphs, most of them indecipherable to me. And opposite them the words in English. "In the eyes, in the heart, in the genitals resides the power and the vitality. In them is the force of the magick. In those organs of the ones sacrificed is the secret to life unending."

It didn't seem to make sense. In a very small typeface there was a footnote to the English version. "According to many ancient reli-gions, the bodily organs of those sacrificed carry enormous magi-cal power. Cf. Lucan, *Civil Wars*, vi. 540–8 and Apuleius, *Golden Ass*, iii. 17. F.P."

This didn't clear it up at all. I'd have to ask Danilo about it.

Instead of the polonaises I worked on the waltzes. They had always seemed lightweight to me, trivial even. That day they fit my mood perfectly.

Except…why wouldn't he let me see him till after the weekend? I was terrified there might be someone else. Why did I keep find-ing men who had wives, or who used to?

I needed him. I needed…I didn't know what I needed. On a mad impulse I left a note for Justin, packed a few things, and headed down-town to the bus station. "Ebensburg, please. Round trip."

The Greyhound traveled slowly, more so than I would have liked. It seemed to stop at every town and wide spot in the road, Salt Lick, Pennsylvania; Gas Pit, Pennsylvania; Eighty-four, Pennsylvania… By the time we reached Ebensburg it was after dark. I found a pay phone and dialed Millie's number.

"Jamie." She sounded tired. "You decided to come home after all."

"Just for the weekend, Mil, just for a visit."

"Oh."

"I'm at the bus station. Can you come and pick me up?"

"I'll be there as soon as I can."

I stepped out of the station to wait. It was nearly 11. A large moon lit Main Street. Small town, narrow streets, streetlights so old they might qualify as antiques. There weren't many people in sight; they tended to go to bed early. It had been nearly a year since I had seen it.

Half an hour later Millie showed up in her battered old station wagon. She honked the horn as she pulled up, and I jumped in. I leaned over to kiss her cheek, and she pulled away from me. So much for my homecoming.

We chatted as she drove to the farm. I asked about her other kids. The younger ones were fine. When I asked about the oldest, Bobby, she changed the subject. Her husband Harry was, she said, "still Harry." He and I had never much liked each other.

"Everybody expected to see you at Tim's wedding."

Oh. "I couldn't come. Late finals." I hoped the lie would be convincing enough for her to drop the subject.

"We all knew what close friends you were when you were in school. Everyone was so happy he was getting married."

"To tell you the truth, Millie, we're not as close as we were. He didn't even invite me."

She looked me up and down, as if to say, well, what did you expect?

I kept talking. "How's Coach Harrison?"

"Not well. He had a stroke last month. The day after the wedding, in fact."

"That's too bad." I hoped she couldn't see me smiling in the dark car.

"What happened between you and Tim?"

"Nothing." I said it firmly. "Nothing happened at all. I think he just decided he had outgrown me, that's all."

"That's all?"

I made an exaggerated shrug. "We never really had that much in common. Can you imagine him at a Chopin recital?"

"I can't imagine anyone at a Chopin recital." She meant it.

When we reached the farm it was dark, no lights in the windows. Farmers go to bed early, get up early, work long days. I had gotten so used to living in a city it seemed strange to me.

Bobby and I had always shared a bedroom. I told her I'd be careful not to wake him.

She stiffened. "Bobby's in jail."

It didn't surprise me.

"He was caught selling drugs. A lot of them. You'll have the room to yourself."

"Is he okay?"

"That's why we were hoping you'd come home for the summer to help. I don't want to talk about it." She was pretty clearly resentful.

I headed to the room. Moonlight filled it; I didn't need a light. The bed wasn't made up. She had stacked some linens on it. I made it quickly, got undressed and tried to sleep.

Danilo. Could he find me here? I wondered. Would he come to me here?

When I finally slept my dreams were of a falcon-headed man. Lean muscular body, beautiful body. But the falcon was eating raw flesh. Blood dripped from its mouth. Welcome back, Jamie.

In the morning Harry said hello, then ignored me. Their two other kids were a lot younger. They regarded me as a curiosity. After breakfast I offered to wash the dishes.

The farm was dry. I could see how parched the earth was.

Harry spent the morning irrigating the fields. Corn, wheat, none of it as high as it should have been. Living in the city, I had barely noticed there was a drought.

Lunch was huge. Harry ignored me. I was eating his food and not helping on his farm. I did the dishes again, Millie went off to run errands, the kids played in the backyard. I went into the basement where the spinet was kept. It was badly out of tune; no one had touched it since I'd left. How had I ever lived there?

In the afternoon I sat on the back porch. There were hawks circling in the sky over the corn field.

Finally in the evening I found Millie in a friendlier mood. Her favorite TV program was preempted for a baseball game; I was the next-best amusement.

"Mil?"

"Hmm?"

"What was my father like?"

"Why do you want to know that?"

Unexpected question. "He was my father."

"You were never curious about him before."

I shrugged. "I am now. Tell me about him."

She obviously didn't want to.

"Please."

"Well…" I could tell she was reluctant to talk about him. "What do you remember about him?"

"Practically nothing. I wouldn't recognize him if you showed me a picture."

She got up and went to a drawer in the desk. There seemed to be a stack of old photos. She thumbed through them and found the one she wanted. "Here."

It was a stranger. A short, thick man, mustached, wearing an ill-fitting suit. I looked from the photo to her. In a thousand years I would never have guessed he was my father. "This is him?"

She nodded.

"I don't remember him at all."

She got another picture. "Here. This is your mother."

A plain girl in a plain dress. She looked sad. I couldn't have recognized her either.

"Why do you want to know about them, Jamie?"

I didn't quite know. "They're my parents."

"You never showed any interest before."

She was right. I didn't know why.

"Your father was a preacher. He had a little church down the valley. When he made your mother pregnant he blamed her for tempting him. And I guess it really was her fault for not being on the pill."

"Did they love each other?" Absurd question.

"How can you ever know who loves who?" She said it pointedly. I wasn't sure why. But then she pressed on. "When Tim was here for the wedding he told people things about you. Shameful things."

I went numb. One more betrayal. I had loved him. Why?

"I don't think it would be good for you to come back here anymore, Jamie. Harry doesn't—"

"Don't worry. I'll leave first thing in the morning."

"Please do. Take whatever of your things you want. I'll sell the rest."

I didn't want to let her know this hurt. But I couldn't keep it inside. "You can burn them for all I care."

That night I needed Danilo. Of all nights, that was the one I needed him to be there with me, if only in dreams. But I couldn't sleep. I even remember saying a short prayer to Horus, the god with the head of a falcon. Doing it made me feel a bit foolish.

I had never had a home. That was so clear to me now. I had merely had a place to live, which is not the same thing at all. But when I closed my eyes and conjured up an image of Danilo I thought, yes, my home is there, in him. What will I do if he doesn't love me as much as I love him?

First thing in the morning, before breakfast, I packed all my things and Millie drove me back to the bus station. She was quiet; her face was stone. Everything that needed to be said between us had been said, and there was an end to it.

Waiting for the bus I got myself a fast-food breakfast. There were hawks circling above the town. I stood and watched them for a while. Graceful, beautiful, predatory creatures. A few people I knew saw me waiting there. None of them were friendly; most ignored me completely.

When the bus came I got a window seat so I could see the last of my hometown. Then I slept for the rest of the trip.

At the station back in Pittsburgh I got off the bus, yawned, and stretched. It was 11 o'clock. Then I noticed the headline on the newspaper in the vending machine: "Three More Corpses Found on West Penn Campus."

Three.

When I got home it was just after noon and the apartment was empty.

"Justin?"

Bubastis came up to me, happy to see me. I picked her up and she licked the tip of my nose.

"Jus?"

He wasn't in. There was no food in the cat's dish, and no water for her either. It wasn't like Justin to ignore her. I fed her, gave her some water.

Suddenly I had an awful feeling. A shot of panic went through me. Could he have been one of the three? He couldn't be; it couldn't have happened to him.

Quickly I turned on the TV and tuned in to the local news channel. The story was just coming on. "Only one of the victims has been identified," the reporter said. "He is Timothy Johanssen, a swimmer on the West Penn team."

It was so completely unexpected. I sat and stared at the television, not knowing what to feel or what to think.

I don't believe love dies. It changes into something else. I had loved Tim so deeply, so much, even to the point of following him to the college he chose. It had turned ugly, or he had. But underneath what I felt for him was still that substrate of love. I suppose on some small level I had never stopped hoping things between us might… But I was being foolish. I knew that. Tim had been what he had been, and hoping otherwise had no point.

Almost without thinking I turned on my keyboard. Chopin, inevitably Chopin. I had never imagined I might actually play the funeral march for the death of someone I had loved. All the things that could have existed between us but never did and never would…I put all of them into what I was playing. The rest of the sonata didn't matter; I played the funeral march again and again.

After God knew how long I felt a hand on my shoulder. I kept playing. "Danilo."

"No, Jamie, it's me." I took my hands off the keys and looked. It was Justin.

"Jus!" I got to my feet and put my arms around him, and kissed him. "Oh God, Jus, it's so good to see you."

He let me get it out of my system, then took a step away from me. "You were only gone two nights. I can't wait to see how you greet me after a vacation."

"I thought…I thought you might be one of the new victims."

He seemed slightly astonished. "I'm fine, Jamie. Why would you think that?"

"Paranoia, I guess. I seem to be losing everything that matters to me. Home wasn't exactly…well, it wasn't exactly homey." I told him about my brief unhappy visit.

"Oh. I'm sorry, Jamie. You deserve better. Of all people, you deserve better."

"Thanks." I wanted to add, "It's nice that someone cares about me," but it would have been too corny. "And then the news about Tim. I mean, it's not like I loved him anymore, but still…"

"What news?"

He hadn't heard. I told him.

"Oh. Jamie, I'm so sorry."

I couldn't say anything.

"I have a bottle of wine. Should I open it?"

I nodded. "Thanks."

"Stop thanking me. We look out for each other, remember?" He went into the kitchen and got the corkscrew. "If you hadn't been there for me when Grant…" He cut himself short. The word about Tim was bringing up unpleasant things.

He poured large tumblers of wine for us. We sat on the couch, close together, and got drunk. Neither of us was much of a drinker; it didn't take much wine. At one point I got up and tried to play some more, but my fingers wouldn't respond. When I went back to the couch Justin kissed me, like a brother, not a lover.

I closed my eyes and thought of Danilo.

That night I sat at my bedroom window and watched the moon and the stars, exactly like the silly romantic I tried so hard not to be, and thought of all the things I had been feeling, all those emotions in so short a time.

The last of Ebensburg; I knew I would never go back again.

The last of Tim; I knew…hell, I didn't know what I knew about Tim and me. I knew there had not been an end to it, not a neat simple one, and I wasn't certain it was over even yet.

Justin. No one had ever cared about me before, not the way he seemed to.

And all of it was connected somehow to Danilo. My future was with him, I knew it, I was determined to make it so. If there was such a thing as love, what I felt for him was that thing. I wanted to see him again. Yes, tomorrow I'd go to class, but tomorrow was a million years away.

It even occurred to me fleetingly that somehow, in some way I didn't understand yet, he was involved with the deaths and the disappearances, involved with what happened to Tim. But that was nonsense, it had to be—literally, it made no sense.

And I remember having another fugitive thought: that even if it was true, I didn't care.

Danilo was to be mine.

CHAPTER 5

Scarabs, dozens of scarabs.

A whole pile of them on my desk.

All the scarabs in the world.

Being Danilo's assistant wasn't quite what I'd expected. I spent hours doing exactly what he told me I'd be doing—cataloging drawers full, rooms full of artifacts. I actually saw him far less often than I'd hoped. When I did, I was working, or he was. Our only time together was at night, and he often had things to do.

But when we were together it was wonderful. It was love. I kept asking myself if it was only because I had never had a father that I was attracted to an older man. And I'm certain that was part of it. But there was more. Danilo understood me in ways no one else had, not even Roland. And he was always gentle with me.

Justin used to tease me about having a daddy. "You only want to collect his insurance money."

"Danilo," I told him jokingly, "is never going to die."

"No, he'll just get older and older, till he falls apart like the monster at the end of one of those old movies of yours."

When they finally met he changed his tune. Danilo and I were at dinner one night. Justin came in with his new boyfriend. When he saw the handsome man I was with his eyes widened. His boyfriend was a center on the basketball team, Greg Wilton. He was clearly upset that Jus wanted to join us—it was perfectly obvious why.

Danilo was all charm as he invited them to sit at our table. "Justin, it's a pleasure to meet you. Jamie talks about you all the time."

"Really?" He seemed surprised.

"He says your housekeeping is even worse than his own."

Greg had a good laugh. Danilo offered to treat everyone, and the two of them ordered heaps of food. I was a bit embarrassed.

We made small talk till our orders came: the summer, the term, what courses they were taking. Greg didn't strike me as all that bright. At one point I jokingly suggested he should try a remedial reading course. Jocks. Justin shot me a dirty glance.

"So," he finally asked Danilo, "Why ancient Egypt?"

Danilo smiled and shrugged. "Everything about it has always intrigued me. Fantastic civilization. I think they knew how to live."

Greg chimed in. "Isn't it all, you know, really gloomy?"

"These people used to sing greetings to the sun every morning. They painted all their buildings in the most vibrant colors."

"I only think of mummies and shit." Greg wasn't exactly making a good impression. "I mean, you know, they're all dead now. Like, who cares?"

Danilo put on his most engaging smile. "Ancient Egyptian civilization flourished, unchanged in its essentials, for more than 3,000 years. And here we are, two millennia after its decline, still discussing it. Do you think that will be true of America?"

Greg didn't like the sound of this; I could tell he was having trouble digesting it. I decided to get between them. "So, are things are getting serious between you two?" They had been dating for nearly a month.

Greg looked around, mildly alarmed. "Not so loud."

"We don't want people to know." Justin mirrored him. "You know how people talk."

"Having dinner like this is good." Greg hadn't stopped looking over his shoulder. "I mean, you know, the four of us. This way nobody'll know."

Finally Danilo spoke up. "'Know'?" he asked coyly. "Know what?"

"You know." Greg looked around still again. "About us."

"What about you?"

"About us being—" Suddenly he caught himself. It had finally dawned on him that Danilo was playing with him. "You know what I mean."

"Yes, I suppose I do."

"The guys on the team wouldn't…" He smiled weakly.

"So it is their fault you're ashamed of yourself?"

I quickly steered the talk into more neutral ground.

That night Justin was home alone. "Where's Greg?"

"Not here. Your boyfriend freaked him." He made a sour face. "Talking like that."

This surprised me. Coming from Greg, it seemed natural. I had never imagined Justin might be quite so…circumspect. "What do you mean? Talking like what?"

"Jamie, Greg and I both have scholarships. So do you. You know what the administration's like. If we want to go into the pros, we have to—"

"Why?"

"Because…because…I don't know. That's just the way it is."

"You told me once you wished the world could know about you and Grant."

"Grant's dead. We made sure nobody ever knew. Not for certain."

"Even so, that's what you said."

"Things change. Grant would have agreed with Greg. So do I."

That was that. He went to his room and stayed there for a while.

When he came out he was in a brighter mood. He told me, "You said Danilo was older. I was expecting a guy in his sixties with a limp and a cane."

I shrugged. "I told you how good-looking he is."

"He can't be more than thirty. Jamie, he's gorgeous."

"It was pretty clear you thought so."

"Was it?"

"Even Greg picked up on it, if you can imagine."

"Greg's not dumb."

"Oh, like, I mean, you know, for sure."

"Bitch."

I actually didn't know how old Danilo was. It never seemed important enough to ask. There were times when he seemed to be in his forties or fifties; other times he seemed hardly ten years older than me. Tricks of the light. Anyway, Justin acted more than a little bit jealous, which pleased me. He pouted and pretended to read a magazine. Then finally he asked me point-blank, "Are you in love with him, Jamie?"

I didn't want to say yes. Love seemed so corny to me. "Are you in love with Greg?"

"Greg's my age."

"What does that have to do with it?"

"Well, what I really want to ask is, is he in love with you?"

"He hasn't said so, not in words. But I've never said so to him either."

"Aha."

I was starting to feel irritable. "There has to be a downside, doesn't there? He talks to me like I'm an important part of his life, Jus. He talks about what we'll do in the future. And about all the things he'll show me. I want that."

"All Greg talks about is hoops."

I couldn't resist. "He's your age."

The summer term was a short one; class sessions lasted three hours instead of the usual one. Finals were coming; papers were due. I had been Danilo's assistant for nearly a month, and I was learning. And everything about ancient Egypt had begun to fascinate me, as it did him. The style, the way they expressed themselves, it all felt…I don't know…right, in some way.

So even though my job was drudgery, I enjoyed it because I was learning. There had been papyri to organize, fragile things I had to handle very carefully; amulets to categorize; and now these scarabs. I had to sort them, measure them, classify them according to what they were made of, limestone, faience, lapis lazuli…and I had to make sketches of what was inscribed on them. It dawned on me, working on them, that a month before I had never even heard of faience and lapis lazuli; the thought pleased me.

Sketching wasn't easy for me. I had never had any artistic training. The first few times, Danilo stood over me, helping me get the hang of it. Most of the hieroglyphs and symbols could be made with a few simple pen strokes. At one point I was having trouble getting one right, the figure of an owl. Danilo put his hand on top of mine and guided it. As always when we touched it felt wonderful. I took hold of his T-shirt and pulled him toward me and kissed him.

"Danilo, I—"

He kissed back, hard, deep. "Jamie, do you know what I'm giving you?"

"Yourself, I hope." He meant something else, something more. He always did in our intimate moments. I only half guessed what he might mean. We lay across the tiny desk in my office and kissed and held each other. When I stood up there were scarabs stuck to my cheek and arm. We both laughed and he brushed them off.

As passionate as we had been, we had never made love, not real love. I was beginning to wonder if…I put it down to his position, and mine. If there was a scandal we could always say, quite truthfully, that we had never—but I wanted him so much.

There had been some talk among the other students in my class when Danilo announced he had hired me. A few of the girls, in particular, shot me unpleasant glances; one of the guys looked like he wanted to spit on me. But that passed.

I had spent a lot of time in the museum library working on my research paper. Naturally I chose to write about the Set cult, what I could learn about it. There was plenty of material about the god but nothing explicit about the secret cult Danilo had mentioned, at least nothing in the open stacks. But what I found tantalized me.

Set was the brother of the great god Osiris, the greatest of the Egyptian deities. Horus, the son of Osiris and the divine embodiment of the king, was his nephew. And Set and Horus made love.

There was a long mystical text called "The Contendings of Horus and Set." At one point in it—yes, uncle and nephew became lovers. Only briefly, and it seemed to be more a matter of them trying to get one up on each other than anything else. Typical relationship; Set was the seducer.

I asked Danilo about it. "You would find that text."

"Yes," I was pleased with myself, "I would."

"Have you also learned about the negative confession?"

I hadn't come across that. "No, what was it?"

"When an Egyptian died his heart was taken out and weighed in a balance, to see if he was fit to enter heaven. Part of the ritual was a long list of sins he had to assert he had never committed."

I knew what he was going to say.

"And one of those sins was same-sex love."

I didn't seem to make sense. "But Danilo, the gods made love. Set made love to his nephew."

"Yes." He shrugged. "Egyptian religion was hardly the last to be caught in that contradiction."

"It doesn't make sense."

"Like all religions, the Egyptian belief system was a crazy-quilt of ideas and attitudes that accumulated over centuries. How could there not be contradictions?"

I found myself wondering how seriously he himself took the old gods. When he talked about Set he always sounded...But before I could think of a way to ask, he shifted tone.

"I've been ignoring you, Jamie."

"No."

"Well, not spending as much time as I'd like. It's been a busy summer. For both of us."

"I don't mind." I minded.

"When the term is over, let's go away somewhere. Be together, just you and I."

I was completely surprised. "Where?"

"Does it make any difference?"

"Not if we're together, Danilo."

"Let me think about it, then."

"I thought that was a definite invitation."

"Let me think about where, I mean, not if."

I kissed him. "Someplace romantic."

"We won't be staying in Pittsburgh, then."

Roland seemed quite pleased that I was warming to twentieth-century music; he didn't make it a secret it was his favorite. A lot of it was beyond me, though. Some of it for technical reasons—it was simply too difficult for someone at my level. I tried Stravinsky's piano version of *Petrouchka* and made a complete mess of it. It would be ages before I was that good.

Other pieces I tried—like the second Shostakovich sonata—were simply beyond my understanding. On the surface the music was fairly simple. But there was something there, between the notes, that I couldn't hear. I played recordings of it and listened as carefully as I could, and the music was filled with passion. When I played it myself it was so flat.

"You need to keep working on it," Roland told me. "It's not a young man's music, but you're beginning to find its heart."

I had no idea what he meant, and I said so. "I feel like I'll never play it properly."

"Do you know much about Shostakovich?"

I told him I didn't. I should have; I should have learned what I could.

"He was the quintessential outsider, Jamie. Isolated, lonely, never knowing who he could trust."

"I'm not sure I want to understand that."

"You will anyway. Sooner or later we all do."

I wanted to ask him who exactly he meant by "we." Before I could he changed gears. "Why don't we work on the Poulenc for a while?"

A week before finals Danilo took me to dinner, an expensive place. I was moving up in his esteem, it seemed. Even though I was underage he ordered a bottle of wine for us. I resisted making any jokes about him trying to get me drunk. He didn't have to.

The place was dimly lit. I thought I saw touches of gray at his temples. We mostly made small talk. Halfway through dinner he reached across the table and took my hand.

It made me a bit nervous. I found myself thinking about Justin, Tim, my scholarships. But it felt so warm.

"I've never invited you to my house, Jamie."

He hadn't. It didn't bother me. I had always put it down to how busy we both were. "That's okay."

He took my hand and kissed it. "Tonight. It's high time."

I had never had anyone do that before. It felt…it felt as exhilarating as all Danilo's kisses felt. For just the briefest instant I was self-conscious about it. Then I didn't care.

It was after dark when we left the restaurant. He took me home. His house was a large Victorian with vibrant stained-glass windows. I told him how beautiful I found them.

"I left the lights on so they'd be shining for you when we got here."

On closer inspection the windows had Egyptian motifs. One had a shimmering scarab at its center; another was adorned with lotuses. "Did you have these made?"

"No, the house came like this, believe it or not. The Victorians went through a period of Egyptomania. How could I not take this place?"

Inside there was incense burning. I had never much liked incense, but this smelled, I don't know, pungent, almost bitter. It took a moment to get used to the aroma, but then it was fine. The rooms were fairly dark; there was only accent lighting, in one room a Tiffany lamp with more lotuses.

I had expected his place to be filled with Egyptian things, papyri, statuettes. Instead there were beautiful antiques, heavy wooden tables, overstuffed Victorian furniture, shelves of old books. There was a first edition of Byron's *Manfred*. It must have been worth a fortune. "Where are the scrolls and amulets?"

"At the campus museum, where they belong."

On the walls were framed portraits of men from different ages, in different styles. I recognized some as medieval, some as Renaissance, some as more modern than that. Some of them wore crowns. The modern ones were photographs, some signed. Some of them were labeled, or were familiar enough for me to know who they were; most weren't.

"Kings, Jamie, all of them. Richard Lionheart, James I—"

"The king who did that Bible?"

"Exactly. And Alexander. David and Jonathan. And Frederick the Great, Julius Caesar and his nephew Augustus, Hadrian and Antinous, Henri III, Franklin Pierce, James Buchanan…" There were dozens of them. He told me about the lives and achievements of some of them. It became clear they were all men who had loved men.

And there were some women too, Queen Christina of Sweden, Queen Anne of England, and a few more that were not labeled. Christina I knew from the Garbo film.

Another corner held portraits of men who seemed to be popes, or at any rate were dressed that way. One was labeled JULIUS II. Another was of a pope with his arms around a beautiful young boy; the label read, JULIO III ET INNOCENZO.

He began telling me about the ones I didn't recognize and weren't labeled. The Holy Roman Emperor Boris II. Chinese Emperors Ai, Qianglong, Xianfeng. William Rufus, the second king of England. Goshirakawa, Emperor of Japan, and the shoguns Yoshimochi, Yoshimitsu, Ieyasu… There were scores of them, hundreds of them, and I found it more than a bit overwhelming.

On one wall, prominently spotlit, was an image of the Kissing Kings.

In other rooms were portraits of artists. Michelangelo, Leonardo, Erasmus, Feng Wenglong, Melville, Saikau, Handel…philosophers, Wittgenstein, Erasmus. There were signed photographs of Poulenc and

Eisenstein, and others I didn't recognize and whose handwriting I couldn't read.

Among them I instantly recognized Chopin. In one corner there was a grand piano. I opened the keyboard and played a few notes; the tone was richer than any I'd ever heard. Above the keys was the logo: Bechstein. The best, the cream.

"I can have it tuned for you, if you like, Jamie."

It was a shrine, the whole house was a shrine. It struck me as excessive, in a way; in another way…most decidedly not. I knew Danilo was more open about himself than most of the people in my circles, and I knew he loved the past, but all this…

I felt light-headed, almost as if were underwater. I had no idea why.

He touched my cheek. "I am the keeper of their flame. The last one left."

I didn't know what to make of all this. For the first time in Danilo's presence I was genuinely…not uncomfortable, exactly, but a bit bewildered.

"We have always been kings, Jamie. We have wielded power. We have made the art that shaped whole ages."

I stepped way from him. "Where are the athletes? Where are the scientists and the auto mechanics and the trash collectors?"

"You tell me where they are. Would your friend Justin want his portrait here, among the others?"

"N-n-no."

"And would his friend Greg?"

"No. You know he wouldn't."

He kept silent so I could realize what he was trying to tell me. I wasn't quite sure I did.

"We have the blood of kings in our veins, Jamie, you and I. We are part of their line. We are one with them, in a way Justin and Greg and their like will never be."

"No, Danilo, that can't be right."

"Close your eyes and feel it," he whispered. "It is right."

I looked around the room. The kings and presidents, the artists and composers all seemed to want something from me.

And some of them were moving. Yes, they were moving.

I realized the incense must be masking something else, some drug. Unlikely as it sounds, I had never been high before. It didn't matter. All I wanted was Danilo.

He put his arms around me and kissed me, and I knew we were finally going to make love. His bedroom had more portraits on the walls but I hardly noticed them. He let me undress him, his firm, smooth body. There was hair on his chest and legs; not much, just enough to define the muscles and make him even sexier. I kissed every part of him. Tenderly he undid my shirt, my shorts, my sneakers.

Nothing I had ever experienced prepared me for the intensity of what I felt that night. Wave after wave of sex engulfing me, making everything else in the world melt away.

"Danilo." I spoke softly. "Do you love me?"

He kissed me again, harder and deeper than before. "Jamie, I love you."

And I told him I loved him too.

The words had been said.

There was, I knew, no turning back.

What he was trying to teach me, I wanted to learn.

In class we learned about the heretic pharaoh Akhenaten. He had dismissed all the priests of the traditional gods and instituted a new religion, the worship of the god he considered the one, true One. He even moved the capital to a new place called Amarna to diminish the priests' influence even more. It caused an upheaval in Egypt: twenty years of chaos and unrest.

"The more romantic historians like to believe he worshiped the Judeo-Christian god," he told us. "But Akhenaten was more original than that. And more subversive. Here is an image of him, with his son and successor."

He showed it to us. It was the Kissing Kings.

There were giggles around the room. One of the girls, Jane, spoke up. "So he was a fag?"

"If you want to be picturesque about it. He was also married, to one of the most beautiful women in history, Nefertiti."

"Then why was he gettin' it on with his kid?"

Danilo smiled a faint smile. "We all have to be true to our natures."

"Not fags." She was becoming more and more upset by what she'd learned.

But Danilo had had enough of her. "To deny your nature is to commit a kind of suicide. To deny your nature is voluntary death. Are there any other questions?"

No one seemed to want to know more about the pharaoh's personal religion. But I had understood what Danilo was telling me, alone among the students: the "heretic pharaoh" was the key to understanding the Set cult.

A few afternoons later I was working in my little office, sorting through some scrolls. Professor Feld knocked on my door. "Have you seen Semenkaru?"

"Danilo? No, not for a couple of hours."

"He's never here when I need him."

Lucky Danilo, I thought. Feld had never quite stopped being suspicious of me. He obviously regarded me as a potential thief, and maybe not so potential. I decided to bait him. "Do you know anything about the black market for antiquities?"

"No. Why?"

"I'm just curious, that's all. I mean, I wouldn't know where to begin to sell a hot mummy, but people do. It's hard not to wonder."

"If I were you, I'd be careful, young man." He left, slamming the door loudly behind him.

The antiquities department only had four professors: Danilo, Feld, a Greek specialist, and a specialist in Persia and Babylon. There was no chairman; they operated independently and made decisions democratically. It gave Danilo a lot of autonomy; as much as Feld disliked me, he couldn't do much about the fact that I worked in his department. Even so, I knew toying with him wasn't the smartest idea. But I could never resist.

One of the scrolls I was working on puzzled me. It was in a style I hadn't seen before. I knew that besides formal hieroglyphics the Egyptians had had a less arty, less ornate writing called hieratic. This scroll wasn't like that. I'd have to ask Danilo what to do with it. He said he'd be down in the catacombs.

This time I was able to step over the cordon without fear of being stopped by anyone.

The basement was filled with Greek and Roman objects. The first subbasement held a group of smaller things from those societies and several rooms of Babylonian relics. The second was where the Egyptian collection began; it was by far the largest collection and extended two levels farther down. Danilo told me the university had been caught up in that same Victorian Egyptomania and had amassed a considerable collection back then.

I switched on the light and descended. On the first level I heard voices and paused. It was unlikely Danilo would be there, but... After a moment I was able to make out what I was hearing. It was Feld, talking to himself. In Latin.

I continued downward and reached the second subbasement, the place where he had shown me those mummies way back when. It seemed a thousand years ago. I had been down there a few more times, mostly just looking for Danilo, but once or twice I had had to work there, sorting through stacks of papyri, recording the inscriptions on mummy cases, that kind of thing. So it wasn't exactly familiar, but it wasn't as unsettling as it had been that first time.

I paused at the landing. The electric lights, as always, didn't provide much illumination. But at least I was used to the dim place by now. I stood and listened. Everything was perfectly silent. The doors to the various rooms were all closed.

After a moment I decided to call out. "Danilo?"

My voice echoed down the corridor.

A bit louder. "Danilo?"

He wasn't there, it seemed. I took a few steps down the passageway and knocked lightly on the doors, knowing it was useless.

And it was. There was no one.

I headed back to the stairs. No use lingering down there when there was work to be done. I switched off the lights in the corridor and put my foot on the first step.

There were voices.

It took me a moment to realize where they were coming from: below.

I called down the steps. "Danilo?"

There were whispers, just at the limit of my hearing, so faint I wasn't even quite certain I was hearing them. Not at all sure it was the right thing to do, I took a few steps down. "Danilo?"

The voices went silent. Then in a moment they began again. I shouted his name still again, and again they became quiet.

I had to see. Danilo had always been so emphatic that I wasn't to go below the second sublevel. But there was someone there. If it was him, he'd be angry, but I had seen his anger before and I knew he wouldn't stay that way very long, not with me. And if it was someone else, someone who shouldn't be there…I had to see.

Carefully I descended, a few steps, pause, a few more, pause. Listening. Voices. I knew better than to call his name; there would be no answer. Among the murmurs I thought I heard my own name.

The lights strung along the stairs were farther apart the lower I went. Still I continued.

Sublevel 3. I found the switch for the lights along the corridor there; they were so dim and so far apart as to give practically no light at all. Something made me keep my voice low. "Danilo?"

Nothing. The voices were from lower down still.

I hesitated. I had never been so far down into the catacombs before. It was a bit frightening. I remembered how on edge I had been that first time. But I was being foolish. What could happen? Even if there were rats or a garter snake, they'd be more afraid of me than I would be of them.

Down I walked, slowly, gingerly, as quietly as I could manage.

The voices whispered, murmured, seemed to call me. At the fourth, final sublevel there was another light switch. It was lower on the wall than the others and I had to grope to find it. A row of dim lamps came on along the corridor, faint lights, twenty feet or more apart.

"Danilo?" My voice was a whisper.

My presence seemed to disturb whoever was there. Everything became still. I took a few steps along the corridor. Finding my resolve, I raised my voice again. "Who's there?"

Nothing. I began to walk. Slowly, cautiously.

Doorways opened to my left and right as I moved along. There were no doors on them; they gaped, empty. The rooms were black as midnight. Anyone could have been hiding in them. Or anything.

The corridor made a turn. I looked back the way I had come. I was quite alone in that gloom, and I was beginning to find it oppressive. I should go back.

From ahead of me came a whisper. The words were almost inaudible. It seemed to me they whispered, "Come to us."

"Who's there?"

Another whisper, quite incomprehensible.

"I said who's there?"

The corridor widened out into what I took to be a large storage area. The walls opened out, the floor became rough, or at least uneven under my feet. The lights were hardly any help in that huge black space, just faint glows along the bottom of the wall, far apart. But there was enough light for me to see the room was empty except for some stacks of things in the corners and along the walls.

Empty. There was no point staying there any longer. I turned to go back.

There was a soft click. The lights went out.

Everything was pitch black. Not the least glint of illumination.

I froze. Involuntarily I dropped the scroll I was carrying. The wiring was old, maybe as old as the building. There must be a loose connection. Maybe they would flicker back on. The blackness was absolute.

Stay calm, Jamie, don't panic. You know where you are, you know where you came from. You can feel your way back along the corridor till you reach the stairs.

I inched carefully toward the wall; I reached out and touched it. Rough stone, cool, solid and reassuring. Slowly I reoriented myself in the darkness and began to move back the way I had come.

Something touched me. Something tugged at my shoelace.

A rat. It must be a rat. I kicked. There was nothing, my foot didn't make contact with anything. I kept moving.

Something grasped my shirt and pulled at it. I cried out and pulled free. Doing it, I spun around and away from the wall. Suddenly I had no idea which direction to move in.

A hand touched my leg, ran along my thigh. I swiped at it with my fist and missed.

A whisper. A voice out of the blackness. "Jamie. You are ours now."

I found the wall and began moving along it again, hoping I had chosen the right one, and the right direction. The thought that I might be heading deeper into that room almost paralyzed me with fright.

There were more hands, running all over my body. Touching my face, my chest, my legs. One of them groped my genitals.

Voices all around me whispered.

"Jamie, be with us."

"Jamie, so lean, so beautiful."

"We will have you, Jamie."

I fought but there were too many of them. They pinned me against the wall. I felt lips touch my cheek. A tongue ran along the side of my throat. I swung my fist. And struck only empty air.

"You are ours, now, Jamie."

A hand stroked my backside, another caressed my crotch. Unseen faces kissed me, licked me, caressed my cheek. I felt a tongue force its way into my mouth.

Finally I found the resolve to scream. "Danilo!"

For a moment they all backed away from me.

"Danilo!"

The unseen whispering things laughed softly. "Danilo cannot help you, Jamie. You are ours."

Hands pushed me against the wall again; others worked at my belt, undid the button on my shorts. I pulled free of them and ran along the black corridor. And tripped, fell.

They were on top of me, groping, fondling, touching, caressing, kissing. Despite my fear I felt myself becoming aroused. The realization sickened me.

"Danilo! Please, Danilo, for the love of god, help me!"

I felt my T-shirt being torn off.

And then, abruptly, the lights come on. Dim lights, but enough to dazzle my eyes. When they adjusted I saw the corridor, quite empty. My T-shirt lay on the floor not far from me, torn to ribbons.

Someone was coming down the stairs.

"Danilo?"

It was Feld. He walked briskly down the corridor to where I was still sitting on the floor. "What exactly is the problem, Mr. Dunn?"

"There was someone here. In the dark."

He smirked. "Of course. Get up."

Slowly I got to my feet and picked up what was left of my shirt. "Professor Feld, I'm telling you there's someone else down here."

"Nonsense. The light went out and you panicked. Are you on something?"

"No."

"Why don't I believe you?" He was so smug I could have hit him. "I'll have to tell Semenkaru about this."

"So will I."

"I warned him it was a mistake to take you on." He turned his back and headed back the way he had come.

Alone, I realized how badly shaken I was. To have been raped, or almost raped, by...by...I couldn't think about it. But I was trembling. I could hear voices again, snickering faintly at me. "Poor Jamie," I thought I heard one say.

I left as quickly as I could, headed back up the stairs without bothering to turn out the lights again. Somehow that would have been…I don't know, inviting them to follow me or something.

Just below the second sublevel, I heard Feld and Danilo talking, quite heatedly. I went back down a few steps and listened, hoping it would pass quickly. It did. Feld shouted something and stomped up the stairs above me.

I stepped up into the corridor. "Danilo?"

From one of the rooms his voice came. "Yes, Jamie, I'm here."

I went to him. He was standing beside an alabaster sarcophagus, obviously waiting for me. He was not smiling. But he put his arms around me and held me.

"Are you all right?"

"I…I don't know. I think so." I was still shaking.

"I warned you not to go down there."

"Yes. But I thought it was because there were valuable things there."

"There are." He looked me up and down. "Jamie, you're crying."

I hadn't realized it, but I was. He stroked my hair. "Here, let me." He took the tatters of the shirt out of my hand and dabbed my eyes with it. Then he kissed me on the cheek. "You mustn't again. Do you understand?"

"What's down there? What?"

"You'll understand in time." He put his arms around me.

"Danilo, I was almost…"

"I know. They could have done worse than that. Promise me you won't go there again till you're ready. Next time no one may hear your cries."

I leaned against him. It felt so good to have him hold me. And yet… "Danilo, I want to know what is down there."

He touched his lips to the side of my face. "In time."

"Now. I want to know."

"No." His voice was as firm as I had ever heard it.

I let him hold me more closely. "Tell me I don't have to be afraid. Tell me I won't have dreams about this."

"Jamie, I wish I could." He held me so tight. "Come home with me tonight. I'll fix dinner, and we'll talk."

"I think I need to be alone."

"No, you'll feel better if you talk it out. And, Jamie, I'm the only one who'll understand. You know that."

I stepped away from him. "I'm not sure what I know."

"Come upstairs. We can talk better in the light."

We went up to the museum. The large gallery was empty. Late afternoon sun fell on the statue of Horus. I loved Danilo so much, and now I was so afraid.

"There are mysteries, Jamie. Deep ones. You'll understand in time. In time you'll have—" He seemed to think better about what he was going to say. The stone god looked down on us.

Finally I broke down completely. "When I was a boy, Millie's husband used to fly into drunken rages and beat everyone in the house."

"You?"

I nodded. "It was terrifying. I never thought I'd know anything worse. But today, down there—"

"This is different. You couldn't control that."

It was such an unexpected thing for him to say.

"Danilo, I don't know what's happening to me. I don't know what's happening between us. I'm so scared."

"As I told you, you have the blood of kings. In time you'll learn to use it, and all the power it carries."

I kissed him. I wasn't sure why, except that I needed human contact.

"Come home with me tonight."

His house seemed less strange to me this time. All the portraits and photographs...after the horrible day they seemed, I don't know, reassuring.

Danilo made me comfortable in the parlor, on the sofa, and went off to the kitchen to make dinner. I fell asleep almost at once. And dreamed.

I was in a vast, dark, empty place, the kind that seem to exist only in dreams. Everything was silent. I lay on an ornate divan. From out of the night came a man, short, thin, with huge whiskers. It was Frederic Chopin. He bent and kissed me.

And I awoke. I had been asleep long enough for Danilo to have cooked an elaborate meal and set the table. When he saw I was awake he smiled and said, "Perfect timing."

There wasn't much talk over dinner, and what there was, was about everything but the museum and Egypt. He asked about Justin and Greg.

"They're the same, I guess. Greg really doesn't like me."

"Is that a loss?"

I laughed. "No, I guess not."

After dinner I helped with the dishes, as I had always done at...not "home," but at Millie's.

We settled in the parlor and cuddled for a time. The talk turned to music. Danilo asked me to play for him.

I moved to the Bechstein, adjusted the seat, tried a few notes. It needed tuning but it wasn't too bad. I played the opening bars of the Schubert C-minor allegretto. Danilo stood behind me, rubbing my shoulders as I played—not helpful but it felt wonderful. Then I played a few of Chopin's nocturnes. He sat beside me and listened attentively.

When I was finished he told me, "Chopin never played them more feelingly himself."

I laughed. It had to be a joke. "How could you know that?"

He avoided the question. "I have something for you."

"Really?" I've always loved getting presents.

"Wait here."

While he was gone I played a few more pieces of Schubert. Lovely tunes, easy to get lost in. The day's tension was finally beginning to dissipate.

Then he came back, carrying a sheaf of large old scrolls. At first glance I thought they must be papyri. But they didn't quite look like any I had seen. He handed them to me and I unrolled them.

It was sheet music but ancient. I had never seen notation like it before. It seemed to be a collection of songs; there were lyrics written under the notes. It must be centuries old; the ink had faded badly.

"Love songs." Danilo said it with quiet confidence. "I was going to give you this for Christmas, but today seems right."

"Christmas isn't for five months. Thank you." I kissed him.

"Can you make out the script?"

I studied it and shook my head. He pointed to a signature at the bottom of the last page. "Blondel."

"He was a poet and signer. The lover of Richard Lionheart."

I looked at him, startled. "This must be worth a fortune."

"He wrote these songs of unfulfilled love when Richard was held captive by the King of Austria."

"Is this...are these...in our musical notation?"

"Something like it. Why don't you try and play one, and see?"

The notes were odd, rectangular things. The staffs were only partly there. There were no key signatures. But I thought I might just be able...

The notes came. I played one of Blondel's songs. It was sad, mournful, the way love often felt to me.

"Transpose it downward."

I did. It sounded better.

Danilo began to sing.

> *Though the universe part us*
> *I am with you, sweet man.*
> *Like the universe,*
> *Like the gods,*
> *Love is eternal.*
> *Life without you is death.*
> *Life with you never ends,*
> *Like the universe.*
> *Like the gods.*

I knew he was singing it to me. For me.

Nothing else mattered.

CHAPTER 6

I wanted to learn more about the Set cult. It was more and more obvious to me that it was a large part of what drove Danilo, what gave him his passion. But equally I wanted to know more about the Kissing Kings. Why had Akhenaten had himself portrayed that way? Even in the ancient world, where human sexuality was understood and accepted so much better, it seemed…well, not quite the thing. And so I dug into the Egyptological stacks at the campus library, at the city library, and online.

I discovered that the portrait I knew was far from the only one. Akhenaten and his son Smenkhare were portrayed in intimate contact in one depiction after another. There was one in the Berlin State Museum that was quite frankly an image of a sexual embrace.

And this was somehow bound up with the Set cult. I had a lot more trouble finding information about it. If what Danilo had been telling me about it was at all accurate, it had been kept quite remarkably secret for four millennia.

I asked him about it one afternoon, but typically he was evasive. Or at least not as informative as I'd have liked.

"What do you want to know?" He smiled his professorial smile and settled behind his desk.

"I want to know what Akhenaten really believed."

"It isn't possible to know what anyone 'really' believes, is it?"

"Don't dodge the question."

He hesitated, then seemed to decide to be a bit more open. "They were lovers, yes. And they were both murdered."

"I know that." Akhenaten died in secrecy, his fate quite unknown. His wife Nefertiti vanished from the historical record. Their son Smenkhare ruled briefly, continuing his father's religious reforms, then died under mysterious circumstances. His body was found in an unmarked tomb in the Valley of the Kings. He was succeeded by his nine-year-old brother Tutankhamen, who was dominated by a priest named Ay, and the revolution came to an end. It was all in the books.

"Then what are you asking, Jamie?"

"It was the Set cult, wasn't it? What he really believed? The contrarian god, the god in opposition to the natural order as most people understand it."

Danilo smiled. "Is there a natural order? When I look at nature I see chaos. Animals sire young, then devour them. Plants grow filled with poison. Babies come with cancer. Galaxies collide and destroy one another."

"Danilo, will you please stop evading my questions?"

"I'm not." He said it emphatically.

"Then I don't understand."

He sat back. He was enjoying this more than I was, it seemed.

"Have you ever been to the observatory, Jamie?"

"No. What does that have—?"

"You should go sometime. You should have them show you Mars."

"Mars? Danilo, this is—"

"You wanted an explanation. I'm giving one."

It slowed me, made me stop and think. "All right, so I go and look at Mars. What then?"

"You might see the canals."

"And?"

"There are none."

I was completely lost.

"People see canals on Mars, even though there are none. The eye takes random markings on the planet's face and connects them, makes them into a coherent pattern. But there is none. There seems to be something inherent in the human mind that tries to find order in things. Even when there is none."

I thought I was beginning to understand his point. "And Set?"

"Set is the god who represents that understanding."

"Chaos."

"No, not that. Simply the recognition that the patterns human beings see are illusions, or may be. The only nature we can ever really understand for certain is our own. Set is that."

It made a kind of sense, but… "I'll have to think about this."

"Do." He picked up a sheaf of papers and riffled through them. "Have you ever read the Bible?"

The abrupt change of tack caught me off guard. I laughed. "No, of course not. Nobody does. I mean, Millie used to read it at me, but—"

"You should."

"Be serious, Danilo. Nobody reads the Bible. I've never even met a practicing Christian who's read the whole thing through."

"All the more reason, then. You might learn things about their beliefs that they don't know themselves."

My impulse was to think he was toying with me, but somehow I didn't think he was.

"The Bible is the best preserved book from the ancient world, Jamie. It contains all kinds of things we'd never know otherwise. Myth and ritual, for instance. Sacrifice, for instance."

I was completely lost. "And this has something to do with Set? And Akhenaten and his son?"

"I didn't say that."

"Yes, you did. Just not in words."

"Go and read, then. Get yourself a good King James Bible, not one of these preposterous modern translations. And read the stories of Jephthah, one of the Judges of Israel, and of Kings Ahaz and Manasseh. And while you're at it, take a moment to thank the king whose efforts preserved them for you."

King James. Since that night at Danilo's I had learned that his lover was the Duke of Buckingham, the man for whom Buckingham Palace was built. "I've never heard of those stories."

"Of course not. As you said, no one actually reads the Bible anymore, except for a few familiar, comfortable bits. There's more truth in that book than the Christians are capable of realizing."

All of this was more than I had expected to learn. But I told him I'd go and read.

"Good. And when you read those passages, remember one other one: 'The blood is the life.'"

I had so much new to think about. I kissed him and started to leave.

"Oh, and Jamie?"

"Hmm?"

"In ancient Egyptian astronomy, the planet we call Mars…"

"Yes?"

"Represented the god Set."

Bubastis had grown quickly, more quickly than I had expected her to. But she was still a kitten with that playfulness in her. I loved her like no pet I'd ever had. When she climbed into my lap and purred, it was almost as sweet as being with Danilo.

The night before my final I was in the living room, going over my notes, trying to decipher my own handwriting. I had a CD on, the late Schubert quartets. It was gray and rainy, a good night to be inside. It was, in fact, the first night in two weeks I hadn't spent with Danilo. Justin wasn't around.

There was a knock on the door. Carrying Bubastis, I opened it. It was Greg. He was soaking wet. I smiled at him. "Real men don't carry umbrellas?"

"Don't be a shit."

"Justin's not here." It gave me pleasure to tell him so. Things between Greg and me had gotten steadily more unpleasant.

"I need to come in. I'm drenched."

"Come back when your boyfriend's home."

He pushed his way past me into the apartment. We hadn't gotten along since that first night when he and Justin met Danilo. Obviously I threatened him in some way, even though Danilo was the one who had played with his head.

He shook himself, like a wet dog. "It's raining."

"I kind of guessed, yeah."

"You have any clothes I can change into?"

"You're a foot taller than me, Greg."

"Why aren't you out with that old man?"

"And miss the pleasure of your company? Look, I've got my final tomorrow. I have to study."

"Go ahead."

He stomped into the bathroom and closed the door. I got my notebook and sat down again. Bubastis sniffed at the bathroom door, curious what might be going on inside. I wanted to ace my test, not just for myself of course but for Danilo.

After a few minutes Greg came out, wearing nothing but his shorts, drying his hair. He rather pointedly sat down in a chair opposite me. Evidently I wasn't to be allowed to study. Bubastis scampered ahead of him and jumped up into my lap.

"That's my towel, Greg."

He smiled a smart-ass smile. "Thanks for letting me use it."

I tried to concentrate on Middle Kingdom politics.

"So, you still boffin' your prof?"

"If you want to be cutesy about it, yes."

"He any good?"

I looked up from my notebook. "Look, Greg, I'm trying to study. Don't you have a final too?"

"Yeah, but it'll be a piece of cake."

"What are you taking?"

"Sports medicine. We learn to bandage sprained ankles and shit."

"I knew how to do that when I was ten."

"We learn how to do it right."

"Oh."

For a few moments we fell silent and I was able to concentrate on the list of ancient kings. Mentuhotep, Amenemhat...

"Do we have to listen to this fag music?"

I didn't bother looking up. "We're fags, right?"

"You better shut up."

"Look, if you don't like it here, why don't you just leave? This is my place."

"And Justin's."

"He's not here. Why don't you go out and look for him?"

"Fucker. Where's the remote?"

"Leave the TV off. I'm studying."

"And listening to pansy music."

I could have ended it. I could have gone to my room. But it was my place, damn it, and I couldn't let him dominate it that way. Instead I just kept reading and hoped he'd get bored.

Bubastis jumped off my lap and headed for her water bowl. I flipped back a few pages and went over something Greg had distracted me from. The music swelled to an agitated "Death and the Maiden."

When the kitten came back into the room she made a beeline for the couch and jumped up beside Greg.

"Get this cat away from me."

I was casual. "She lives here, Greg. You don't."

"Faggot fucker."

I went back to my notes.

An instant later there was a frightened cry from Bubastis. Greg had picked her up by the throat. She was struggling, swiping at him with her little paws, but of course it was no use.

I jumped up. "Put her down! Gently!"

"I hate cats."

"Then get the hell out of here."

"Only fags have cats."

"Then you should get along with her."

"Fucker!" Still holding her by the neck he threw her across the room at me. I tried to catch her, but she slipped through my hands and hit the wall. She shrieked in pain.

I ran across the room and jumped on him. He had ten, maybe twelve inches on me and sixty pounds or more, but I threw myself at him and knocked him over and started pounding him. "You get the fuck out of here, you goddamned pig!"

He pushed me off. "It's only a cat. Christ."

I punched him again, not that it did much good. "Get your clothes on and get out of here!" He swiped at me, but I ducked.

In the opposite corner Bubastis was crying pitifully. I went and picked her up. It looked like her right front leg was broken.

Greg got to his feet and glared at me.

"I told you to get out of here!"

"Why the fuck should I?"

"Because if you don't, I'll call the police. Cruelty to animals is a crime. And I'll tell them everything. You understand me? Do you want your little friendship with Justin made part of the public record?"

Something like panic crept into his eyes. "Fuck." He headed to the bathroom.

I cradled poor little Bubastis. There was an emergency animal hospital in the neighborhood. I called them, and they said they could take her right away. I went to the closet to get the cat carrier.

A few moments later Greg came out of the bathroom, dressed. His arrogance had left him, at least a bit. "Would you really do that?"

"In a minute."

"You can't."

"Push me again and see." I lined the carrier with soft towels, hoping to make the trip easy on her. She was still frightened, cowering in the crook of my arm.

"The guys on the team would... They can't know."

"Then if I were you I wouldn't pull this shit again. I don't want to see you here except when you're with Justin. And even then you had damned well better behave."

He glared at me. It was obvious how much he hated me. Sullenly he went to the door. "Tell Jus I was here."

"And I'll tell him what you did. Bubastis is his cat too."

"Fucker."

"Get out."

He left, sulking. A moment later there came a faint tap on the door. It was Mrs. Kolarik. "I don't mean to intrude, but I heard raised voices. Is everything all right?"

"There's been an accident with Bubastis. I have to get her to the vet's."

"The one over on Shady? I'll get my car and drive you."

"Thanks."

I got a jacket and umbrella, and Mrs. Kolarik drove us to the emergency vet's as quickly as she could without shaking Bubastis up even more. Her leg was broken, as I had thought, and they put a cast on it; there were a few bruises. Otherwise she seemed all right. When they were finished with her and she saw me she came running to me, as quickly as the cast would let her, meowing happily.

When I got home Justin was there. I told him what Greg did. He defended him. "It must have been an accident."

"Jus, he picked her up by the throat, shook her, and threw her across the room."

"He wouldn't do that."

"Goddamn it, Justin, he did it."

"No."

There was no point. He was in love.

The phone rang. I didn't much want to talk to anyone; my opinion of humanity wasn't especially high right then. But it was Danilo. Hearing his voice calmed me down almost at once. He offered to come over and keep me company.

"Thanks, but I have to finish studying. I have a final tomorrow."

"You have, Jamie darling, an unattractive tendency to be a smart-ass."

"I know it."

"Bring her to my house. I can help." He hung up.

Every time I thought I had his range, Danilo said or did something to surprise me. What he had said made no sense.

I was sitting on the sofa. Bubastis tried to jump up beside me but she couldn't. I picked her up and cradled her.

Justin came out of the kitchen with a packet of cat treats, but she seemed afraid of him. Intelligent kitten.

He was put off by it. "She always likes these."

"She must smell Greg on you."

"Don't be silly. They must have her on some drug or something."

"Right." I didn't try to hide my sarcasm. "That must be it."

Late that night the rain stopped. The sudden absence of sound woke me up. Bubastis was sleeping on the pillow beside me. And I realized Danilo was in the room. He was sitting, watching me in the dark. Like, I thought, a lover. I reached over to the nightstand and switched on a little stained-glass lamp he had given me, a genuine Tiffany.

He kissed me, and I kissed back.

"How did you get in?"

"Where there's a will, there's a way. How is Bubastis?"

She woke up, groggily, and recognized him. She had always liked him, and she limped across the bed to him. He picked her up and nuzzled her.

"Sweet little kitten." She meowed, happy to see him. "Were you dreaming, Jamie?"

"No. For once I wasn't."

He kissed me again.

"Let me take her for a few moments."

I sat up. "Take her?"

"Just for a few moments. Leave me alone with her, all right?"

I was too off-balance to object. He picked her up and disappeared into the living room.

It was odd, even for Danilo. I got quietly out of bed, pulled on my shorts, and went to look.

The living room was empty. The kitchen light was on.

Slowly I pushed the swinging door open a crack and looked in. Bubastis was on the kitchen counter. She was drinking something dark from a saucer. Danilo was at the sink, washing his hands. When she finished drinking he took the saucer and rinsed it off. She scampered to him happily.

Then he took a knife out of the silverware drawer and started to cut her cast off.

THE BLOOD OF KINGS

113

"Danilo, don't!"

He smiled casually. "She doesn't need it now."

Before I could reach them he slit down the center of the cast and pulled it off. Bubastis capered about, glad to have it off. There was no limp, no sign of pain. She jumped down off the counter and scampered past me into the living room.

"What did you give her?"

"I've already told you that, in any number of different ways."

He took a step toward me but I backed off. "Danilo, you know how much I love you."

"And I you, Jamie."

"Then why do I feel like I should be afraid?"

"I took a poor, injured kitten and made her well. Why should you be afraid of that?"

"It isn't just that."

"No?"

I was more frightened than I wanted to admit, not of what he might do, but of losing him. "Danilo, please tell me."

"Tell you what?"

"Tell me what you are. What we are."

He hesitated. "I gave her consecrated blood to drink. I said a spell. And she was healed. You've seen enough of the old papyri. That cannot surprise you."

I was terrified to ask, but I had to. "Do you love me?"

He crossed the room to me, slowly. "Jamie, sweet Jamie, in all the world, in all the centuries, I have found no one to love more." Just as slowly he put his arms around me, and we kissed again. I felt the tip of his tongue touch the side of my throat, and I shivered with pleasure. There was no place I wanted to be but in his arms.

I felt something brush against my leg. Bubastis was there, circling us, rubbing against first Danilo then me, purring sweetly. There were still traces of blood on her face. When she had finished letting us know she was there she sat and began cleaning her face with her paw, carefully, methodically.

The blood is the life.

*

I aced the final. No problem. After class I went to Danilo's office and he graded my paper while I waited. A+. We kissed again. It seemed to me that all we did was kiss and touch and make love. And that was just fine.

Though I hadn't taken any formal piano instruction that summer, I had of course stayed in practice. Roland gave me nothing but praise for my progress at the keyboard. Loving Danilo fired my art, or so it seemed. At the winter recital Roland wanted me to have a go at Schubert's *Wanderer Fantasy.*

The suggestion made me self-conscious. "But Roland, that's such a tough piece. I don't want to bite off more than I can chew, not again."

"You can do it. You've gotten better. This time you won't just have the passion, you'll have the technique."

"But—"

"Besides, I want you to have a real challenge in front of you. You've got the talent to do it. Stretch yourself till you can."

He knew, or suspected, about my affair with Danilo. He disapproved—that was obvious—but he seemed to understand Danilo was good for me, and he never said anything. That meant a great deal to me.

The next morning was brilliant with sunshine. But it was already hot, a hideous August day, and the humidity was climbing. I woke early.

Bubastis was sleeping beside me as usual. She woke, yawned, stared at me, then curled up and went back to sleep.

I headed for the kitchen to make some breakfast. It was a mess. Greg had spent the night with Justin, and they must have gotten up for a snack in the middle of the night. Annoyed with them, I found some clean bowls and a griddle and started a batch of pancakes.

Things between them and me had been tense. When they realized Bubastis could walk, they thought I had invented or exaggerated her broken leg. Plainly there was no way I could tell them how she had been healed. And so in Justin's mind I was the liar, not Greg; I was trying to break up their affair. Villainous me.

The telephone rang.

Danilo.

"Are you packed?"

"Packed?"

"I'll be there to pick you up in twenty minutes."

"What are you talking about?"

"We're going away, remember? I promised."

I had forgotten. It had seemed so…unimportant, I guess. "No, I'm not packed yet."

"Then pack now. I'll be there as soon as I can."

I forgot about breakfast and headed for the bedroom. I hadn't asked him how long we'd be gone. How much should I take?

Bubastis sniffed at my bag. She remembered the last time I packed it and knew it meant I'd be leaving for a time. And she made it clear she was unhappy. The thought of leaving her with Justin and Greg… I tried not to think about it. Despite his ongoing hostility to me, Greg had been on his best behavior. Instead of protecting him, his secretiveness only made him vulnerable, but that wasn't a realization he seemed able to make.

I had just started packing when a car drove up and the horn sounded. I looked out the window to see Danilo. He was at the wheel of a Corvette, a bright red one. I had never seen him in a car before. I was so used to seeing him in an ancient setting, full of papyrus and alabaster, that the sight rather startled me. He smiled a breezy smile and waved.

I ran out to meet him. He put his arms around me and we kissed for a long time on the sidewalk. There was a time when it would have made me self-conscious. Now I didn't care.

"You didn't say how long we're going for. I don't know what to pack."

"The skimpiest clothes you have. I want everyone to see."

In bright sunlight his hair always seemed grayer. And his eyes greener. I swear, I would have made love to him then and there if he'd asked me to.

"I'm serious. What should I bring?"

"Enough for a week. Nothing too dressy, all right?"

I ran back inside while he waited on the sidewalk, polishing his car like a good suburban husband. It was so incongruous. Ten minutes later I nuzzled Bubastis to say goodbye, left a note for Justin, and we hit the road.

He avoided the Interstates. We traveled one back road after another. I hoped we'd keep going. Every town we passed through reminded me of Ebensburg.

After a while he asked why I looked so gloomy, and I told him it was reminding me of home—what I smilingly called home, because I had no choice.

"Should we stop and visit your relatives?"

"God, no. They'd lynch us."

"Or try to, and live to regret it."

"Thanks, but I'd just as soon never see Ebensburg again."

We kept driving northeast. After a few hours we were in the Poconos. Lush, green, rolling hills, giving way to even lusher, greener mountains. Eventually he turned off onto a dirt road.

"Where on earth are we?"

"A million miles from Greg, and even farther from your relatives."

It was mid afternoon. Shadows were stark and the sun beamed brilliantly overhead. We crept slowly along the road. Trumpet vines blossomed bright orange among the trees, and vivid purple wisteria cascaded everywhere. Among the trees here and there was a dead rotted one.

The road led to an old stone house, almost a small castle, tucked among the hills. A turret soared up to the treetops; rainspouts carved into gargoyles adorned the four corners. Dark green ivy climbed the walls and the tower. Heavy leaded-glass windows looked out onto the mountains and the forest. A house out of Poe, I thought.

"Danilo, it's incredible."

"It's ours for the next week."

I mentioned Poe, and almost before I had the words out he said what I somehow knew he would, that Poe was one of us too.

"How on earth did you find this place?"

"Online. How else?" Again, hearing something so contemporary from him seemed…not quite right…out of place, maybe.

He seemed to know what I was thinking. "We have to change with the times. We have to use what the times give us. Come inside."

We walked to the door, holding hands. Large door, eight feet tall, heavy wood, stained-glass coat of arms in the center of it. He pulled out a set of large, heavy old keys and opened it. Then, quite unexpectedly, he picked me up and carried me across the threshold. Part of me felt silly, like a kid or a girl. Another part fell more in love than I had been before.

"Jamie, welcome home."

Inside, the house was a wonder. There were the most fabulous antiques everywhere, eighteenth-century things mostly. I couldn't stop grinning. "Danilo, it's perfect, it's a museum. We have our own private museum."

"With no Professor Feld prowling around."

In one corner was a piano, a concert grand. I ran to it, opened the cover, and played a few notes. It was in perfect tune. Even more excited, I sat down and played the opening bars of the "Minute Waltz." Danilo moved behind me and put his arms around me; it hampered my playing, but I didn't care.

I found myself wondering whose house it was.

"No one's. The owner's dead, and all his family. Old money from Philadelphia. They owned a department store. The last of them died twenty years ago. The estate rents it out to help cover the taxes."

I played some of a brief nocturne. The dark tone seemed to reflect the dark forest outside.

"I had them tune the piano for you, made it a condition of our lease."

I had never been so excited. I stopped in mid bar and ran to the largest of the windows. "This is wonderful. You could live here for years without seeing another human being." I turned to look at him. "Just you and me. We're the only ones in the world."

"Well, not quite. There's a caretaker. Part-time."

"Oh." I didn't want anything to bring me down. "Well, tell him to stay away."

"He has a room, in the basement around back. But I think he usually sleeps at his own place."

"Danilo, I don't want to see anyone else. Just you."

That night we went for a walk in the woods. There was a quarter moon and more stars than I had ever seen. The Milky Way arced high overhead. We held hands and ambled without much aim. The mountain air was cool, even in August. I was a bit chilly in my shorts.

"Do you know the sky, Jamie?"

"Not on a first-name basis, no."

"Do I love you despite the fact you're such a smart-ass, or because of it?"

"Face it, professor, I'm irresistible."

He ignored this. "Only in Egypt, in the middle of the Great Desert, have I seen a sky so vast, filled with so many stars."

"It's marvelous, Danilo. I used to think Pittsburgh's sky looked empty after living in the country. But Ebensburg nights were nothing compared to this."

"You Americans have lost touch with so much."

It was still another of his odd comments, but they hardly seemed to register anymore. "Where are you from, then?"

He smiled. I could see it clearly in the moonlight. "The Old World."

"Would you like to be more specific?"

"My parents were Egyptian."

It surprised me. "I thought you were from somewhere in Eastern Europe."

"Europe is where I've lived most of my life." He put an arm

around me and gestured with the other. "That bright star over there—the one with a reddish cast to it, just above the moon?"

I looked where he was indicating.

"Mars," he said. He stroked my hair in his familiar way. "Or Set, if you prefer."

"Let's honor him, Danilo. Let's shatter all the patterns."

"I thought we were already doing that."

"Make love to me here, where he and all the stars can see us."

Slowly he began to undress me. "Do you understand what the ancients saw in the stars and the planets?"

"They thought they were gods." His touch warmed me.

"Not exactly. The ancients understood the soul and the body are not necessarily one."

I opened his shirt and kissed his chest. "I don't know what you mean." The gods were the last thing on my mind just then.

"The lights in the sky are the gods' souls."

Despite myself I had to ask him, "Then your soul can be somewhere other than in your body?"

"Of course. Why not?" He never stopped teaching me. Or teasing me. There were times I wasn't sure which.

I got the last of his clothes off. We put our arms around each other. From the corner of my eye I could see the moon and, just above it, Mars, tinged with blood, shining steadily.

Suddenly there were headlights shining through the trees. We quickly got back into our clothes. Danilo seemed more disappointed than I was. Our first night together in our own world. I had meant it when I said I never wanted to see another human face.

We went back to the house as quickly as we could in the dark woods. A jeep was parked at the back of the house. There was a man knocking at the front door. Danilo strode up to him. He must have been six foot six and he was overweight, dressed in jeans, a flannel shirt, and heavy work boots.

"Good evening. Can we help you?"

"You Mr. Semenkaru?" He had trouble pronouncing it.

"Yes, and this is Mr. Dunn. What can we do for you?"

"I'm Albert Little Bear." He looked from one of us to the other suspiciously.

Danilo looked at me and mouthed the words, "The caretaker."

"I just wanted to make sure you got here and everything's all right."

I spoke up. "Everything's perfect, Mr. Little Bear. You're Native American?"

"One eighth. This land used to belong to the Iroquois." He stared at us. "You shouldn't go out in the forest at night. It's easy to get lost."

"We didn't go too far." Danilo didn't want him there any more than I did. "Is there something you need?"

"No. Like I said, I just wanted to make sure you got here okay." He looked from Danilo to me again, not seeming to approve of us. "What are you planning to use this place for?"

"Just rest and relaxation, Mr. Little Bear."

"Albert." He took a step toward us, then stopped. "This is a quiet region. People don't like anything funny."

"I'll try to restrain my sense of humor, then." I pointedly crossed to him and shook his hand.

It seemed to startle him. "I think you know what I mean. How old are you, Mr. Dunn?" He leaned on the "Mr." with heavy sarcasm.

"Twenty." I decided an extra year couldn't hurt. "Want to see my driver's license?"

Danilo quickly got between us. "You've stocked the pantry for us?"

"Enough food for a week." He smiled to show he didn't care if we starved. "You want me to light a fire before I go?"

"We'll manage." Danilo smiled back at him, a polite "screw you." "Why don't you stop back in a few days?"

Without saying a word Albert got in his jeep and drove off down the road.

I couldn't help smirking about the encounter. "It's so hard to find good help nowadays."

Danilo watched till his tail lights disappeared. "He could be trouble."

"For you?" I didn't believe it.

"For us. I wanted this trip to be a break from that kind of thing. You get enough of it at home." He took my hand and we went inside. The night air held a chill. "I should have had him start that fire."

"We can warm each other up."

And we did. We made love again and again. When the night became too chilly we lit a fire and made love again, there in front of it. Then we sat, spoon-wise, his arms around me from behind, and we talked about our lives, and about our life—together.

At one point I felt him get a bit tense. When I looked over my shoulder he was staring at the window.

"What's wrong?"

"Nothing." He didn't sound convincing, and I said so. "I thought I saw our Albert looking in the window at us."

"Oh."

"He's gone now. He ducked away as soon as he knew I'd seen him."

"Another closet case?"

"Maybe. He could merely be a generic brute, or a lunatic."

"I saw the look on his face when we came out of the woods. He's a closet case."

"I don't want him to ruin this, Jamie."

"He won't. No one could."

The next few days were paradise. There was me, there was Danilo, and there was out little castle in the mountains. If anything else existed, I didn't want to know about it.

We made a few trips into a nearby town to eat at a little diner that had surprisingly good food. Especially pies, which Danilo seemed quite partial to. On our third visit, the owner mentioned Albert Little Bear. It seemed our caretaker had been spreading gossip. The owner didn't exactly tell us we weren't welcome in his diner, but that was what came through.

I played for Danilo every night.

The third night Albert was at the window again. This time I was the one who saw him. He grinned at us like a vicious animal. We got into our pants quickly and went out to deal with him. But he was gone. He knew the woods better than we possibly could; he even knew the house better, if it came to that. He could have been anywhere.

Two more nights we had to ourselves. Our interval of solitude, or near solitude, was ending. Late, very late, Albert was at the window again, watching us make love, leering and grimacing. This time when we saw him he stayed there for a long moment and held up a huge hunting knife. The threat could not have been more clear.

Danilo jumped to his feet and headed for the door, quite naked. "Stay here, Jamie. I have to deal with this."

"You can't go like that."

"Yes, I can. I don't want him to get away again. Stay here. I'll be back."

He took a flashlight and went outside. I rushed to the window, but all I could see was the light, heading into the moonlit woods.

I climbed quickly up to the turret. All week long I had been too preoccupied to go there. The steps spiraled. The top room was empty, full of dust, debris and boxes; a storeroom, nothing more. The moon's light poured in. At the window I could see Danilo's light heading into the forest.

I should have gone with him. Albert was a large man. Against him, two of us would have been…I didn't know what. I was afraid he'd do something to Danilo then come for me. We should have fought together.

Then Danilo's light went out.

Terrified, I waited.

It was forever. I was so worried what would happen to my Danilo, my lover, my…absurdly I found myself thinking *father*. And I knew in a way that's what he was. After all my life I had found him, and now he was in the dark nighttime forest with a hateful fiend. I pressed my hands against the window as if that could have made me closer to him.

Then I saw a figure emerge from the trees. Large, enormous in fact, but moving quickly and with a kind of grace. When it finally entered a patch of moonlight I realized the shadows had created an illusion.

It was Danilo.

He seemed unhurt, no evident limp or wound. He was naked. Then I saw something dark on his face and throat.

I was afraid to move. He stopped walking and looked up to the turret. He knew where I was.

I waited there. In a moment he entered the house; I heard him climbing the steps, and he came into the room. He stood there naked and beautiful in the moonlight. There was a large smear of blood from the corner of his mouth down to his chin, then down the side of his throat.

We stared at each other for a time. Then he said softly, "Albert will not bother us anymore."

He had beaten a man who was much taller and heavier, who must have been stronger. I felt so many conflicting emotions. Danilo had fought him for me. To protect me. In all my life no one had done such a thing. In that moment I knew he truly loved me. Yet there was blood.

"Danilo, I want to know who you are."

He stayed silent.

"Please, Danilo. I love you, but part of me is terrified."

He took a step toward me. I tensed. He sensed it and stopped. Very gently he said, "Achilles was the first. I was there when his mother hid him among the women, to keep him out of Agamemnon's insane war. I saw his rage when his lover Patroclus died. I helped bury him.

"And there were all the others, long, sad generations of them. Socrates and Pericles, Marc Antony and Dellius, Erasmus, Richard Lionheart, Ludwig of Bavaria, who they called mad."

Hearing him say this did not surprise me. I had known, in a way.

"We were not the first, Jamie, my father and I. There had been Gilgamesh, who loved the warrior Enkidu. There had been…" He stopped and smiled. "But by now you know the catalog. My father and I were not the first to have the blood. But when they killed him—"

"Your father?"

"My father was Akhenaten."

Smenkhare. I don't know why the similarity in names had never struck me before.

"You have their blood, Jamie. The royal blood, the blood of kings. I've told you so before."

I had thought it was love talk, the kind of silly thing an older man would say to a younger one to flatter him.

"We were not the first. No. But when they killed my father, when they did the most awful things to his corpse, right in front of me…" He looked and sounded lost. "Then two years later, when it became clear how much I was my father's son, they decided to do away with me too. I escaped; I honestly don't remember how. I had been trained as a priest. I knew what the ancient scrolls said. A cousin of mine had died recently. We looked alike, and I dressed him in some of my things, so when they found him they thought he was me.

"Then I lived for a generation like a desperate hermit in an abandoned rock-cut tomb, collecting all the papyri, learning the spells, mastering the words. Some of them are even in the Bible. 'The blood is the life.'"

All of this…I had suspected something, but nothing this immense, this timeless. "And I…?"

"There are more of us," Danilo said. "More than anyone guesses, more than even I know. But you…I have mentored so many men, hoping to revive the power we once knew and the pride we once took in it. Keeping the flame alive, however dimly. You are the one love of all the ones I've known. You are the one, the blood prophet who can—"

"I am not. I am no such thing."

"You are. A thousand generations of kings and prophets speak through you. When you play, I hear the hand of Frederic Chopin himself."

The universe was in a whirling chaos. I could not make sense of it. I could not know what to say.

"The power will be yours, Jamie. Only take it. You have the blood of kings."

Across the moonlit room he stood tall and naked. I knew he loved me. And I heard in his voice that he was terrified I'd reject him and what he was offering.

All my life I had been alone, no family, no one to love who loved me in return, no one, even, who understood the passion I felt for my music.

I took a step toward him. He was afraid to move or say anything, I could see it. I crossed the room to him and touched his chest. He was sweating. From the struggle? From fear of what I'd say to him?

But I didn't say a word. I touched his face. It was still wet with blood. I pulled him to me and licked the blood from his lips. It was sweet, much sweeter than I'd expected.

We made love, there in that empty, dirty room, and it was more intense, even, than the most intense things I had felt before. Right then we were the Kissing Kings, and I knew something of what he meant. I could feel the blood of a hundred artists pounding in my heart; I felt the power of a thousand kings.

When we were finished we slept in each other's arms, there on the dirty floor. It didn't seem to matter.

Then, very late, when I was certain he was sound asleep, I got up quietly and got dressed. There was something I had to do, something I had to see.

It took me a few minutes to find another flashlight. On a table just inside the door I noticed a knife, the golden one I had seen in Danilo's office once. It was soaked with blood. Then I headed out into the woods. The moon had wheeled round to the other side of the sky, making everything look different. It took me a moment to get oriented and find the place where, I thought, he had come out of the trees. Even so it took me a time to be quite certain. My flashlight and the moonbeams pouring down through the branches were not really much help. Mars shone brightly.

But finally I found what I was looking for. Albert's body. I shined my light on it and saw at once that it was cut open, exactly like the others. But this body was mutilated even more. I realized the foxes had been at it already. I could hear them—could hear something—moving around me in the dark woods. Were there wolves?

I suddenly felt foolish and vulnerable, standing there alone in the darkness. But I had had to see.

And still did. I took a step toward Albert's remains and bent over to look more closely. There were a few shreds of clothing still around his ankles and wrists; otherwise he was naked. His genitals were gone; his eyes were gone. The vast gash that tore him open was filled with blood and shredded flesh. Where his heart should have been there was a gaping black cavity.

Danilo had done this. This was not like finding Grant. I had known Grant. Finding him dead had been…but Albert had been a stranger, and a hostile one. Danilo had killed him. He had kept trying to tell me why, but I was too slow to understand. Something about *The Book of the Dead*, something about the Bible, something about an immortal life…

Looking at Albert's corpse, knowing Danilo had done this for me—*for me*—I felt a thrill, a sexual thrill. I could have gone back to the house and made love to him again that moment. Instead I got down on one knee and pushed a finger into the body. The blood was congealing; it was thick and sticky. But I raised my finger to my lips and licked it clean. It was nowhere near as sweet as it had been on Danilo's lips.

Some mad impulse made me do it. I leaned down and kissed Albert's lips. For a moment I thought I felt it his body twitch under my caress.

There were foxes in the dark woods around me, or raccoons,

or...I could hear them moving. I was interfering with their unlooked-for feast. I got up and dragged the body farther into the trees, then went back to the house.

Danilo was still sleeping.

He was quite as naked as Albert had been. Asleep, he had an erection. I kissed him till he woke up, and we had hot, wild sex. It seemed to last forever, the night seemed endless, before we finally fell asleep again.

And in the morning the first rays of the sun woke us. Danilo was young and vibrant, more so than I had ever seen him. I could have eaten him with a spoon, I loved him so much. And I was also still scared. He sat up and yawned and kissed me.

"Danilo, I don't know whether to feel guilty. I don't know what to feel."

"Should we go and bury Albert, then?"

"No." I stood and stretched. "No one will ever find him. The bears and foxes will see to it. They were already at it last night. People will suspect, but..."

"Let them. They won't have any proof."

I had an ugly thought. "The ones in Pittsburgh..."

"I wanted them to be found."

"Why, Danilo?"

"So that people would know."

"You killed them all? Tim? Grant?"

He nodded. "It was necessary. For us. If I hadn't done it, we would not be here now, together."

It didn't make sense to me. Albert had threatened us. But Tim...I suppose I had never quite stopped loving him. How can you? "Did you kill Tim because you knew he had been my lover? Were you jealous?"

"I didn't know it was him at the time, no."

"I still have mixed feelings about him dying, Danilo."

"I did not kill him, Jamie, nor any of the others. They themselves chose to be dead. What I did was merely a postscript to their empty lives. Let's go downstairs. I should get some clothes." He headed down the staircase and looked back to make sure I was following. "All of them threaten us, Jamie. Not always as directly as Albert. But they would deny our nature, they would have us deny it ourselves, as they deny theirs."

I made hotcakes for us and fried a pan of bacon. Danilo ate like he hadn't been fed in weeks.

"You still have some of Albert on your chin."

"I'll get a shower."

"No, Danilo. We will."

The next afternoon was cool and rainy. We headed back to Pittsburgh. I switched on the radio to hear a forecast. It was supposed to rain all day.

Danilo picked a different route than the one we had taken on the way up. After a while it became clear why. I realized he was heading for Ebensburg.

"Danilo, please don't."

"I'm curious to see where you came from. What kind of place produced you. We won't stay, if you'd rather not. We'll just drive through."

I knew it sounded foolish, but I didn't want to see the place; it carried too many unpleasant things for me. But I couldn't make myself say so.

Late in the afternoon we drove into town. Danilo coasted to a stop in front of the bus station. The streets were nearly empty, just a few scattered people with umbrellas. The rain was coming down fairly heavily; sidewalks were flooded, water cascaded through the streets. Overhead there was a flash of lightning.

Neither of us said anything. He sat behind the steering wheel, taking it all in, seeming to study it. A woman came out of the bus station carrying an old, battered suitcase and looked around, not seeming to recognize anything. She looked lost. After a moment she lugged her bag off along the street and disappeared into a little restaurant.

"Are you hungry, Jamie?"

"Not for anything here."

"You told me once about a swim coach here, who—"

"Danilo, can we please go?"

He fell silent and looked up and down the street again. "That church there. Is that where your father—?"

"I don't know. I don't remember." I knew it sounded petulant but I added, "I don't want to."

Slowly he said, "Of course. I should have realized." He started the car and we left Ebensburg, slowly. He seemed still to be studying it, or looking for something. I couldn't imagine what.

When we reached the main highway the rain started to come down even harder. The wipers were hardly keeping the windshield clear, and I thought we might have to stop. But Danilo kept driving. After a time he told me he was sorry for taking me there. "I didn't understand how painful it would be for you."

"I've told you often enough."

"I'm sorry. But seeing it…I had to see it. It's part of you, even if it's a part you've closed off. I'd like you to see where I was born someday."

"Egypt?"

"Yes, of course."

I touched his hand, then pulled back. "You know I'd love that."

"Then we'll go."

"Next summer? I can't go while I have class. Neither can you, for that matter. You have to teach, don't you?"

He nodded.

"Are you teaching any advanced classes? I can rearrange my schedule and I could…"

"No, nothing but intro courses this fall. In the spring, though…"

"I'll be in the front row. I'll dust your erasers."

When we finally reached Pittsburgh it was twilight and the rainstorm was just ending. There were a few flashes of distant lightning, that was all. The city was quiet with that after-the-storm stillness, no one in sight, only the sound of water guttering its way through the streets. We pulled up in front of my place. There were lights on. Justin and Greg. I didn't want to see them, either of them.

"Come inside with me. I want them to see us kiss."

He smiled. "Just kiss?"

"Yes, professor, just kiss. I have some modesty, after all."

"Pointless emotion."

He helped me carry my things inside. There was no sign of them; they were in Justin's room. I put my arms around Danilo, and we kissed and held each other for a long moment. Bubastis came scampering out of the kitchen and rubbed against our legs, obviously happy I was home.

CHAPTER 7

The fall term began. Some of the other students I knew made a big deal about not being freshmen anymore. I had more substantial things on my mind.

In some ways the new school year was much like the first had been. Classes—I had to take economics, which I hated—studying and practicing, working out in the pool. But of course it was different too: I had Danilo.

We had a practice meet against Villanova, and the three days I spent in Philadelphia, with no real contact with him, seemed endless. While I was gone there was another killing, another young man found dismembered, organs missing, an acting student this time. The killings were happening when I wasn't around. I wasn't at all certain whether to be grateful.

The administration and the police finally realized that the only way to deal with the rising wave of rumors and fear was to issue warnings to students and staff that "there may be a serial killer" on the loose. FBI experts were on the case, constructing a psychological profile of the killer. Needless to say, nothing in their reports came close to the truth. But the campus was tense.

Roland told me my piano skills had slacked off during the summer—"You're getting sloppy"—which wasn't something I'd expected to hear. Love is supposed to fire your art, not hinder it. But then I was still a boy in so many ways, still caught up in all the romantic patterns we're taught to expect. I resolved to work harder.

"Are you still determined to do the Chopin second again?"

I told him I was.

"It's such a bear. It might be better to shoot for next year."

"I can do it, Roland. I know I can."

"Why don't you work on something else too? Some Poulenc, maybe. So you'll have something else prepared. Just in case, I mean."

I knew what he meant.

He also suggested I stop using my keyboard. It was a discussion we had had before. The touch of an electronic piano is nothing like the touch of a real one; if you get too used to it, your playing suffers. But there were so many times I felt the urge to play, to express what I was feeling in a concrete way. In the middle of the night, in the early morning hours, whenever I needed to release what I was feeling. The music department, like everything else on campus, got locked down. But I also knew Roland was right, so I decided to spend as much time as I could practicing at the department.

When I told Danilo about it, he responded by giving me a set of keys to his house. "Play on the grand here whenever you like."

"I don't want to bother you."

"You couldn't."

"That sounds like a challenge." I grinned.

"Just once, young Mr. Dunn, couldn't you rein in your penchant for being annoying?"

"How would you know it was me, then?"

But the offer was made, and I was only too happy to take him up on it. His instrument was so much better than the ones for student use at the department.

The first night I went there to practice, he came up behind me and put his arms around me. I felt his lips on my throat. Then the tip of his tongue.

"Really, professor, I thought I was invited here to study your etchings."

"Sorry. I didn't mean to interrupt. But every time I see you, I…" He smiled sheepishly. "You'd think I'd be past this kind of thing."

"Is anyone, ever?"

"I mean, at my age."

"Face it, Danilo. We swimmer boys are irresistible."

He laughed, tousled my hair, and headed off to his study. I went back to the Chopin sonata. I was determined to get it right at the winter recital.

Later, after two hours of only the slightest progress—I tended to be impatient with myself, in ways Roland found frustrating—I found Danilo on the leather sofa in his den and sat beside him. In a moment we were snuggling.

"I've been wondering…" I had needed to discuss something with him for weeks.

"Hmm?" He was busy nuzzling my cheek.

"How can I explain to Justin what's been happening to me—with us?"

He pulled back from me. "That wouldn't be a good idea, Jamie."

"He's my friend. My best friend."

"That's hardly the point. You don't know you can trust him, not with this. He couldn't understand. Even men like him, who share our bloodline, don't understand much more often than not. Or don't want to."

"He's my friend."

"I know. But really, do you think he could understand? How long has it taken you? And he seems so…" He let his voice trail off, not wanting to say anything insulting.

"Dull? Yes."

"Let's just say analytical thought isn't his thing."

"He's a typical jock." I saw his point. "It's awkward, not being able to tell anyone about it."

He got up and poured us each a glass of red wine. "As I said, even men who have the blood frequently don't understand, or don't want to. Justin's friend Greg, for instance."

He handed me my glass and I sipped. "You're saying Greg is part of our bloodline too, that he's one of us?" It caught me completely by surprise. "I thought he was too—"

"Kings do have idiot cousins, Jamie."

We fell silent for a moment.

"What about Roland?"

He shook his head.

"Then it's not merely a matter of who you love?" It was an unexpected thought. I had taken it for granted that we were all, more or less…

"It's not that simple. As a mathematician might put it, we're a subset."

"Oh." The wine was good burgundy. Danilo always had good wine on hand. "So Jus shares our blood, but he couldn't understand. Does that mean you're going to kill him and eat him?"

He sighed an exaggerated sigh. "It's just my luck, after 3,000 years, to fall in love with a brat."

"Danilo?" I had a sudden serious thought. "I thought Roland must have the blood. He seems to understand me so well." They had met several times, briefly.

"No. That, he could never understand." He refilled my glass. "It's about blood. It is both that simple and that complex. The ancient bloodline has been kept alive all these centuries, sometimes in a more or less pure form. More often than you'd expect was possible. It is the driving force, the spark that made James I defend his love for Buckingham against their critics in parliament. That made Camille Saint-Saens defy society and tell the truth about himself. That made Pope Julius III take the beautiful boy he fell in love with and make him a cardinal." He paused for what seemed a long time. "But very often it is watered down, so to speak."

I sipped my burgundy. "I always knew I was different. Even when I was a kid."

He smiled. "Different from the people in Ebensburg? What a tragedy."

"Different was the only thing I knew how to be."

"The blood is the life, Jamie. And the power. You've read the Bible and the ancient scrolls. You understand that. You know the magic that lies in the organs of men who have been sacrificed. The Christians never..." He shrugged and made a vague gesture. "They do not even understand why guards had to be put on the tomb of their Christ. The power in his body that had to be protected."

It was still another new thought. "Jesus Christ was...?"

He nodded slowly. "You have seen the mention of his Beloved Disciple. And what do you think their holy communion commemorates?" He stopped and took a long drink. "The blood has kept me alive all these long millennia, so that I in turn could protect the bloodline, keep it vital."

I pulled his arms around me, buried myself in them. "Like a dragon swallowing its own tail."

"You are the blood prophet, Jamie. The one who will revive the power, and the greatness."

"You keep telling me that. I don't even understand how—"

"You will. You've learned a great deal, very quickly. More quickly than most people are capable of. You will learn more." He got up and refilled our glasses still again. "One day we will be able to proclaim our love to the world. And the world, or at least the part of it that matters, will honor us. As they did Hadrian and Antinous. As they did Alexander and Hephaestion."

I wasn't sure I wanted to be honored. It seemed so…undemocratic or something. "Danilo, will you stop these killings?"

"I can't. That would mean death. My death, and perhaps yours. A thousand generations of our fathers and brothers need us to justify them."

I put my head on his shoulder. Despite his warmth and his tenderness with me, I couldn't help being a bit frightened. "Will you make me one promise, Danilo?"

"If I can, of course."

"Promise me you won't hurt Justin."

"We may have to."

"'We'? No, Danilo, I don't think I could ever do that. Not to him."

For a moment neither of us said anything. Then, involuntarily I found myself laughing. "If you have to take someone, let it be Greg."

Danilo looked directly into my eyes and kissed me. Through the haze of three glasses of burgundy I wanted to put my mouth on every part of him, blood or no, killings or no. He inhaled the bouquet from his wine. "Greg is most emphatically one of us. But the odds that he would ever admit it, or comprehend what admitting it means…" He smiled. "You could scan him with an electron microscope and not find a particle of understanding."

"Sacrifice him, then."

"I think," he said, settling back beside me, "we can find more productive uses for him."

Bubastis continued to grow, like the happy cat she was. There were no signs the incident with Greg had left any residual trauma, though she tended to hide when he was at the apartment. Intelligent creature. But now and then, every once in a rare while, she would wake from a sound sleep, obviously terrified of something. Dreaming. She would come to me, nestle in the crook of my arm and be calm again.

Justin won the state title for the high platform. There was a lot of publicity, at least on campus. The local news programs did stories too, covering him as an Olympic hopeful, but they forgot about him pretty quickly. All the attention, all the cameras and reporters, made Greg stay away, which was fine with me.

"You really love Danilo?" We were alone one night, studying for our classes.

I nodded. "I never thought I'd fall for an older man. But after Tim…" I fell silent. The memory of him always left me uneasy.

"Do the police tell you anything?" He set his book aside. "About what kind of progress they're making, I mean."

I shook my head. "They come around now and then with questions, do I remember such-and-such. I don't think they'll find who did it." This was not a comfortable topic.

He groped for the right thing to say. "Some fiend, some psycho…"

"Maybe. Someone who is lost, at any rate."

"I worry about you, Jamie. A man that old…it doesn't seem right."

"I would have thought so too, last year at this time."

"Don't you know any guys our age who…"

"No." I said it emphatically.

"It's because you never had a father."

"Maybe. I've thought of that."

"I don't like the way he looks at me, Jamie. He's a chicken hawk."

"I don't think so. He says he's as amazed by our relationship as I am, and I believe him." This was less and less what I wanted to be talking about.

Justin shook his head and went back to his textbook. "If you're happy with him, that's great. I wish I could find someone who really…" He broke off self-consciously.

"Greg isn't the one, then?" It was the nicest news I'd had in ages.

"No, I don't think so. He's too…too…I don't know what. But you and Danilo. The two of you really kill me."

After a few weeks all the attention for Jus died down and Greg started hanging around our place again. Mrs. Kolarik didn't like him, ever since the night he hurt Bubastis, and she told him he'd better behave or she'd call the police herself. When he complained about it to Justin, Jus was obviously nervous about it.

"She's a fucking bitch, Jus," Greg said. "We need to teach her to mind her own business."

I couldn't resist cutting in. "She likes us. Both of us, Justin and me. I think she feels a bit motherly and protective toward us."

"Fuck her."

I smiled. "If she's your type, Greg."

I wasn't really afraid of him, not anymore. But I knew he could still hurt me. He walked across the room and got in my face. "I'm talkin' to my boyfriend, bitch boy. You stay the fuck out of it."

I laughed, "Oh, yes, sir!"

He pushed me and I stumbled a few feet back.

Justin quickly got between us. "Why don't the two of you stop it? We all have to get along here."

"Tell him to stop riding me." Greg said the words into my face, not directly to Justin.

He forced us apart. "I want this to stop, Greg."

"Then fuck you too." Greg got his jacket and stomped out of the apartment.

For a moment neither of us said anything. But I couldn't resist adding a smart-ass footnote to it all. "And you have doubts about my relationship. Has he ever hit you, Jus?"

"No." I think he was lying.

"He will."

"No, Jamie, he wouldn't."

"You see how he behaves."

Mrs. Kolarik interrupted us. She had just baked a chocolate cake, and she brought us the first two slices. It was delicious.

Archaic Egypt, the very earliest times, before the pharaohs, even. Danilo asked me to catalog a collection of pots and fragments of rock with inscriptions on them. They'd been sitting in the subbasement for years, maybe decades, unlooked at.

The writing was crude, not the hieroglyphs I was becoming used to. And the art was too; the standards that defined Egypt's art so beautifully for three millennia had not jelled yet.

I sorted through them at a work table in the catacombs. At my insistence Danilo had had more lights installed. It was a bit of a strain on the department's budget, but it made sense and it was long overdue. Even so, I was still uneasy when I went down there alone. Hell, I was even nervous when I was there with Danilo. On edge constantly. The slightest sound made me jump. Danilo had promised me I'd be safe as long as I avoided the lowest subbasement, but…

Among the collection I found a piece of granite with part of a relief cut into it. It appeared to be of two men kissing. I thought I could make out the name of one in the archaic script: Set. The other one must be Horus. The story of their love—or rather, of their sexual relationship—must go back to the beginning of recorded time.

I took it to Danilo and showed it to him. He inspected it carefully, with a magnifier.

"You can make out this ancient writing?" he asked me.

"Just a bit. Mostly I'm guessing."

"You're a good guesser. And this is quite a find." He switched on a reading lamp and inspected it more closely. "Yes. This must be the earliest depiction of them ever found. I'll have to write a monograph." He looked up at me and smiled. "Or rather, we will. You found it."

"I'm not an Egyptologist. No one would take anything seriously if it had my name on it. It would be like you playing Poulenc."

He got up from his desk and straightened his clothes. "You're probably right. But even so, you're the one who found it. And recognized what it is. Otherwise it might have sat in the catacombs for more long years. Most undergraduates would have simply put it back in storage. You deserve at least a mention."

There was a quick knock at the door. It opened and Feld came in. He had a student with him, a pale, slight, red-haired boy. For a startled instant I thought he was Grant.

Danilo beamed at them. "Professor Feld, I'm glad you're here. Look at what Jamie's found."

Feld examined it, turned it over in his fingers. He looked dubious; it wasn't very impressive at first glance. "What is it?"

Danilo explained what it was and why it was important. "A vital contribution to our understanding of the development of Egyptian religion."

"Oh." He looked at me from the corner of his eye. "So Mr. Dunn has made a lucky find."

"Luck was a part of it, yes." Danilo was finding his obtuseness or stubbornness amusing, I could tell. "But he recognized it for what it is. He understood at once how important it is."

Feld ignored this mild dig. "I wanted to introduce you to my new research assistant." The young man took a step into the room. "Professor Semenkaru, this is Peter Borzage."

Danilo said hello and introduced him to me. We shook hands. He was queer, I was sure of it. "So you found something important?"

I smiled a smug little smile and nodded.

"I hope I can."

"If you are as lucky as Mr. Dunn, you will. Let's go." Feld took him by the arm and they left.

I stared after them. "Love in bloom."

"I wouldn't have thought Feld had it in him. He's married and says he's Christian. He seems to think the Greeks and Romans were only important to the extent they paved the way for Christianity. Working with all those statues of naked athletes must have finally gotten to him."

"Little Peter is one of us." I hesitated, not quite sure of myself. "Isn't he?"

"You're learning. Quickly." Danilo smiled and examined the relief again. "This really is an extraordinary find. Your name will be under mine on the paper, quite definitely."

"Now I belong to the ages."

He sighed. "Brat."

"Everybody gets the lover they deserve."

He swiped at me playfully, but I ducked and ran out of his office.

I had never really spent much time in the Greco-Roman part of the museum. But as I was leaving I saw Peter there. He was looking up at a sculpture of a nude discus thrower, slightly larger than life-size. I had noticed it before myself, once or twice. It was a Roman copy of a Greek original. The lines of the body were perfect. Even the way the pubic hair was rendered seemed sensuous. It was hard to mistake his interest in it.

From the doorway I said, "A long way from Feld, isn't it?"

When he saw me, he smiled and waved. "Come on in."

I joined him and we shook hands again. "Borzage. Are you related to the director?"

"What director?" His bafflement showed.

"Nothing."

He was shorter than me, with a much slighter build. No one could mistake him for an athlete. His eyes were pale blue, and his hair was the most shockingly bright red. I couldn't resist saying something about it. "They say King David had red hair."

"King David?"

"You know, the one who loved Jonathan?" It was as bold as I had ever been with anyone.

He blushed rather alarmingly. "I—I—I—"

"Relax. You're among friends."

"F-friends? I—I—"

Oh. Oh dear. I hadn't realized he was so easily flustered. "Never mind. How did you come to work for Feld?"

"I'm in a few of his classes." He was still looking at me as if I might bite. "I'm majoring in classics with a minor in archaeology."

Not exactly a career move, but then I was a classical pianist. He was a sophomore, like me. A native Pittsburgher. He lived at the Delta Kappa Tau frat house. He kept mentioning his "brothers." I resisted asking the obvious question about life there, much as I wanted to know.

My eyes were drawn back to the discus thrower. "These old statues are so beautiful."

He nodded. He couldn't seem to find any words.

"I'm on my way to lunch. Want to get a sandwich?"

"No, thanks." He looked over his shoulder. "I'm eating with Professor Feld."

"Oh." I tried not to make the word too insinuating, but he caught my meaning.

"We're teacher and student, that's all."

"Danilo and I seem to have started a fashion around here. Feld's not the easiest man. I hope you get along with him."

"I like him."

Oh. No arguing taste. "Well, I guess we'll be seeing each other around. Will you be doing any work down in the catacombs?"

"I don't know yet."

"My office is down the hall from Danilo's. If I can be of any help—you know, getting oriented around here—just let me know."

"Thanks." He shook my hand, rather stiffly. I don't think either of us had any idea what to make of the other. But something told me…

He looked so much like Grant.

Peter and I did see each other around the museum, quite a bit actually, over the next several weeks. And I was more and more certain what I had in mind was the right thing to do. It wasn't too hard to con-nive for Justin to meet the two of us "by accident" at the Z. And they hit it off exactly as I'd hoped they would. On our third get-together Jus asked him for a date. When they thought no one was looking they touched hands under the table. It was all so sweet. And better yet, it meant Greg was history, or would be before long.

Danilo worked on his monograph. When it was nearly done he asked me how I'd like my name to appear.

"You mean I get to choose, like a movie star? Call me Cary."

He laughed. I knew what he was going to say, and the words came out of our mouths simultaneously. "He was one of us."

Again he laughed. "You know me too well."

"That isn't possible. I could never have enough of you."

"Flirt. Nearly all the great screen lovers were. Valentino, Gary Cooper, Chevalier…"

"I already know all that. I've been a movie buff since I was a kid."

"And a gossip." He grinned. "See? I know you pretty well too."

"You're the one with all the backstairs news about Erasmus and James Buchanan, Danilo."

"Yes." He was smug. "I am. But it's hardly backstairs. First-hand would be more like it."

"You knew them? All of them?" I knew his passion for history, and it was fast becoming mine too. He told me how Leonardo had spent time in prison for making love to an underage boy. He even had a photo of Clyde Barrow, autographed "To Danilo, with Love."

"As many as I could."

We headed to the Z, which neither of us liked. Actually no one liked it, but it was so damned convenient to everything on campus. Jus and Peter were there. The blush of new love was hard to mis-take. We stopped at their table and chatted for a few moments, then left them to themselves.

"I was asking seriously, Danilo." I couldn't let go of what we'd been talking about. "You seem to have known so many of our…" I found myself borrowing his phrase, "our fathers and brothers."

He smiled a gentle smile. "A lot of them weren't exactly fatherly. Or brotherly. But even without television and the Internet, news traveled. When I heard about a king or an artist or a philosopher who, people said, was…" He grinned playfully and made a twisted little gesture with his hand. "I made it my business to seek him out and make his acquaintance and educate him." He scanned the menu, as if everyone on campus didn't know it by heart. "Some were grateful, some not. Scott Fitzgerald was unpleasant. Dag Hammarskjöld was cold. Nero was, well, Neronian."

I had to ask. I had no illusions that I might be his first love, but I had to ask. "Did you sleep with all of them?"

"Not all, no." He broke into a mischievous grin. "Most of the popes only liked boys. Let's get something to eat."

It seemed so implausible. There were moments when I had my doubts about Danilo's sanity. But I had seen him heal Bubastis. I had seen him go from older to younger time and again. Any scruples I had about him—about the way he stayed alive—disappeared when I was with him and felt his touch.

There was a disturbance at the other end of the restaurant. It was Greg. He was at Justin and Peter's table, shouting and banging his fist. There was some commotion and a campus cop escorted him out. Jus looked a bit startled. Peter's pale complexion had turned bright red.

I told Danilo I'd be back right back and went to their table. "Are you both all right?"

They both nodded but didn't say anything. I was tempted to tell Jus "I told you so," but what would have been the point? He surely understood. "Why don't you come and join Danilo and me?"

They said no thanks. They got their jackets and left. They weren't talking to each other.

Sometimes I worked out in the pool late at night. I liked it when no one else was around; when I needed to think it made concentration easier. The water was a bit cooler, and I could swim for hours. My butterfly always needed work. I frequently thought of

Tim then, always with mixed feelings. His blood, his death had helped continue Danilo's life. How could I know what to feel?

One night after a long practice at the music department I decided I needed to work off some energy. The finale of the sonata still wasn't coming, and I was angry at myself. Roland always told me it would take time. "There aren't more than a handful of players in the world who can really do justice to that last movement, Jamie. I've told you. Ashkenazy, Pollini, Argerich."

"I'm not in their class."

"You will be one day. But you have to take it slow, give it time."

I understood perfectly what he meant, but I was too impatient. Working on it always left me frustrated. I headed for the pool.

The athletic complex always seemed strange to me when there was no one there, uncharacteristically peaceful, devoid of the usually abundant testosterone. And cool. There were only work lights on, so it was pleasantly dark. I stripped and got into my Speedo and plunged into the water. Almost at once I could feel myself relaxing, the tension dissipating.

I swam for half an hour, and I felt wonderful. The rush of the water along my body was always so exhilarating.

There was someone else in the building.

I didn't make anything of it. One of the divers had had the same idea I had, maybe, or one of the runners wanted to use the track. Then I realized who it was.

Greg Wilton was standing at the side of the pool, staring at me, or rather glaring, the hatred plain to see. His hands were folded behind his back. I hung motionless, watching him. I could tread water for hours, and he could never reach me in the pool.

"Get out of there, faggot."

I laughed at him. "Come and get me."

"I said get out of there."

"Is that menace you're trying to convey, Greg? You're not doing a very good job."

He moved his hands. He was holding a baseball bat. "You fucked with me and my boyfriend."

"He's not your boyfriend anymore."

A security guard came in on his late-night rounds. Greg glared at him, then at me. "Later, Dunn."

I knew he was violent. I'd have to be careful. I chatted with the guard, who knew me from all the nights I swam there. After a while, when I was sure Greg must be gone, I got out and headed for the locker room.

Greg was there, waiting. He swung the bat and hit me square on the head. Everything spun. I fell.

"Don't ever fuck with me again, queer boy."

He raised the bat. I winced, bracing myself for another blow to my head. Instead he hit my fingers. I felt them crack and I cried out in the worst pain I had ever felt.

It wasn't enough for him. He caught my fingers and bent them back till they were all broken. He twisted them.

"Let's see you play your goddamn fag piano now, cocksucker."

I cried out. The pain was terrible.

Then everything went black.

Hospital room. Hospital smell in the air.

I woke and looked around.

Justin was at one side of the bed, Roland at the other. My hands were in casts. There were IV tubes in my arms, and some kind of monitoring device whirred and hummed on a stand beside me.

Seeing me awake, Roland stood and kissed my forehead gently. "Jamie."

I looked up at him. Jus came close and touched my cheek.

Then I remembered what had happened. Greg. My fingers shattered, destroyed. There would be no more Chopin.

I felt tears coming. I didn't much want to cry in front of them but there would be no more piano for me, no way to express myself. They would never heal they way they had been.

"How do you feel?" I could read the pain in Justin's face. He blamed himself. He was still stroking my cheek.

"I want to die. That's how I feel."

"Jamie, that's no way to talk."

"Isn't it?"

"They caught Greg. The security guard caught him beating you, even though you were already unconscious. You have a concussion." I saw a tear in his eye. "This is my fault, Jamie. I'm so sorry. I should have listened to you about him."

Roland looked at him. "The thug who did this was your…?"

I could see a slight panic in Justin's eyes. He was being asked. After a moment he swallowed hard and said, "My boyfriend, yes."

Roland didn't seem to know how to react to this.

Where was Danilo? I tried to move my fingers, but of course I couldn't. Still there was awful pain. I cried out, not loudly.

They both stared at me. Neither seemed to know what to say. How could they?

My Chopin was gone. I cried and could not make myself stop.

"Professor Semenkaru had to go out for a while. He'll be back soon." Roland seemed not quite to approve of what he was telling me.

"He was here?"

Jus nodded. "Some lovers really are lovers."

Roland shifted uncomfortably and tried to put on a professional air. "The guard called Justin. He called me and Semenkaru."

"Don't let him go after Greg." I tried to adjust myself in the bed but couldn't. Roland helped me shift my weight.

"Go after him?" Roland smiled. "He's an archaeologist, not a gunslinger."

I looked at Jus. "Don't let him, okay?" Then I turned to Roland. "I guess I never will get that last movement right, huh?"

"For God's sake, Jamie, stop doing this to yourself."

"I can't help it. The only thing I've ever wanted to be is a pianist. The only thing I've ever loved is the music I play. That, and Tim, and Danilo." We all fell quiet for a moment. "When will he be back?"

"He didn't say." Jus tried to give me a drink of water, but I wasn't thirsty and pushed the glass away. At least my hands were good for that.

"This room is his doing." Roland was sounding more and more like a professor. He must have thought it would help. "Your student med insurance wouldn't cover a private room. He told them he'd make up the difference. He insisted."

I stared at him, hard, as if to tell him, *Don't say he doesn't love me.*

"The police have Greg. Everyone on campus is relieved, now that they know who's been behind all the attacks. They're questioning him now."

This startled me. I almost laughed. Greg, the fall guy for Danilo and me. It was too perfect. "They think he...?"

Jus nodded. "It could have been me he went after next. I told them how he screamed and threatened me."

"So you're a bit of a hero." Roland smiled for the first time. "You helped put an end to the nightmare this school has been through."

I looked at my hands. "Big deal. Big goddamned deal. What do I get?"

"It could have been worse, Jamie. You could be dead."

"Without my hands, I am."

"They can fix them. There are wonderful new therapies. I'll have you at the keyboard again in no time."

All I could do was cry.

Danilo had not come. I fell asleep wondering why.

Then, in the smallest hours of the night, I woke and saw him standing in my doorway, carrying a wooden chest under one arm.

We kissed. He held me. The pain seemed not so bad.

The light in the room was dim, but I could see tears on his face. "I thought there would be time. I thought we could delay this. I never thought..." From his chest he took a large candle. He struck a match and lit it. "Pure beeswax," he whispered, "like the ones they use in church."

There was an empty part of me. Danilo loved me, I loved him, it gave meaning to my life, but there was a hole in me now and always would be.

A nurse came to the door and saw us. "It's past visiting hours."

Danilo turned and stared at him. "Leave us."

He took a step into the room. "You have to go. And that candle is a fire hazard. Put it out now, or else I'll call security."

"You will not."

Danilo spread his arms wide. The nurse's eyes followed them. He seemed to go into a trance. Danilo told him to leave and forget he had seen him there; and he did.

Then he lit a second candle beside the bed and began to chant in what I knew was the language of ancient Egypt. The flames rose and turned red.

He made gestures over me. I didn't understand why.

He pressed his lips to my eyes, then to my heart, then to my genitals, and chanted more.

Then he produced a shallow bowl. It seemed to be made of gold. By the candlelight I could see a row of hieroglyphics inscribed on it.

From one of his pockets he brought out a bottle. Ancient glass, a piece from the museum; I thought I had seen it, or ones like it, in the display cases. It was filled with bright red blood.

He poured it into the golden bowl. I understood now. As he said more prayers over me, I drank.

When I bled from cuts as a little boy, my blood had always tasted salty to me. This blood was sweet. It tasted like Danilo.

I drank greedily.

He prayed to the gods, or to one god; I knew which.

And I felt life and energy flow through me like a river. My hands tingled, my fingers were alive with electricity. And I had an erotic reaction; I felt myself become erect.

"Feel the power, Jamie." He whispered. "And this is nothing compared to what you will feel when your own power reaches its height." He put his hand on my thigh. "This is only the beginning."

We both fell silent. He studied my face. "It has worked, then," he said into my ear.

"I don't know. I felt something. They don't hurt."

"Quietly, Jamie. The things we do must be done in stillness and the dark."

He bent down and kissed me.

In the candlelight I saw that there was a trace of blood on his own lips. He was young and beautiful. We had shared communion, then.

"You must keep the casts on for a few weeks, perhaps a month or more. The healing will seem miraculous, but they will be able to rationalize it then. An overnight healing…that would be too much."

He placed his hands on mine. "You will play again, Jamie, more beautifully than before."

"I never thought I would. Danilo, I—"

He held up a finger. "Shh. Quiet now. Your body needs sleep. I'll spend the night here beside you."

I wanted to ask him who he had taken that night, whose blood…but it didn't seem to matter.

Two weeks later, Danilo had to go out of town to attend a professional conference in Chicago. The University of Chicago has an Oriental Institute, the most important center of Egyptological studies in America. He wanted to show some colleagues, experts on Egyptian religion, the relief I had found.

It seemed that quite without wanting to, I had become a bit of a hero on campus, the one who survived the campus killer. There were notes of sympathy from the dean and the chancellor, from my teachers, from students I barely knew or couldn't remember. I was on the news. Inevitably, the story of Justin and Greg's affair came out.

Roland arranged for me to take the rest of the semester off, and I could take another one if I needed it. The university was prepared to be as generous and forbearing with me as I needed. He kept telling me I'd play again. I didn't believe him; I believed Danilo.

Justin kept fussing over me, taking care of me. It took me hours of argument to persuade him he didn't have to feed and dress me. His guilt was so touching. It occurred to me in the middle of one of our little exchanges that I'd never had a real friend before.

He and Peter had been dating. I don't think either of them knew how serious it was, or how serious they wanted it to be. Then when the facts about Jus and Greg made the news, Peter was obviously shaken by it. "I can't have people know," he told Jus. "I couldn't do that to my family. And my frat brothers would…well, they wouldn't understand." So their affair ended.

Each night, Bubastis slept beside me on my pillow, purring gently. Mornings I'd wake to find her licking my nose, wanting to be fed.

Greg was being held without bail. The police were doing everything they could to prove he was the serial murderer. He kept saying I was the only one he wanted to kill, as if that would let him off the hook. And he kept insisting he and Jus hadn't been boyfriends, claiming rather desperately not to be gay. There was a lot of coarse humor around town at his expense; I wasn't sure how I felt about it.

At first, his basketball coach had tried to deny that Greg could possibly be queer; when that got laughed at, he just kept telling everyone, "No comment." I found that very entertaining.

In two weeks I hadn't left our apartment. Jus had tried to get me to go out, saying it would be good for me. But I refused every time. My hands were clumsy in their casts, and the concussion had left me a bit light-headed. The doctors said that would pass.

Then one night he suggested the campus observatory. "Neither of us has ever gone up there, Jamie, and I keep hearing it's a really cool place."

"I'm not sure I feel like it."

"I called them. When I told them you were coming they offered to give us a private tour. They said Mars is at its nearest approach, and would you be interested in seeing it?"

Mars. I didn't hesitate. I told him we should get going.

There was a private shuttle bus waiting for us outside. The university ran them all over campus, but I had never heard of them sending one for just two students before. I was more of a celebrity than I'd thought.

The driver, an astronomy grad student named Mark, fussed over me, made sure I was comfortable. "Would you like me to put on a classical CD?"

"No, thanks."

"I have some jazz, then."

"Sure."

Ella Fitzgerald serenaded us. It was a half-hour drive to the northern part of the city. For part of the way I leaned on Justin, and he put an arm around me. The observatory sat on a high hill. There were three domes, an enormous one flanked by two smaller ones. Mark told us it was the highest point in the county. "This place was built back in the 1800s. There were no houses or stores around then. This was pure country."

"As long as the music isn't." Smart-ass Jamie.

And we got our tour, again by Mark. He showed us the two refractor telescopes in the side domes and the gargantuan reflector in the main one. There were rooms full of computers, rooms full of lenses and other optical equipment, huge archives of old photos and research notes. In the basement we saw, somewhat to our surprise, the tomb of the man who had built the place. It was under a red granite monument inscribed with a quote from the Bible: "And the morning stars sang together."

"And now," Mark announced dramatically, "it's show time."

He led us back up to the main dome, the one with the enormous telescope. There was a paddle with electronic controls. The huge dome began to rotate, slowly, making a low rumbling sound. The telescope swung around, following the slit in it. It was all impressive, even a bit awe-inspiring, like the parting of the Red Sea in *The Ten Commandments*. "We don't normally let the public look through this one," he said. "It's reserved for research. But you're a hero."

"A hero?" I laughed. "Try victim."

"If it wasn't for you, Greg Wilton would still be loose."

I let it go. The dome and the telescope danced above us then came to a quiet stop. The slit in the dome opened. Mark switched off the lights and wheeled a stepped platform into place at the eyepiece. "Gentlemen, take a look at Mars, the Great God of War."

There was a little platform on wheels with a ladder attached. Mark positioned it by the eyepiece and I climbed the steps and put my eye to the lens. It was there. The fact he had been able to point the telescope at it without seeing it seemed a bit magical to me. The planet was a ruddy orange disk. There were darker markings across it, some dark green, some brownish like dried blood. I could just barely make out one of the polar caps.

Mars. Set. Watching it, I tried to remember what Danilo had told me: The ancients believed the planets were the souls of the gods. Seeing Mars, it was hard to believe. There seemed no real mystery about it, strange and even beautiful as it was. The markings were random. I thought I could understand how they might seem ordered, connected, but they clearly weren't.

"Mars has always been associated with war, blood, and death." Mark gave us what sounded like a canned lecture. "The Persians, the Syrians, the Greeks, the Romans, even the Druids saw it that way. Every primitive society we know of."

"Primitive?" I decided to goad him a bit. "Isn't that politically incorrect?"

"Well, early, then. Scientifically primitive. You know what I mean." I noticed a wedding band on his finger.

"Yeah, I guess I do."

Jus tugged on my pant leg. "Do you mind if I get a look?"

"I'm the hero here, remember?"

"Oh."

I was only kidding. I stepped down and let him take my place at the eyepiece. I asked Mark, "And what about the Egyptians? What did they make of Mars?"

His face went blank. "I…I don't know. Same as the others, I guess."

Jus stood and stared for a moment. "I think I can see the canals."

"There are no canals," Mark explained quickly, "just random surface markings."

"I can see them."

"It's just a trick of the eye," Mark told him. "An illusion."

Jus looked down at us, then back into the eyepiece. "I could swear…"

It made me surprisingly uncomfortable. "So much for Mars," I told Mark. "How about the goddess of love, now?"

"Venus isn't visible just now."

"Oh."

He showed us more—galaxies, nebulae, the planet Pluto, which looked like just another faint star. When we'd seen enough, we thanked him and he drove us home.

Justin made a late dinner, pasta and a salad, and we sat down to eat. He seemed out of sorts. "I think I'm sorry we went up there."

"Why?" I asked him.

"I felt like a damned fool. Having him tell me what I know I was seeing wasn't there."

"You're not the first to see canals on Mars, Jus."

"Even so. He made me feel like an idiot."

"I'm sure he didn't mean to."

We ate without saying much more. Just as I was about to get up from the table he said, "And I saw all kinds of things in Greg that weren't there. What's wrong with me?"

"Nothing. Not a thing."

"I'm stupid."

"No, Jus. You're human."

"Is that supposed to make me feel better?"

I paused. "No, I guess not."

Later, in the living room, as I was reading, he went on. "I hate feeling stupid, Jamie. I know I'm not. But everybody thinks because I'm a jock I'm an airhead."

"I don't."

"It's different for you. You play the piano, and those sonatas and things. People know you have a brain."

I held up my casts.

"Oh. Sorry."

I set my book aside. "Look, you're the best friend I've ever had. I don't know how I could have gotten through this without you."

"You wouldn't have gotten into it without me."

"You don't know that."

For the thirtieth time, he apologized. Then we fell silent. Nothing I could think of could make him feel better. I only wished he'd get over it. Maybe, I thought, when my casts came off and I could play again, he'd stop feeling so awful.

"Jus?"

"Hmm?"

"You ever think about dying?"

"On this campus? And with Greg in my life? How could I not?"

"I mean your own death. The end to your existence. The nothing we all face, sooner or later."

"Life is nothing now. Peter won't come near me. No one will."

Justin was twenty years old, a college diver, and gorgeous. He could have lovers by the score if he wanted them. But there was no way to tell him that. He didn't want to hear it.

I made myself smile at him. "If you could live forever...if there was something you could do to become immortal...would you do it?"

He laughed, rather bitterly, I thought. "Like what?"

"I don't know. Just say there was something."

"I wouldn't want my life to go on one minute longer than it has to. No."

Oh. It had only been a thought. He got up and headed for his room. I went back to my book.

As much as I loved Danilo, and as much as I trusted him, it was hard to believe my shattered fingers would play again, at least not well.

After another month the doctors x-rayed my hands and found the bones had knitted perfectly. They were pleased but rather obviously baffled by it. "You must have good genes," one of them told me, as if that explained anything. They said they wanted me to keep the casts on for another week, "just to be sure," but that my hands looked perfect. Word of the "West Penn medical miracle" spread, and I found myself the object of attention again. Not that I wanted it; all I wanted was to get the casts off and get back to my music.

Danilo cooked dinner for me most nights; Justin did it when Danilo couldn't. I kept hoping Danilo was right, that I would play again; it seemed to be all I could think of. But I could hardly talk to anyone about it—not Jus, not Roland, certainly not Danilo. How could I tell him I wasn't sure I believed what he was promising?

On the day I was finally to have the casts off, Danilo offered to cancel his classes and come with me. But it seemed pointless. "I'm only going to get them cut off. It's not like I'm having surgery or anything."

"Will you promise to come to my office first thing?"

"Sure." I found his concern touching but a bit funny.

In the hospital waiting room I ran into Peter, of all people. He wasn't exactly someone I wanted to see. At least he and Jus hadn't gotten too serious before he panicked and hid in his closet.

He asked how I was, said he'd read about my healing in the news, all the stuff I'd been hearing from everybody. I wanted him to go away.

"Why are you here, Peter? Did you stub your toe on your closet door?"

He mouthed the words "HIV test."

"Isn't that a mighty bold step for a cautious guy like you?"

"I think I need it. I wish you wouldn't make fun of me."

"I can't help it. Shame and timidity always strike me as funny."

"Oh." He fell silent. "I've been getting more than my share of that from my frat brothers. They heard about Justin on the news, and…"

"And?"

"Well, they knew he was the guy I had been hanging out with. The fairy jokes still haven't let up."

"I thought they were your brothers."

"Don't rub it in, okay?"

I felt no sympathy for him. He had hurt Justin. Not badly, but he had hurt him, and for nothing that seemed at all reasonable to me. I pretended to have to use the men's room, and when I came back I sat pointedly as far away from him as I could.

He refused to take the hint; he got up and moved beside me again.

In a confidentially low tone he said, "There are rumors that all Greg Wilton's victims were…" He seemed not to want to say the word. "Like us."

"Us? You and I don't have much in common, Peter."

"You know what I mean."

"Do I?"

He ignored my deliberate obtuseness. "I don't see how that can be, though. A lot of them had girlfriends, or fiancées even. One of them was married."

"Well, that settles the matter, then."

"I even went to a meeting of the campus gay group. When I asked, they laughed at me, the way you've been doing."

"Then stop being laughable."

"Jamie, I'm afraid. If my family finds out…"

"I won't tell them, okay? Now will you leave me alone?"

He got up and moved away. But he kept staring at me across the room. If I hadn't been so anxious to get the casts off, I'd have left.

After another ten minutes, awkward ones, the nurse called my name. They did another quick set of x-rays, "just to be a hundred percent sure," then cut the casts. For the first time in six weeks I was able to move my fingers. It felt wonderful. The doctor warned me to take it easy with them, but I wanted to get to Danilo's and play.

Just as I got back to the waiting room they were calling Peter's name. As we passed each other he caught hold of my arm. "We can't all be as brave as you, Jamie."

"I'm not all that brave."

"If I were you, I'd wouldn't be out and about today. Not after the news."

It was the first thing he'd said that caught my interest. "What news?"

"Haven't you heard? Greg Wilton escaped from the police this morning."

He went inside. I hadn't heard a thing about it.

Greg, loose.

I had no idea what to think or feel. I headed straight for the museum. Danilo was between classes. He held my hands. "How do they feel?"

"I'm not sure. I haven't used them for so long, I've forgotten what they're supposed to feel like."

He massaged my fingers. His touch was wonderful. I told him about Greg.

"Oh." He hadn't heard either. "If he has any sense at all, he'll leave town. Do you know where he's from?"

"Someplace in Indiana, I think."

"That's where he'll head, then."

Walking home, I couldn't think of anything else. Everyone Greg was queer now. He would blame me for that.

I stopped at Mrs. Kolarik's, wanting to show my newly free hands, but she didn't seem to be home. So I headed upstairs to our place.

The door was open. It was unlike Jus not to close it. When I got inside I called Bubastis. She was gone.

"Jus?"

He must have had a late class or a date or something.

"Jus?"

Nope, he wasn't home.

Bubastis had run away. I prayed she'd come back.

I felt restless. Danilo's. I needed to play. Feeling the response of the keys under my fingers after all that time would be paradise.

The day was a slight bit chilly. Jus had borrowed my sweatshirt. I went into his room.

He was on the bed, his throat slit. Blood soaked everything.

I heard a movement behind me and turned. I caught the briefest flash of Greg's face, filled with rage or hatred or both. I saw the knife in his hand. Then I felt the blade cut into my throat. Slowly.

I needed to vomit. But all that came out of my mouth was blood.

CHAPTER 8

Darkness.

Night.

Cold.

No dreams. There were no dreams.

And then…

Stone. The coldness and hardness of stone, chilling and invigorating my body.

Fire, filling my eyes.

A rush of pleasure, the most intense surge of sexual pleasure I had ever felt.

I awoke. Danilo stood over me, smiling gently. "Jamie. Welcome. Or should I say, welcome back?"

I was weak and disoriented. Instinctively I put a hand to my throat, to feel the wound. There was none.

There was something around me. It took me a moment to focus. I was lying in a sarcophagus. Alabaster, I thought. Pure white, at any rate. Danilo took my hand, then bent down to kiss me. "Are you all right?"

"I don't know. I should be dead. Or in a hospital under intensive care."

"If you were anyone else, and if you loved anyone else, you would be." His hand felt especially warm.

Groggy, stupid, I muttered, "I love you."

"Why do young people always feel the need to belabor the obvious?"

There were candles burning all around the sarcophagus and in the corners of the room. And torches too. Their light seemed impossibly bright. I tried to block their glare with my free hand, but I was too weak to hold it up for long.

The world went black again.

And again I woke to find Danilo watching over me, holding my hand, and smiling like the father-lover-protector that he was.

Had Greg been a dream, or was this?

I reached up once again to feel the wound on my throat. There was none. No blood, not a bit of tenderness, even; no trace of what he had done to me. "Danilo?"

"Relax. Sleep more if you need to."

"I should be dead. I saw my blood spill, a lot of it."

"Yes."

"I felt the knife go all the way through my throat. I felt it tear muscle and shatter bone."

He smiled at me.

"And…" I remembered Justin, his eyes wide open, lying in a bath of his own blood. I remembered that my cat was gone. What horrible thing had Greg done to her?

Danilo held a golden cup to my lips. "Here. Drink."

I pulled away instinctively. "Is it more blood?"

"No. You've had enough of that for a while."

"Then…?"

"Drink it."

I sipped, cautiously. It was wine, good red wine. It warmed me. I looked up at him and he touched my face. "It wasn't possible to lose you, Jamie."

"You wouldn't have been the first to give me up."

"Time has made me a skeptic." He stroked my cheek. "Do you know that?"

I didn't know what he was trying to tell me.

"Cervantes wrote that love is a force too powerful to be overcome by anything but flight. But I've waited too many centuries for it. I couldn't lose you, not after the years I've waited and the things I've lived through."

He held the cup to my lips and I drank a bit more.

"I was there when the bishops passed the first law to condemn us. I was there when the Knights Templar were tortured for loving each other. To have lived through all that was awful enough. But losing you, Jamie, would have been worse." He bent down and pressed his lips to mine.

I was still lying in the sarcophagus. My back was beginning to feel a bit stiff. The torches and candles still burned brightly all around me. "Danilo, where are we? What is this?"

Very quietly he said, "You will never die. Not until you want to."

The blood. The prayers. The ancient inscriptions. "You have made me…?"

"Yes."

"I wasn't sure I wanted that, Danilo. You should have—"

"It was that or lose you. To lose you, Jamie…as I said, that I could not do."

"Then what I saw…Greg. Jus. It was real, not a nightmare."

"I'm afraid so." He paused. "He slaughtered your landlady too."

"Mrs. Kolarik. She was a nice lady." I felt tears coming. "Justin. Poor Justin."

"I know how close you were."

"Bring him back too, Danilo. Please." I could feel tears running down the side of my face. The stone was beginning to be more and more uncomfortable. I tried to get up.

And I lost consciousness still again.

When I woke I was alone and lying on my side. I tried to sit up again, unsure I'd be able to.

For the first time I got a good look at the room I was in. It seemed I was in an Egyptian tomb, or in a place made to look like one. Torches and candles still burned everywhere.

The walls were stone, and they were covered with painted reliefs of gods and demons. The great god Osiris and his consort Isis, who resurrected him when he was killed by Set. Maat, the goddess of truth, who weighed the purity of people's souls when they died. Anubis, the god of the graveyard. There were winged serpents, insects with the wings of falcons, men with the heads of frogs and lions. A ship filled with the dead sailed overhead across the ceiling.

It was a shrine, a holy place. From what little I had learned I recognized that every image in the room had to do with death and the underworld. A fit place for me, I thought.

I was still weak. Carefully I moved some of the candles that were burning immediately beside my sarcophagus, stood up and climbed out.

"Danilo?"

I was quite alone. I saw that the sarcophagus's lid was sitting on the floor, propped against it at an angle.

There was a door. Not a carved stone door of the kind you'd find in a real Egyptian tomb. Just a typical wooden door, with a doorknob and keyhole. I tried it, and it opened.

There were steps going up. I climbed.

And I was in Danilo's kitchen. It was so unexpected I laughed.

He was at the stove. Wearing, absurdly, an apron. I smelled bacon and eggs. When he saw me, he beamed. "Good morning."

"Good morning." I was so disoriented. "We're in your house."

"Keen observation."

"How? Why?"

"I was wondering how much longer you could sleep. The rites tend to take it out of a man, but…" He grinned. "You're hungry?"

I realized I was starving, and said so.

"Sit down and have some breakfast. It is the first morning of your new life. Your second life."

I was still feeling weak, light-headed. "I was…I really was dead, then?"

He nodded. "Fascinating, isn't it?"

I didn't know. "Really dead?"

"Yes, Jamie, you really were dead."

"And you…?"

"Yes." He smiled a tight little smile. "And I…"

"But…" My head was spinning. "But it isn't possible."

"He that believeth, though he die, yet shall he live."

"Stop it, Danilo. I need you to be serious about this."

163

He set two plates, poured hot tea, and we sat down to eat. The bacon smelled wonderful. I tucked in.

"I got to your place not long after you must have on Friday." He forked a slice of bacon. "I saw someone running away, I couldn't tell who. The door was open, and I went in. Blood was still flowing from your throat when I got to you."

"And Jus?"

"He's dead, Jamie. There was nothing to be done for him."

"You brought me back."

"But not him. It wasn't possible. You had already tasted the blood of the sanctified when you were in the hospital. That prepared you; that made it possible."

I fell silent.

"You died in my arms, Jamie. I've been alive all these centuries, and all I could think was, my love should be able to keep him alive. My love should be strong enough. But you died in my arms. I sat there crying and holding you for I don't know how long. Then I came to my wits. There was a way to bring you back. I knew it only too well."

It took a moment for this to sink in. "You have…" I groped for the word, "resurrected others, then?"

He nodded and ate. "They were, well, let me only say they were disappointments to me." He bit a slice of bacon in half.

Like him, I stopped talking and ate. Then I had a realization "You said once that Jesus Christ was… Is he one of the ones you…?"

"I'm afraid so, yes." He took a sip of his tea. "I have a great deal to account for. It has been his followers, by and large, who have stripped us of our birthright. If you could have seen the persecutions… Good men imprisoned, tortured, mutilated, burned alive even."

"Where are they now? The ones you resurrected?"

He shrugged. "They're around someplace, sharing their self-hatred. Spreading it, like the malignancy it is."

He told me he had waited till nightfall, then carried my

corpse to his house. He left a note addressed to Justin, signed with my name, telling him I was going out of town for the weekend, to a conference, with Professor Semenkaru. It was for the police to find. Then he phoned them, claiming to be a neighbor, saying there was something wrong at our house. And so they went and found Jus and Mrs. K.

The story was that Danilo and I were at a professional conference, discussing the Kissing Kings relief I had found. When the police called him to ask about me, he waited while they left a message. Then after a few hours he called them back to tell them we were out of town and would be back on Monday evening. It was now Tuesday morning.

"But Danilo, what if they check?"

"They will not." He said it with perfect confidence.

I remembered how he had dealt with that nurse at the hospital. "You have that kind of power over people's minds?" He had hinted at it often enough. No one will ask questions about us, no one will try and get me fired for making love to a student... I asked him how he did it.

"One step at a time, junior. You have only just been born."

I grinned. "Do you want me to wear diapers? Would it turn you on?"

He tried to swat me playfully, and I ducked. The sudden movement made me dizzy. "I...I think I need to lie down again."

He helped me into his den, to the sofa. There, sleeping at one end of it, was Bubastis. When she heard us she looked up. Recognizing me, she ran to me, purring excitedly.

"How...?"

"He didn't hurt her. He must have left the door open when he went in, because she ran away. I went back to your place a second time, late that same night, to make certain there were no traces of your being there. She was hiding under a bush. When she saw me, she came out."

I stooped to pick her up, and the world spun. Danilo helped

me to the couch. She climbed happily into my lap, and I fell asleep yet again.

The police came around that afternoon to question me. Two detectives; not the ones who had questioned me when I found Grant. I followed Danilo's lead and told them we had been out of town.

"Out of town, where?"

"New York. A miniconference at the Metropolitan Museum."

Danilo interrupted to tell them about that little relief I had found. "A few experts got together to examine it."

They were puzzled at the amount of blood they had found, enough for two people, apparently.

I pretended not to understand it either. "Was it his own?"

"No, we checked. He was AB positive. This was O negative."

"Maybe he had someone else with him and took the body away."

"Why would he do that?"

"He's crazy."

The detective seemed a bit suspicious, but Danilo had a private little talk with him and he left satisfied.

My house, or rather Mrs. Kolarik's, was off-limits, sealed off with police tape. It gave me a perfect, suspicion-free excuse to move in with Danilo "temporarily." Not even the university administration would question it. I had to live someplace.

The police let me in to get some things; clothes, sheet music, and books. I'd be able to get the rest of it later. Greg had poured blood over my keyboard. My own blood, I imagine. It was ruined. Just as well.

And so I was in the news again. Or rather, Greg and I were: "Manhunt for Serial Killer Wilton. Dunn Escapes Massacre." And on and on. I knew the media would get bored with me soon enough, but it was still quite unpleasant dealing with their vacuous questions. I refused to play their game.

"How did you feel when you heard about the killings?"

I smirked. "How do you think?"

"Are you sorry you weren't home?"

"What kind of stupid question is that?"

"Justin Hollis was a homosexual. Were you and he lovers?"

"No. He was my best friend."

The reporter was suspicious. "You mean to say you were best friends with a homosexual?"

"Yes, I mean to say that."

"And you were not lovers?"

"We were friends. If we were lovers, I'd say so."

This seemed to confuse him.

It went on for a few minutes more. I quite deliberately made myself into a bad interview, and they finally went away.

There was a guest bedroom in Danilo's house. He had made it over for me while I was unconscious. My favorite colors, a wonderful soft bed, even a spinet, for when I wanted to practice in privacy. On the keyboard was a music manuscript. From the look of it, it was ancient. I picked it up carefully and examined it. Yellowed, slightly torn. Twenty-four preludes for piano. At the top of the first page was the composer's autograph: F. Chopin.

To hold it, actually to handle it and own it, thrilled me so much that I started shaking. I had the best lover in the world. And I went to tell him so.

He was in his den, writing something. I looked over his shoulder and saw that it was in hieroglyphics. He looked up at me and grinned, a bit sheepishly, I thought. "My memoirs."

"Like the emperor Claudius."

"He was most emphatically not one of us." He shuffled a few pages and set them aside. "Too feeble-minded."

"Kings have idiot cousins, remember?"

"Not him. He was the only one of the first twelve caesars who didn't understand the power they held. In themselves, I mean. Even Caligula, mad as he was, seemed to grasp the truth. When he announced to a startled empire that he was a god, he was only telling them the truth, more or less."

"You knew them? All of them?"

He shrugged. "Rome was where the action was back then. Rome and China. I moved back and forth a lot."

I held out the Chopin manuscript and kissed him. "Thank you."

"You're welcome. It is part of your birthright, after all. Or should I say your rebirthright. It only made sense to give it to you."

"The caesars themselves could have known no better lover, Danilo. Not in Athens or Byzantium or Babylon can there have been such a wonderful man."

"Yes, there was, Jamie." He laughed with unusual heartiness. "And I was that man."

Bubastis and I adjusted to our new home quickly and happily. But I was haunted by the image of Justin, his throat gaping, his blood covering everything in sight. There were nightmares. I pictured him reaching out to me, begging me for life. Danilo held me in the night till I calmed down again.

In odd moments I played. My fingers felt strange, weak. But they responded. I thought I'd get back the full use of them. Danilo assured me I would. "You'll play like a god."

I was never quite comfortable with the talk of us having that mystical blood, of us being the sons of divine kings and so on. It felt, I don't know, presumptuous or something. There never seemed a polite way of telling him so, but I did now.

"You were dead, Jamie. Now you're alive. What more proof could you need?"

"If we men with 'the blood' are so special, how do you account for Greg?"

"You've said it yourself. All kings have mentally defective blood relatives. Psychotics, morons. Read a good history of any dynasty you like."

"I don't feel very royal. I just feel wasted."

"You haven't begun to exercise your power yet. You don't have your wings. Wait."

Waiting was all I could do. The nocturnes had never felt so right to me.

Justin's funeral was at a Catholic church in Zelienople on a dark, cloudy, windy day. Danilo went with me. There was quite a crowd of people. His diving coach and most of the team. Representatives of the administration and a party of faculty members. Roland was among them. Justin's parents were there, of course; it was the first time I had met them.

We arrived a bit late; the requiem Mass was just beginning. There was a choir singing sad hymns. There were candles and flowers everywhere. Jus had been a bit of a hometown hero.

Afterward we went to the cemetery. It was high autumn, and the ground was thick with dead leaves. Now and then the wind brought a slight spray of rain, but it never really developed into a steady shower. The campus chaplain said prayers over the grave. When everyone else joined him, I stayed silent. Jus had never been religious in the time I knew him.

His mother was a gray-haired woman in middle age. She wore a black suit and veil and looked rather like a stern nun. Mr. Hollis was a bit shorter than her, quite trim, and even a bit handsome. I forced myself not to think that. Older men. It wouldn't do for that to develop into a habit. I remembered Jus telling me once that his father had been a diver too.

After the service Danilo joined several other faculty members and started chatting. Mrs. Hollis, seeing me alone, came over to me. "You are Jamie Dunn?"

I told her yes.

"Justin liked you."

"I liked him, ma'am. He was the best friend I've ever had." Quite against my will I felt tears welling up. I fought them back.

"You weren't praying, Jamie. Why not? Don't you think you could have prayed for him? Justin liked you."

It caught me completely by surprise. Why had she been

watching me instead of the funeral rites? "I pray my own way, Mrs. Hollis," I said. "And to my own god."

"You should have prayed with the rest of us. And why are you telling people he was a homosexual?"

I was even more off balance. I couldn't think of a thing to say.

"He was a good boy. He was not a deviant."

Jus had told the police about himself and Greg. I never would have. At least I didn't think I would. And I was grateful I had never had to make the decision.

Her husband joined us. He smiled and shook my hand. "Jamie. Thank you for coming."

But she was not to be distracted from what she'd been saying. "Justin was a Christian, a Catholic. He was not a sex pervert."

I was completely out of my depth. I thought I remembered him telling me once his parents knew about him and Grant. And I was still weak from what I had been through; I felt myself becoming light-headed.

Roland stepped out of another knot of faculty people. He had been watching all this from a few feet away. It was the first time I had seen him since the killings. He crossed quickly to us, put a hand on my back and interrupted her. "Jamie, it's so good to see you. Are you all right?"

I nodded and smiled at him, mouthed the word "thanks," then introduced them.

Mrs. Hollis glared at him. "You are a friend of this...this..."

"This fine young man. Yes, Mrs. Hollis. I'm Jamie's teacher, advisor, and friend."

It felt good to hear him say it.

"Then why are you permitting this kind of indecent talk?"

Roland smiled, ignored her, and turned to me. "Greg's still at large. Are the police protecting you?"

They weren't. Their best guess was that Greg had left the area. What they based that on, I had no idea.

"They should be. Let me see your hands."

I held them out. He took them in his and carefully worked

them, to feel how they had healed. "I thought you'd stop by the department when the casts came off."

"It was the day Greg escaped. I—since the murders I've been—"

"No need to explain. Have you played at all?"

"A bit."

"You'll have to let me hear."

"Sure. I'm living at Danilo's for now." I told him the address. "Stop by any time."

Mrs. Hollis, obviously unhappy at being ignored, stepped away from us. She walked to the open grave and began to cry. "My boy. My baby."

Her husband followed her and put an arm around her.

Danilo joined Roland and me. "The mother," he said.

"Yes."

He and Roland knew each other slightly. They shook hands, and I told Danilo I had invited Roland to come to the house to hear me play. That afternoon was Mrs. Kolarik's funeral. I had to go. We arranged for Roland to come by that evening.

I took him to the parlor and sat down at the grand. Danilo left us to ourselves. The C-minor nocturne, sad and lyrical, had always been my favorite. I played.

Roland listened without comment. I could tell he was pleased. When I finished I didn't give him the chance to say anything. I launched into the finale of the second sonata. Furiously I played. And fumbled. Shamefaced, I couldn't look at him. "I'll never get it, now."

"You played beautifully. Nearly as well as before. And with even more feeling. With some good physical therapy…" He put an arm around me. "You're good. You'll be better. There can't be many players who'd do that well after having their hands smashed. Anyway, I wanted to let you know, there's absolutely no problem with your taking the rest of the semester off. And as much more as you might need. I've got administration approval."

"Thanks. I feel…I think it's been worse on me emotionally than physically."

"Do you need me to arrange for some counseling?"

"No, thanks. I'm seeing someone privately." It was a convenient lie.

Danilo joined us and offered us some wine. Roland refused. He seemed to stiffen a bit when Danilo came into the room. But he smiled cordially. "Jamie's been telling me how well you've taken care of him."

"Anyone would."

"Hardly. I never see you at faculty meetings."

Danilo shrugged. "I always seem to have a class when they're scheduled."

"Good planning." Roland laughed. "I'll have to remember that next semester."

I was happy the tension between them seemed to be easing. Ronald had never quite approved of my relationship with Danilo. They chatted for a few moments, mostly faculty gossip. Danilo seemed bored with it, but he listened politely; he knew how important Roland was to me. After a few minutes he left us alone again.

I played a bit more, one of the Dvorak humoresques. But I was overdoing it. The joints in my fingers began to feel sore. "I guess I'll have to ease back into this."

"Don't overdo it, Jamie. Play what you can, when you can."

Bubastis came in. She had never seen Roland before, and she sniffed his cuffs and shoes curiously. I picked her up and nuzzled her. "I thought I had lost her. She ran away when Greg…the night he…"

Roland shifted uneasily.

"Danilo found her and brought her here."

"Danilo's quite something."

I laughed. "I needle him all the time."

"That's all right. We older men have to be kept on our toes. Have you ever met Geoff?" Geoff was his boyfriend.

I told him I hadn't.

"He's ten years younger than me."

"So that would make him, what, seventy?"

He laughed and poked me in the ribs playfully. "If you're back to being a smart-ass bitch again, I know you'll be all right."

My fingers were aching. I rubbed them.

"We'll arrange for that physical therapist and get you playing again. You come and see me. As soon as you feel up to it, hear? I promise you'll be better than you were before."

I promised him I would. I wanted to believe it.

"The department will support you any way we can. You have my word on it."

"You can speak for the department?"

He nodded smugly. "I haven't told anyone but Geoff, but…I'm to be chairman starting next term. Baxter's retiring, and my colleagues elected me."

"Roland, that's great!"

"We've discussed you. What you've been through, I mean. And the entire music faculty's behind you. Anything you need, anything the school can do for you to help you get over this…you only have to ask."

It was wonderful news. Not quite wonderful enough to off- set the sadness of seeing Justin and Mrs. Kolarik buried, but it helped.

After he left I tried the finale of the sonata again. And muffed it again. There was power in my fingers. I could feel it. But how could I ever master it?

Next afternoon I went to the museum. I was still weak and had to rest a lot, but I managed to make it and sat down in Danilo's office. He was teaching; he should be back in a few minutes.

A moment later Peter Borzage stuck his head in. "Jamie. Are you all right? I mean, should you be here? I heard you were taking the semester off."

"I'm still weak, Peter, but I'm on solid food."

"You were on a liquid diet?"

"Joke. How are you, Peter?"

"Never mind me. How are you? When I heard about your roommate and your landlady…I was afraid something might have happened to you too."

"I'm okay. Shaken but okay. It was pure luck, but thanks."

"I'm glad." He smiled at me in a more than friendly way. What would his frat brothers think?

"I was looking for Danilo."

I looked around, then picked up the desk blotter and peered under it. "I don't think he's here."

He was puzzled. What makes some people so literal-minded? He held out a sheet of paper. "Memo from Feld."

"I'll give it to him."

He started to go, then hesitated. "I really am glad to see you."

"Uh, thanks." It was my turn to be baffled. "You too."

"Thanks. Can I— Can I—" He turned the most alarming shade of red.

"Can you what, Peter?"

"Can I give you a hug?"

"Sure." Why the hell not? He put his arms around me, squeezed, and then left without saying another word. I looked after him, wondering what to make of it. At least he wasn't as crazy as Greg, or didn't seem to be.

When Danilo got back to the office he was in a breezy mood. "You should be home, resting."

"It's just the gypsy in my soul."

He ignored it. "I like saying 'home' for the place where you and I live."

"I like hearing it."

"Good." He sat down and put his lecture notes in a drawer. "Do you have a passport?"

"Me? A passport? What for?"

"They're for travel. I thought you knew."

"I'm having a bad influence on you, Danilo."

"I'm serious. Do you have one?"

"No. For heaven's sake, you don't need a passport to travel from Ebensburg to Altoona."

"We'll have to get you one, then." He put his feet up on the desk and folded his hands behind his head.

"I've never been farther away than the Poconos."

He got up, poured himself a cup of coffee, offered me one, then sat down again. "That relief you found is generating a lot of interest. Word's getting around about it. I think we can use it as an excuse to travel, with the university footing the bill."

"Travel where?"

He grinned like a fox. "Why, to Egypt, of course."

"You're kidding. Danilo, that would be so fantastic!"

"With, I think, stops in London, Paris, and Berlin on the way."

A thought cut through my mood. "You planned this."

He became a sphinx.

"Danilo, answer me."

"You didn't ask a question."

"Did you plan all this? Is it all your doing?"

His face might have been made of stone.

"It always seemed so odd that I found the relief the way I did. So odd that no one else had ever noticed it."

"Hundreds of people, dozens of archaeologists had walked directly over the entrance to the tomb of my brother, Tutankhamen. It took Howard Carter to find it."

"And he was one of us." I spoke the by-now predictable words. "Yes."

"Don't evade my question."

"I thought I had answered it."

"You know perfectly well that you didn't. When I found that relief…it was your doing, wasn't it?"

He nodded slightly. I had the impression he was a bit ashamed. Was it at pulling such a pointless trick, or because he had been caught out? "It accomplished so many things so neatly."

"You should have told me the truth. You've never played with me that way before."

"It was a step in your education, Jamie. And it will lead to many more."

"Even so."

"To live the life you have ahead of you requires depth and resiliency. You have both. Realizing what you just realized is one more indication of it."

I wasn't at all certain I liked being tested in that way. But once I was over the jolt of realizing my "luck" had been manufactured by Danilo, I started feeling better. London. Paris. Egypt.

That night in bed I was still excited. Danilo and I made small talk, then he rolled over and went to sleep. I was restless. There had been too many new things to think about. I switched on a little lamp and opened the book I had been reading.

He opened his eyes and yawned.

"I didn't think I'd wake you. Sorry."

"It's all right."

"Danilo?" It was a foolish question, but I had to ask. "All those men you've known, all the emperors and poets…you've slept with them, right?"

The question seemed to catch him unawares. "Some of them."

"Many?"

"Jamie, I've been alive for more than 3,000 years."

That was that. But I couldn't make myself stop. "And now?"

"I don't know what you mean."

It was difficult to ask. After 3,000 years could one man possibly satisfy him? "Will you be faithful to me?"

He looked at me, apparently surprised at the question.

"Will you, Danilo?" I had been without love for so long. The thought that the love I had now might be conditional was too sad for me to want to face.

"I made love to a great many of them, yes, Jamie. But only you have I loved."

It didn't really answer my question, not quite. But I knew him well enough to know I couldn't get him to say more, not if he didn't want to. Danilo, when he wanted to be, was even more impenetrable than a real sphinx.

I switched off my reading lamp, and we held each other in the night. He was warmer than anyone I had ever known, or imagined. And we slept.

Dreams. There were always dreams. At times I could not shake the feeling they were prophetic. At other times they merely disturbed me, or excited me.

There I was, playing Chopin. I was at the base of the Great Pyramid by night, and the full moon bathed everything in its light. The pyramid was still cased in gleaming white alabaster, as it was in the ancient world, and the moon made it almost seem to glow. Bubastis, now a large, fully-grown cat, sat atop the piano, watching me. Justin was there, listening to my music, crying. And Tim, and Mrs. Kolarik.

The moon turned blood red. The world turned blood red.

I woke. The bed was empty. Danilo was gone. I did not want to know where.

I got up and went to the window. In the real world as in my dream, the moon was full. I had never asked for the life Danilo was giving me. Or had I asked for it, indirectly and without realizing it, when I began to love him? I wished he had given me the choice.

Bubastis began to rub herself against my legs, purring.

If he had offered me the chance to choose, what would I have done?

I had been alone and without love so many years.

His manuscript, his memoir was on the desk in his study. What did it say about me?

I switched on the reading lamp. It was a thick, heavy manuscript. Page after page was covered with hieroglyphs. I wasn't good enough to read it all. Not even most of it, really. But here and there among the pages I could pick out words and even sentences. And there were familiar cartouches, framing the names of kings. Not all of them were pharaohs. I could decipher the names of the caesars, of Alexander, of Richard Lionheart…

Then, near the end, I saw my own name, framed in a cartouche like the other royalty.

CHAPTER 9

December was colder than anyone could remember, and there was constant snow. I wondered how effectively it would cover the bodies of the dead, or the sacrificed.

For two months I had had physical therapy, and my fingers were responding. The only actual studies I pursued that semester were with Roland under the supervision of my therapist. Slowly my fingers got stronger and more responsive, and they both agreed that my piano playing was improving every week, almost to the level of skill I'd had before the attack. But when the weather grew especially icy my hands turned sore, and nothing anyone could do seemed to help.

"You're punishing yourself." My therapist was on the sports faculty but had worked with a few musicians too for some reason. His name was Michael Columbus. Roland had known him for years, and he told me I could trust him. I knew what he meant. "You should think about going a bit easier. Let them heal for a few months before you really start pounding the keys."

"What I pound, Michael, is my business."

"And being a little bitch won't help." It hadn't taken him long to get my range. "Let me see your gloves."

I got them out of my coat.

"These are too thin. Get some that are thermal-lined. Keeping your hands warm will help."

"Yes, Auntie."

He was holding my hands in his, putting slight pressure on them to see if they hurt. "Watch your mouth, Rubinstein, or these might get broken again."

It bothered me that my hands were still hurting. It hadn't seemed that Bubastis remained at all sore after that awful incident with Greg. I asked Danilo if there were ancient remedies, or even spells. But there was nothing. Michael kept telling me the condition would improve in time, but I wasn't sure I believed him. I would be a warm-weather pianist, it seemed, at least in the short term.

Somewhat to everyone's surprise, swimming helped. Fighting the resistance of the water strengthened and toughened my fingers. When I realized that, I really began to believe I'd be whole again.

But there was still pain. Finally Michael and Roland got together and applied some tough love. "No more piano. You're barred from the department till at least the first of the year." Roland was smiling as he said it, but I felt as if the ground was quaking under me. "Maybe till springtime."

"I have a grand at Danilo's."

"Jamie, please. You need to let yourself heal. If you push too hard, you'll only do more damage."

Michael seconded this. There wasn't much point arguing. I left, feeling as if I'd had my tongue torn out.

On the third of the month Greg Wilton was captured. He was hiding on an aunt's farm in rural Indiana near the Illinois border. His lawyer was fighting extradition. The district attorney was confident he'd get him back to Pittsburgh. I was notified I'd be needed to testify against him. Since I hadn't actually witnessed the murders it didn't make much sense, but apparently testifying about what he had done to me would help convince the jury to convict on the more serious charges too. His lawyer would fight that too, so I might not be needed at all in the end.

When his lawyers told him I might be testifying against him, he reportedly freaked, claiming I was dead or should be, that he had killed not only Justin but me. Everyone took it as part of the groundwork for an insanity defense.

I told the D.A.'s office I was planning a trip to Europe and Africa. "We leave just before Christmas."

They replied that I should keep in touch with them, but that the case was unlikely to go to trial before next autumn at the earliest.

They were determined to find evidence linking Greg to all the campus murders.

The campus murders.

I don't know if it was the cold weather, or if he simply wasn't as hungry, but Danilo became more circumspect. When he began to age he left Pittsburgh. He sacrificed victims in West Virginia, in southeast Ohio, even in the Maryland panhandle, not as frequently as he had before. And he was careful to cover up his killings. Most of them weren't found. The two that were discovered were put down to a convenient but imaginary "copycat killer."

Weren't found. So many of the victims around campus had simply vanished. Where were they? I wanted to ask him, of course, but I was afraid of the answer. Besides, I thought I already knew. I did not want to have it confirmed.

And then my world began to open. To blossom.

The semester ended on the 18th. Danilo gave his class their papers and turned in their grades. I met him at the department that night; we had dinner, went home, and began to pack. We were to leave for New York city on the 20th, sailing on the *Queen Mary* on the 23rd, first stop London. Crossing the ocean had me a bit apprehensive, but I didn't tell him so. I wanted the winter to end, but there was no sign of it.

It seems incredible, but I had never seen the ocean. Or, needless to say, an ocean liner. Except in movies, of course. I found that conjuring images from films I loved helped me get past my nervousness. Fred and Ginger in *Shall We Dance?* Alice Faye and John Payne in *Week-end in Havana*. I would have been embarrassed to tell Danilo so.

I wasn't quite prepared for New York either. And *On the Town* didn't help much. A city so huge, so busy, so full of energy. I had always imagined it a larger version of Pittsburgh, but the difference was not simply of size; it was one of kind. There was nothing like it in the world. Once I got over feeling intimidated I fell a bit in love with it.

The icy wind never stopped, and the snow hardly did. I missed Bubastis. Danilo's next-door neighbor had offered to look after her. I called him and he told me not to worry, she was fine.

Danilo showed me as much of the city as we had time for, the historic places, the Stonewall Inn and the monument in Sheridan Square. We spent a day at the Metropolitan Museum. Their Egyptian collection was enormous, larger than our campus museum in its entirety. Even deep inside it seemed to me I could hear the wind.

There were a great many objects from the Amarna period, the time when Danilo's father had tried to reform Egyptian religion. The art changed too then. It became much more sensual, more emotionally direct than the conventional, rather formal things we usually see. Was it at the orders of the pharaoh? Or did the change in thought brought about by the king's new religion subtly change the way his artists saw their world? You could feel the sensuality in the pictures of the pharaoh and his family.

I noticed an odd lack, though. "Danilo, there are none of you."

"No." He smiled, but there was a bit of sadness in it. "The priests held the male members of our family responsible for their loss of power. Their revenge was near total. All signs of my father and myself were expunged from the record, or nearly so. Even my brother, whom the priests manipulated to restore the old gods, even he—until Carter found his tomb, there were archaeologists who seriously thought he was a myth. And my own reign was the shortest of all, so it was easy for them to wipe it out."

In a small, unobtrusive case, he showed me a few things from his brother's tomb. "He was a beautiful boy with a smooth, muscular body like yours. I loved him; we all did. But he was sickly. Easy for the priests to dominate. Easier still for them to murder."

I remembered that Tutankhamen's mummy had mysterious, unexplained wounds to the head.

"He was your age when he died, Jamie."

I looked at him. "And Justin's."

"Yes." He turned away from me. "And Justin's."

He told me they used to have a relief of the Kissing Kings on display. But we couldn't find it. Finally Danilo asked an attendant where it had been moved.

"Oh, it was taken off public display, sir." In a stage whisper he added, "Complaints from conservative board members." It was clear he understood why we wanted to see it. "It's down in one of the storage rooms."

Danilo picked up on his lead. "Might we…?"

He nodded, looked around to make certain no one could see, and without saying another word led us down a long flight of stairs. I was expecting dim subbasements, like the ones in the museum on campus, but these were wider and better lit. In a large room there it was, on the floor, propped against a packing case. Akhenaten and his son-successor Smenkhare, depicted in that lush sensual style, their arms around each other, their lips touching. Akhenaten had his hand on his son's hip, in a way I had myself so many times. The resemblance between the two of them—and between the image and the way Danilo still looked—was unmistakable.

The attendant shifted his weight nervously. "You'd be surprised how many people want to see it."

There in front of him, Danilo and I kissed. He looked from the image to us and back again. It was clear he saw the resemblance. It was equally clear he couldn't quite fathom it as anything more than a coincidence. "We shouldn't be down here. I'll have to take you back up, now. You understand."

We understood.

We stayed at the Chelsea Hotel. Danilo told me about the great and near-great artists who had stayed there, the Beats and more.

Then that night he disappeared, heading out into the desperate winter toward what he called the meat-packing district. When he came back he was younger.

The ship was magnificent, much larger than I had imagined. It had a weight, a solidity that seemed at odds with the fact it floated on the surface of the water. Everything was appointed in the most marvelous art deco.

A hundred movies had prepared me for our stateroom to be tiny and cramped. But it was fairly roomy and quite comfortable.

"The best and largest on board." Danilo was pleased with himself.

"And the most expensive?" It hardly seemed possible the university was paying for it.

"They're only paying part."

"Oh." I knew he had money. He'd have to have been a dolt not to have accumulated a fortune over the years. "How much?"

"Enough. Don't be nosy."

I jumped onto the large double bed and stretched out. "Now this," I said grandly, "is the life I was meant to lead."

"Part of it." He unpacked patiently.

"All we need is for Fred Astaire and Jane Powell to do a show for us tonight."

"You've lived your life in a fantasy world."

I nodded happily. "And look where it's gotten me. Into the best fantasy of all."

He went off to leave some valuables with the purser. I decided to explore the ship. Leaving the stateroom I happened to see myself in the mirror. The hair at my temples was beginning to turn gray. Seeing it made me go a bit numb. I knew what it meant, or what I thought it did.

The wind in the harbor was even more vicious than the wind in the streets. I quickly checked out the dining hall, the theater, the gym. There was an indoor pool; I'd be able to swim.

Later, when I asked Danilo about my graying hair, he was offhand. "Yes. I noticed it a day or two ago."

"But…but I'm twenty."

"Or newborn. Your new life has its costs." He stretched out on the bed. "Or perhaps I should say its requirements."

"Are you telling me I have to…?" Somehow, I had known. But I kept pushing the thought out of my mind. Now it seemed inescapable. "Suppose…suppose I don't? Suppose I won't do that?"

"Then you will age and die."

"No."

"You were dead, Jamie. The gods of the underworld will have you, soon or late. You must placate them. Feed them. Keep them happy."

"You serve Set, not Anubis, Danilo." The image of the jackal-headed god of the graveyard had always seemed slightly unsettling to me. Perhaps this was why. I had seen films of real jackals, devouring the carcasses of freshly slaughtered animals. During periods when food was scarce they were known to dig up freshly-turned graves and eat the corpses. The Egyptians chose the forms of their gods only too wisely.

"I serve the gods of Egypt." He smiled. "And they serve me. Or us."

"I don't want them to serve me. I don't want anyone to serve me."

"The alternative, Jamie, is for you to return to that death I interrupted. Do you want that?"

"No." I was twenty years old. I didn't know what I wanted.

He wanted to kiss me. I could tell. But I was too upset. I walked out of the room and left him alone there. The ship lurched. The tugs began pulling us out of the harbor.

I spent long hours walking the decks, lost in troubled thought. It was cold and overcast, and there was still that bitter wind, but I needed to be alone. My fingers ached, despite my thick gloves. I had known from the beginning the time would come. It had come. I would have done anything to have it otherwise.

It was nearly dark when I went back to our cabin. Danilo was lying on the bed, reading. He glanced at his watch and suggested we get some dinner. "Then…" He avoided looking at me. "Then you will have to…"

I sat down beside him. "I don't know if I can."

"You can do anything you want to now. We are making this trip so you can learn that, so you can at least begin to learn the power you have."

"Not enough power to stay alive without doing awful things."

He kissed my cheek, but I moved away from him. "Set," he whispered, "is the god who teaches us the gods do not exist."

Night at sea was magnificent but arctic. The sky had cleared, and ahead of the ship a quarter moon hung in the sky, brighter and whiter than I had ever seen it. There were a million stars, more vibrant than in the mountains even. But despite the fact that the sky was nearly cloudless, there were snowflakes. Not many of them, only occasional ones, but they glittered in the moonlight.

I didn't eat. I couldn't. It was Christmas Day. Not that the holiday had ever meant much to me. I had always taken it for granted that you had to have a family, a real loving family, for it to mean anything. And now I had a family; I had Danilo.

There was to be an especially lavish dinner on board. Danilo said he wasn't hungry, and so I headed for the dining hall alone. But I didn't have much appetite. The other passengers went in to their meal and I stayed on deck. The sky began to cloud up again, and there was more snow and less light. The sea, which had been so lovely, turned black. Finally I went back to our stateroom. Danilo was gone. I knew where.

It would be a young crew member, or that suicidal passenger you see in so many old films. It would be a boy traveling with his grandmother, or.... I sat in the room without turning on any lights, waiting.

And he came to me.

Slowly the door opened. In the light from the passageway he looked sad. "Jamie, it is time." I got up and followed him.

It was late. Nearly everyone else was asleep, or so it seemed. The ship was quiet. Even the rolling of the waves seemed to have subsided, mostly. But the bitter wind still blew. Neither of us bothered to put on a coat.

At the stern rail a young man stood waiting. Young. Hardly older than myself. Dark hair, large dark eyes. He wore a thick parka but the hood was down; the wind blew his hair. Danilo approached him. I stood a few paces away. Danilo touched his cheek, stroked it. He licked the side of his throat, and the boy shuddered with ecstasy.

I saw him take that golden knife out of his pocket. Just as the boy's passion reached its height, quite swiftly Danilo sank the knife into his throat and tore it open. Blood splattered across the deck. For a startled moment the boy stood still. His body shuddered again. I wondered if it was still with pleasure, or…then he collapsed. Crumpled into a heap. Danilo bent down and, with the same golden knife, began his surgery.

It was quick. He gestured to me. I drank. I ate. I could not control my appetites. There was a surge of sexual pleasure stronger than anything I had ever felt, more powerful even than the erotic rush I had felt when Danilo reawakened me.

We dropped what was left of the young man's body overboard.

No one had seen. I almost asked Danilo what would have happened if someone had seen us, but I knew the answer. "They will find a note in his cabin, in his writing. A suicide note." He looked down at the water, but the boy was already gone. "He asked me not to tell his mother."

We went back to our cabin and made love. He did things to my body—I felt things—I had never known before. The wave of pleasure was almost tidal, so intense I forgot everything else in the world.

Later there was a storm. The ship tossed wildly. I didn't care. It was not as wild and exciting as what I felt with Danilo.

In the gray morning light I saw myself in the mirror. I was twenty again.

That night's storm passed, but the fourth day of our crossing there was another one, much larger and more ferocious. The ship rocked in waves taller than itself. Ice coated everything. We passengers were warned to stay in our cabins. Danilo and I made love for what seemed like the hundredth time that week.

When the storm finally passed the sun was brilliant, blinding in the afternoon sky. I looked out our porthole, and the entire ship was encased in gleaming ice. We sailed into Southampton in bright sunlight on a crystal ship.

The European winter was one of the worst on record. London's streets were mostly abandoned. Everything was gray; everything was gloomy. There were practically no other tourists. The Brits had sense enough to stay in out of it. Not us. We were hungry.

Our hotel was in a little street north of Hyde Park called Craven Terrace. Just where it intersected the Bayswater Road a young man had a newsstand. He was handsome and boyish with green eyes and bad teeth and that rosy complexion Brits often have. Danilo bought a copy of *The Guardian* from him.

He smiled. "Thanks, sir." I could see he was looking us up and down, trying to get our range. To my eye, wrapped in his heavy winter things, he looked like a boy.

Danilo got him into a conversation. I didn't pay much attention; I was looking at the enormous park. Even in ice and snow it was impressive. Finally the newsboy agreed to come to our hotel room that night.

When we left him I was alarmed. "Danilo, we can't. Not in our room. The police will—"

"No, they won't. Not if we're careful. After we have sex with him we'll suggest walking to a pub to buy him a drink. We can leave the body in the park. The park is so large, if we hide it well enough, they won't find it till we're out of the country. And it's supposed to snow still more tonight."

He had a lean, pink, beautiful body. He didn't fight us, not that Danilo would have permitted it. I think he wanted to die. When I produced the golden knife and held it to his throat he looked at me, smiled faintly and whispered something I couldn't quite hear.

The next day we went to the British Museum. I asked if there was another depiction of the Kissing Kings there, but Danilo said he didn't know of one.

But there was so much else. Mummies, sculptures of lean,

handsome pharaohs, the Rosetta Stone. And it wasn't only Egyptian things. The Ishtar Gate from Babylon stood tall and impressive. Danilo pressed his hand against it, as if he was trying to convince himself it was quite real. I thought it an odd gesture, and I said so.

"Gilgamesh and his lover Enkidu passed through this gate. They held hands, and the entire population greeted them as heroes. Gilgamesh the immortal." That was all he said for a long time.

In another suite of rooms was the most magnificent collection of Greek vases and cups. They were not something that would normally have interested me, but Danilo knew which ones would catch my eye.

They had figures of men. Loving. Making love. Touching, kissing, stroking. Hercules and Hylas. Idas and Lynceus. Pericles and an unnamed boy. There were hundreds of them, rooms full of them, a vast shrine to love like ours. Their bodies were trim and muscular and quite beautiful. And quite inflamed with sexual passion. They coupled in every imaginable position, even one or two Danilo and I hadn't tried. After the first moment I stopped talking, stopped asking questions and simply basked in the wild sea of male love.

That evening we went to the theater, a performance of Christopher Marlowe's *Edward II*. It seemed to me that the actors played the love scenes between Edward and his lover Gaveston with special heat and energy. During the interval Danilo noted dryly, "Marlowe. Edward II. Double whammy."

And of course that night we coupled again, more ferociously even than we had before. I was more and more in love, and it surprised me, because I had thought the love I already felt was the strongest, deepest love imaginable. But there was more.

In the lobby of our hotel there was a concert grand piano. During the busy hours, lunchtime and dinnertime, a hired musician played lounge music. Sanitized Gershwin and Porter, that kind of thing. Mid morning, the day we were to check out, I sat down and played a few bars of Chopin. The pain in my fingers was less than it had been. It wasn't gone, but I could tell they were healing. Danilo had given me my life. Now he was giving me this. Outside, a snowstorm raged.

I played a waltz, then one of the preludes. I played a Schubert impromptu. Everyone in the lobby stopped and listened. They seemed almost to freeze, as if I were casting a kind of spell over them. After a few minutes my fingers began to stiffen a bit, and I stopped. They all broke into spontaneous applause. I blushed and made a slight bow for them.

I remembered what Danilo had said once: "The blood is the life, and the power."

All the death was healing me.

The Seine was frozen. There were ice skaters just below Notre Dame. Snow and ice were everywhere, piled up in streets and on sidewalks, filling the parks. Vendors sold hot chestnuts. Paris had never looked like this in an Audrey Hepburn movie. In those it was always bright spring. We had winter storms.

There was so much to see. Danilo showed me Poulenc's house, and we went to Versailles, to see the magnificent palace started by Louis XIII. "One of us." We said the words together and laughed; "one of us" had become a private little joke between us, the kind of thing lovers share. Danilo told me about the grand balls Louis used to hold in his "hunting lodge" for his male courtiers.

Next day we visited the Louvre. Wonderful building, magnificent contents. We saw Leonardo's work, and Caravaggio's, Donatello's, Botticelli's, and on and on. "The Renaissance," he said, "was one of our gifts to the world."

There was a suite of rooms with what I thought fairly dull art. But Danilo looked around nostalgically. "This was a palace before it was a museum. These are the rooms where Henri III quartered his various lovers." A twinkle in his eye, he added, "He was even better at lovemaking than at making war."

Finally, at the end of a long day, we went to the Egyptian wing.

Without reading the labels I knew which objects came from which period. I could even identify the royal ones by the pharaoh's names on them. Danilo was pleased that I was able to identify so much. "You've learned such a great deal."

"I have a sexy teacher. That always helps."

There were huge rooms of things from the Amarna period. In one were colossal figures of Danilo's father. I recognized them at once. The features were unmistakable, high cheekbones, large sensuous lips, the family resemblance was impossible to miss. I thought the long-dead pharaoh looked sad.

"He does. He was. I think he knew how he would end. People prefer superstition, fear, and hysteria to the truth."

I looked up into Akhenaten's face. "He must have been a beautiful man."

"He was, Jamie. These figures don't do him justice. His body was so lean and lithe and supple. When he moved it was like bronze flowing. Just the touch of him, the sight of him even, excited me more than anything ever has." As he said it he took my hand, then put an arm around my waist. "Till you."

For what seemed eternity we stood in passionate embrace under the protecting gaze of the king whose blood we shared. And in the next room we kissed again, under a huge relief of Danilo and his father doing the same. Each city, it seemed, brought us closer to our true home.

We stayed in Paris longer than we'd planned to, and we went back to the Louvre three more times. I could not get enough.

There was one more thing I wanted to see before we left Paris. "Isn't Oscar Wilde buried here?"

Danilo's expression soured. "For what it's worth, yes. Oscar was a fool."

"One of us?"

"Most emphatically not. He tried to deny what he was instead of embracing it. And you know how he ended."

It was an unexpected thought.

"Some of us tried to persuade him to acknowledge his true

nature. But he wouldn't hear of it. He was protecting Bosie Douglas, or so he thought."

"I think I'd still like to see his tomb."

"Go alone then."

I did. It was covered in snow and ice. I found myself wishing I hadn't gone. The clouds above me were ominous, pregnant with more snow.

Berlin.

I wanted it to be familiar, I wanted it to look like *The Blue Angel* or maybe *Metropolis*. But all of that was gone, burned or blown up in the war. It was a new city, a modern one. I was disappointed.

There were a few things I recognized, not many. Unter den Linden. The Brandenburg Gate. I tried to see myself strolling on the Kurfürstendamm with Sally Bowles. I found myself humming Kurt Weill as our taxi driver showed us the city under a dark sky in a harsh winter wind. Danilo listed an itinerary of places for the driver to show us; then when we had seen the city he asked him to take us to the Hotel Bismarck.

"You mean we're not staying at the Grand Hotel?"

He seemed a bit preoccupied. "What Grand Hotel? There is no Grand Hotel in Berlin."

"There is a Grand Hotel in every city." I put on my most tragic Garbo. "I vant to be alone."

"Keep that up and you will be."

The city made Danilo uncharacteristically quiet. I think it was haunted by sad memories for him. At the State Museum we saw another depiction of the Kissing Kings, the original of the one I had first seen in Danilo's office. They seemed to be everywhere. I wondered why I had never heard of them before Danilo.

"Because our lives and our history and our bloodline have been denied," Danilo told me. "Erased. The ones who hold the power now cannot countenance the fact that anyone else ever did, or ever could." He looked away from me. "Or ever will."

"A conspiracy?" I found the idea amusing.

"No, hardly that. Denying power to others is the essence of maintaining power."

"Power." I smiled. "Germany would make you think this way."

But he was too distracted, or too sad, for there to be much fun in goading him. "It isn't simply that they don't want to know who we are, Jamie. They don't want us, ourselves, to know who we are. You must be ready to fight for your birthright."

Also in the museum was the famous bust of Nefertiti. It was even more beautiful than all the photographs of it suggested. Sleek beautiful woman, long graceful throat, huge sad eyes, full lips, perfect features. Danilo's mother.

He stood and stared into her face for a long time. Then he reached out to touch it.

"Danilo, no. There are detectors. Alarms."

"They will not go off."

"But—"

He touched the statue. He stroked its cheek gently, almost lovingly. At one moment he leaned forward slightly, almost as if he was going to kiss it. But he took a step back away from it. "They branded her a witch, Jamie. They did everything they could to expunge her memory, as they did with my father, my brother, myself. That this survived, intact, is a small miracle."

He took my hand and we left.

The city was nearly abandoned. People were indoors, hiding from the cold; that seemed to be the pattern all over Europe. The sky was so dark it seemed always nightfall, even at high noon. When, now and then, the sun broke through the clouds, its light was cold and cheerless. It would have been better if we hadn't seen it.

We walked the streets, saw the Reichstag, the '36 Olympic stadium. "There was so much evil unleashed here, Jamie. I knew Ernst Röhm and some of his officers. A lot of them were…" He didn't have to say it: us. "All of them massacred by Hitler. The Night of the Long Knives, they call it in the history books. I was there. I saw the blood. I heard Himmler tell the nation that men like them must be slaughtered. Jamie, we must be prepared to fight, always and everywhere. We must be as ruthless and as vigilant as they have always been. Or our bloodline will die out, and that will be that."

We did not stay in Germany very long, only long enough to see the things in the museum and a bit of the city. It was time for Egypt. We were to cross the Mediterranean on a steamer, bound for Alexandria.

I was aging again. There was a young German man in the steamer's crew, blond, blue-eyed, Aryan, I imagined.

"Call me Horst."

We did. The three of us made love in an unused cabin.

And before long I was my twenty-year-old self once more.

As we crossed the Mediterranean the weather warmed and cleared.

Alexandria. City of Alexander.

Egypt.

We were there.

Modern city. Modern traffic, congestion, noise, overcrowding. And blessedly warm, kept so by the sea, which was a deeper blue than I would have thought possible. To go about in shirtsleeves seemed wonderful. I tried to imagine Alexander walking the streets, with Hephaestion at his side, laying out the city. "Put the library here, and the temple of Zeus over where those streets cross…" But the images were impossible to conjure. Everything was too new.

There wasn't much of the ancient city left. At one place we saw an enormously tall column, remains of what must have been a titanic public building. "The great Library of Alexandria," Danilo told me with a bit of awe, "where all the world's books were kept." He shrugged. "Burned by the Christians. It is the kind of thing they've always done well."

At the waterfront we saw the place where the famous lighthouse had been; it was now occupied by a smallish stone fort. Danilo showed me where Cleopatra's temple had stood and, several hundred yards from it, where Antony had built his "Timonium," where he went to brood or be alone. "He disliked humanity," Danilo told me offhandedly. "Except for women who could give him power. And boys who could give him pleasure."

"That can't be, Danilo. He and Cleopatra were one of the most famous couples in the world. They still are."

"He loved boys. He was notorious for seducing them. We have the word of any number of ancient authors for it. There are records of high officials refusing to let Antony anywhere near their teenaged sons."

I was beginning to understand what he meant about all the things that were kept hidden from us, obscured by a more or less willful silence. "I've been wrong to rely on movies for my sense of history."

He laughed. "You can't help it. You are an American."

"But…but…" I tried to find words for what I was feeling. "It's all the dead past, Danilo. Does it really matter?"

"The past is never dead, Jamie. It is not even past."

As we strolled the waterfront I couldn't get over the deep vibrant blue of the sea. We ate at a little café, the best seafood casserole I had ever tasted, more delicious than I can say. The waiter fussed over us; it was fairly clear he wanted more than a tip. We took him to our hotel, and to my surprise, Danilo let him leave again when we finished coupling, or tripling. Neither of us needed his blood or his flesh. And Danilo said he only wanted to taste the taste of an Egyptian man again. "Just as an appetizer."

The thought of the main course upset me. This business of living off the flesh of others…I had not really adjusted to it yet, except as a necessity. I changed the subject. "Let's go out and see more of the city."

I think he was amused at my reticence, but what could I do?

It was late afternoon. He showed me the Greco-Roman Museum, which held the city's few mementos of Alexander. And he emphasized that most of them probably weren't genuine. "Nothing is anymore."

"Where was Alexander's tomb?"

He hesitated. "The city has changed so much. But if tradition is accurate, we are there."

"This building? It's on the site?"

"I think so. Every last atom of his tomb is gone now, of course. Good heavens, we can't have monuments to powerful pagans here. Especially not one who loved men and boys."

I looked around and tried to imagine what it must have been like. Danilo knew my thoughts and described it, a magnificent temple in black marble. In the sanctuary lay Alexander in his royal armor, preserved in honey, in a glass sarcophagus. Augustus had stood sighing before it. Caligula shattered the glass and stole the breastplate.

His voice turned soft. "I think that may have been the spot." He walked to the rear of the gallery we were in. "You should have seen him. Stunningly handsome man. Perfectly confident of his ability to rule the world. His poise was almost unsettling, till I got used to it."

I closed my eyes and tried to conjure up the image. I knew he had been blond, athletic, handsome. But the thought of him lying in state, covered in honey…it seemed too grotesque. "Why, of all the men you've known, didn't you give him what you've given me, Danilo?"

He circled the spot. I could tell he was trying to imagine it too, that his thoughts were 2,000 years in the past. "I offered. I wanted to." He looked at me. "Think of the glories he could have accomplished. But he refused. When Hephaestion died, I believe he wanted to stop living too. His grief was as imperial as his love and his ambition."

"But he had another lover. That Persian boy."

"Bagoas. Beautiful boy. Quite slim, quite effeminate, quite alluring. No, that was never the same."

"What happened to him?"

"It isn't recorded."

We left the museum not long after that. Arm in arm. No one seemed to notice or care. I tried to imagine that happening in Pennsylvania, even in New York. It wasn't possible. Perhaps a trace of Alexander's spirit lingered after all?

The next morning we traveled to Cairo. Danilo stopped back at that same café before we left and bought several large portions of the same casserole and a few bottles of wine. Then he said he wanted me to see the real Egypt.

We rode on the top of a railway train. Around us were dozens of Egyptians. "One of the reforms Nasser introduced in the 1950s was this. Anyone can ride anywhere in the country for free—as long as he rides on the roof." We had a bit of trouble getting our luggage up, and a young man helped us. Danilo gave him a tip. Baksheesh.

It was a wonderful way to experience the country—to see it better than you could through a window, to smell its smells and hear its sounds. The sky had the most amazing transparency, a few wisps of clouds, no more. And the people were wonderful. Everyone had brought food and wine, it seemed, and we all shared. Our casserole was a big hit. People recognized me as an American and said so. I wondered how they could tell. Couldn't I as easily have been a Canadian, or a Brit, or…? But every last one of them had me pegged. I had never thought being an American was such an obvious thing.

Danilo chatted with a lot of them in Arabic. But most of them spoke English, and quite well. And they talked about current events in the United States with a surprising level of knowledge and insight, even the youngest of them. They knew what the president was up to, and Congress, and even who the presidential candidates from the opposition party were and what they stood for. I have to say it was a bit disconcerting. Very few of my fellow students at West Penn were so well-informed.

The men were beautiful: dark, with the largest black eyes and lean bodies. They wore the robes called galabias; when the breeze blew in off the Mediterranean it outlined their bodies perfectly.

Pairs of them held hands or walked arm in arm. It was merely an expression of friendship, Danilo told me. But I wondered if it was always just that. I knew the atmosphere in Egypt wasn't exactly friendly, but still....

The Nile Delta was more lush and fertile than any place I had ever seen. Fruit, nuts, even wheat seemed to be growing everywhere. We could see little arms of the Nile branching off all around us, making the land marvelously fertile. Canals added to it. When, frequently, the train made stops, everyone would jump off and run to collect apples, limes, grapes...it was all perfectly delicious. It didn't taste like the food I was used to, and I commented on it to Danilo.

"Of course not." He grinned. "It's natural."

For the first time in days he smiled a lot. An exiled king returning to his homeland. But his people could hardly know or recognize him. Exile had been centuries too long. He must have been feeling the strangest complex of emotions. When he seemed to want to be alone, I'd go off and mix with the Egyptians. Several young men expressed an interest in me that I couldn't have mistaken. I'm afraid I drank a bit too much wine.

After a time people slept. The sun was warm and brilliant. The train rocked gently from side to side. I fell asleep myself without really wanting to.

Cairo. The first great capital of old Egypt, known then as Memphis. It had been the world's greatest city a thousand years before Danilo was born. Of its ancient glories, very little remained.

It was late afternoon when we got there. I knew it was the largest city in Africa, but I was hardly prepared for it. The crowds, the noise, the traffic...it made New York look prim and provincial. Danilo flagged a taxi and instructed the driver to take us to the Mena House, the famous hotel at the foot of the Giza Plateau west of the city. Traffic was nightmarish. Cars weaved in and out, horns blared nonstop, pedestrians rushed for their lives. "Is this a typical Cairo rush hour?"

Danilo ignored the question. He was watching everything and everyone, quite intently I thought.

Once, our driver pulled up onto the sidewalk and drove for half a block, scattering people ahead of us.

"For God's sake, Danilo, tell him to be more careful!"

He laughed. I was keenly aware of being an outsider.

On the sidewalks pairs of men walked hand in hand, a great many of them. I asked Danilo how they could be so open.

"You're in a different culture now, Jamie. What Americans would view as shameful and scandalous, Muslims see as an expression of friendship."

I looked again. Men holding hands. I could see the affection. "You're telling me they're just friends?"

He nodded, then added wryly, "Most of them, anyway."

It took half an hour to reach Giza, on the outskirts of the city. Our driver helped us get our bags into the hotel and apologized for not being able to go faster than he had. I gave him his fee and his baksheesh and he left. In the lobby was a huge picture window with a perfect view of the plateau outside.

And there they were: the pyramids, solid and monumental, the oldest stone buildings in the world. Before them sat the Sphinx, gazing into eternity as tourists sat drinking mint tea and smoking, as if this might have been any hotel lobby anywhere. Danilo checked us in and told the desk clerk we had to have a suite facing the monuments. There was a bit of a controversy, but after more baksheesh he found us one.

When the bellhop, a boy of sixteen or so, opened the door to our rooms there they were again: huge, ancient, magnificent. More distant in time from Julius Caesar than he was from us. The sun had just set and they were bathed in golden light, quite artificial, quite striking. I stopped in my tracks and gaped. The pyramids. There. Real. It was like being in a myth, like walking a woodland path and finding a gravestone that read: HERE LIES KING ARTHUR.

I left Danilo to tip the bellhop and went to the window. After the boy left he came and put an arm around me. "Welcome to my home." He kissed me.

They were larger than I'd imagined, larger than anything. But there was something wrong. "You haven't smiled since we got here, Danilo."

He ignored it. "Let's get some dinner, Jamie. Then I want to introduce you to my realm."

The steaks in the hotel restaurant were wonderful, filet mignon cooked with spices I couldn't quite identify. We got sweaters—Danilo warned me the evenings could be cool—and went out.

It was a short walk up to the plateau. Tourists milled everywhere, busloads of them. Vendors swarmed, selling souvenirs, offering camel rides, haggling over prices. Boys begged. Antiquities Service security men kept a careful eye on it all. It was a little chaos. But above it all loomed the monuments.

The pyramids rose, step after step, seeming to reach the sky. The Sphinx towered over us. Danilo told me their history and their legends. He approached each of them in turn and pressed his hand flat against the stones, as if he had to convince himself they were real. An odd gesture, I thought.

"I wish you could have seen them when they were still new. Encased in polished alabaster, gleaming brilliant white in the sunshine. Their tops were plated with gold."

He showed me the swarms of tombs around the pyramids, for queens, for court officials, even some for the workmen who built their pharaohs' monuments. There was a stela between the legs of the Sphinx, promising the benevolence of the gods to whomever would keep it in good repair. There was a building to house an ancient boat that had been found in a pit behind the Great Pyramid. It looked like Noah's Ark to me.

Danilo made a sour face. "That was quite deliberate, so the Christian tourists might feel there was something familiar. You'd think they'd be content with their own myths in their own lands, but they have to import them here too."

A full moon broke the horizon, large and beautiful.

Floodlights came on, illuminating the monuments. But despite all the wonderful things I found myself yawning; the train ride had taken a lot out of me. Danilo suggested I go back to the hotel and get some sleep.

"Aren't you coming?" I wanted him beside me.

"Later. I'll be down in a while. Go and get some rest."

"But—"

"Please, Jamie. I think I need to be alone here for a while."

I looked around. There must have been a thousand people just on the same side of the Great Pyramid as us, and thousands more all around the rest of it.

"They'll go soon enough. Everything turns quite silent here after dark. The Antiquities Service turns off the floodlights, and people leave."

The hotel lobby wasn't so crowded now. I stopped in the bar and had a glass of wine. Then I headed up to our room. The bed was soft and comfortable. I fell asleep quickly.

When I woke the room was bathed in moonlight. For a moment I was disoriented. Then I remembered where I was. The full moon washed the pyramids in its ghostly light. I was alone.

I glanced at my watch: 3 A.M. Danilo had not come back. Or had come back, and then left again. I wanted him.

A beautiful young Egyptian man dozed at the front desk. When I asked if he had seen Professor Semenkaru he smiled, shook his head and closed his eyes again. I thought I knew where Danilo must be.

He had been right. The plateau was quite deserted, so silent I could hear the desert sand crunch under my feet. The moonlight was more than bright enough to see everything by. At four distant places there were small guard houses; lights burned in them; there was no sign of the guards. A slight breeze blew, and I was glad I had worn my sweater.

From the lip of the plateau I looked out over the city. Lights glistened; there was still traffic in the distant streets, all of it sufficiently far away that no sound came to me.

The Nile had flowed at the base of the plateau in ancient times. Its course had shifted over the centuries; now it was off in the middle distance. Its water gleamed under the moon. Keeping an eye out for the guards, moving as quietly as I could, I walked to the Sphinx. Imperious, impassive; no wonder the ancients had thought it possessed a secret. Like Danilo I pressed a hand to it. The stone was cool. Sandstone; it left my palm feeling gritty.

Then I went to the Great Pyramid. The size was mountainous, overwhelming. St. Peter's in Rome could fit inside with room to spare. I knew it was forbidden to climb it, but I had to. There were no guards in sight.

Each step was six feet tall, taller than me. I struggled up three levels, six, ten. The moon seemed to smile on me. To the old Egyptians it had been Thoth, the scribe of the gods. Not at all seriously, I whispered a little prayer to him, thanking him for the light.

I walked along the course of stones and turned the corner. At the far end, a hundred yards ahead of me, just at the next corner, I saw someone else standing in the moon's light, seeming to stare directly into it. Or rather something.

It was not human. It was a man with the head of a falcon. Eight feet tall, maybe nine, muscles rippling, with a beak that could tear a man in half. I froze. I could not be seeing right. It must be a trick of the moon.

It spread its arms, or what should have been arms. They were wings, large feathered wings. It flapped them. I thought it would lift into the air and fly off.

This was not possible. This was Horus, the son of Osiris, the god who embodied the soul of the pharaoh. A myth. There in front of me.

The breeze picked up. A dark cloud crossed the moon. The world was plunged into shadow. It took my eyes what seemed forever to adjust. I moved carefully back around the corner, out of its sight, and stood quite still. I even held my breath. It could not be real.

The cloud uncovered the face of the moon, and the light

returned. I looked around the corner cautiously. In the place where the falcon-thing had been there was a man. And though he was a hundred yards off, I knew it was Danilo.

I had no idea what to do. This was private; he was alone by choice. If he knew I had seen him…but I could not simply go back to the hotel, not after the thing I had seen.

Slowly—sadly, I thought—he sat down on the pyramid's harsh stone. And buried his face in his hands. I thought he must be crying. Slowly, cautiously I took a few steps toward him.

There were guards somewhere close by, and it was quite illegal to be there, but I had to let him know I was there with him. "Danilo?" I hoped my voice would carry to him but no farther. He didn't seem to hear; he kept his face buried. I moved closer. And again he seemed not to hear me.

Finally I was ten yards away. And yes, he was crying. I could hear him sobbing, muttering to himself, or perhaps to his gods, in a language not English. I spoke loudly. "Danilo, I'm here."

He looked up, quite slowly. His face was streaked with tears that caught the moonlight and glistened. For a moment he seemed not to recognize me. "Jamie?"

"I'm here, Danilo." He held up a hand. I walked beside him and took it in mine. "I'm here."

"I don't know what's wrong." He looked away. "I was walking here. I waited till everyone else was gone. I needed to be alone with the past. And then suddenly the most awful wave of melancholy overtook me."

I sat beside him and let my feet hang over the step.

"This isn't at all like me, Jamie. I've been home dozens of times in the past, hundreds. But I've never felt anything like this before."

As he had done to me scores of times, I reached out and stroked his hair.

"I began to cry, Jamie, and I couldn't stop. I'm crying for everything I've lost. And for everything I've found." He put his arm around me and held me tightly. "I'm mourning for what I once was. And for what I have become."

It all made sense to me in a way; in another way it made no sense at all. For a man to be so complicated and to let it be seen— it was a new thing to me. I had no idea what to say to him, or even if saying anything was the right thing to do. And so I simply held him. He buried himself in my arms and cried for a long, long time under that bright Egyptian moon. In time he was still, and I knew that he was sleeping.

I think I must have fallen asleep myself. The next thing I remember is looking up to realize that the sky was beginning to lighten. I shook him gently. "Danilo, it's time for us to go."

He looked into my face groggily.

"Come on. The guards will be out and about. And the morning's first tourists will be arriving."

He stood and stretched; so did I. Then glanced upward. The last bright stars were still shining. He took my hand. "Do you feel up for a good, hard climb?"

I realized what he meant. "But security…"

"They will leave us alone. Come on. We'll both be sore tomorrow, but it will be worth it."

And so we climbed the Great Pyramid, step by difficult step. At times we kept apart, at other times we push-pulled each other up the face of the monument. The eastern sky went from gray to purple. As I had expected, a tourist bus drove up the plateau and parked a few hundred feet away from us. People spilled out of it. Danilo took no notice of them; he seemed determined to get to the top before the sun rose.

Panting, nearly exhausted, we finally reached the top. And stood with our arms around each other's waists.

The sun rose, as swiftly and majestically as if it had actually been a god. There might almost have been fanfares. First the top of it notched the horizon. Its rays reached us and bathed us in brilliant golden light. Then it climbed slowly over the rim of the world and ascended stately into the sky, its proper element. The age-old city stretched out beneath us, the blinding light of the sun above… It was as thrilling a sight as I'd ever seen.

"Is this what it feels like to be a god, Danilo?"

"A king, at least. And it is ours."

I couldn't resist. "When do we take possession?"

"Possession is long overdue. We owned it all once, my family did. My father bestrode this land with all the wisdom and majesty the world could want in a monarch. And insight. He understood so many things. I've always thought that was why they hated him so much. The viciousness of the dull toward the intelligent." He looked into my eyes, then held me even tighter. "And then came myself, and then my poor brother's short imperium, and then...night." He squeezed me tightly to himself. "But as the Bible reminds us, the sun also rises. Next comes you."

"Papa."

"You do not have the right demeanor for a prince, Jamie. No true prince could ever permit himself to be so rude. It's a lucky thing for you I love you."

I knew he was right. Standing there at the top of the world with a future brighter than the sun—or so it seemed to me—I couldn't imagine a more fortunate existence. But of course nothing lasts.

We spent another day in Cairo, at the Egyptian Museum on Liberation Square. I knew the building at once. There's footage of it in Karloff's *The Mummy.*

Gallery after gallery of the most exciting objects, all preserved carefully in glass cases with fine wood frames. I had seen photographs of the more famous ones; seeing them in person was quite marvelous. There was a colossal statue of Akhenaten, not as fine as the ones in the Louvre. The colonial powers had been only too efficient.

On the upper floor were the treasures of Tutankhamen. Rare things, beautiful things. Danilo stood before the famous golden death mask and looked into his brother's face. And so did I. He had indeed been a beautiful boy. His eyes seemed to be fixed on something distant and unreachable, perhaps on eternity, perhaps on the face of Set himself.

Danilo seemed transfixed. He slowly raised a hand and pressed it against the glass. A guard took a step toward us. Danilo shot him a glaring glance, and he stopped.

"He was the sweetest boy. He had a bit of a limp, you know. But he was as athletic as his body would permit. He loved to swim. His limp didn't matter then." The tone of his voice was unmistakable. It was love. I didn't ask whether they had ever actually…no, that I didn't want to know.

He walked me through the galleries, one after another, and told me about the things he remembered: toys, thrones, jeweled collars…ruefully he called them "the family jewels—all that is left of us."

"That isn't true, Danilo. You're here."

"Barely."

"You're worth more than all of this, at least to me."

"Flatterer." Like me, he wasn't much good at taking compliments.

We had dinner at a restaurant on the square, steaks braised with a fascinating complex of spices. The wine had a bitter edge.

"Egyptian wine always does now. I suspect it's because the Nile is polluted." He took a long drink. "Everything is in the modern world."

"How long will we be here? Will you take me to Sakkara?" It was the burial ground of ancient Memphis, the place where the first pyramids were built. It was in use till the time of Cleopatra and beyond.

He shook his head. "No, we have to leave tomorrow. I'll show you Sakkara on our next visit."

There would be a next visit. I liked hearing it. I was falling in love with Egypt.

"But Jamie, we are not here as tourists. We have work."

Danilo hired a felucca to take us up the Nile. I had expected another train ride, but he said that no train would stop at the places we were going.

We left just after noon. The boatman met us near the famous bridge designed by Eiffel, the one that almost looks like his tower lying on its side. Danilo exchanged greetings with him in Arabic; then he greeted me in English. He helped us get our things on board, then took his seat at the rear, holding the tiller with one hand; with the other he hoisted that long, graceful, curving sail, and we were off. We sat in side-by-side seats in the middle of the boat, which was named the *Cleopatra*.

The Nile was busy with traffic: water taxis ferrying people about, tourist boats loading and unloading their passengers, a few small steamers that had made their way upriver from the sea. There were also police boats. They made me nervous; I knew Egypt was not exactly a friendly country for men who love men, not anymore.

I hadn't had much sailing experience, a few trips to Pennsylvania lakes, but not much to speak of. So my first ride in a felucca came as quite a surprise. The long sail seemed to catch the least whiff of wind, and we moved so smoothly there was almost no sense of motion. It was quite startling; if it hadn't been for the scenery moving by, I'm not at all certain I'd have known we were under sail.

The city surrounded us, an enormous metropolis of hotels, office buildings, there were even houseboats moored along the riverbank. All quite modern and not what I thought of when I thought of Egypt. Danilo pointed out a large floating structure, a barge with a superstructure erected on it, and told me it was the art academy where the ancient techniques of painting on papyrus had been revived a few decades back.

After a time the city passed, then the suburbs, and we were in something like the Egypt I had always imagined. Or rather, had always seen in movies. I let my hand trail in the water.

Our boatman was named Mohammed Ali, which Danilo explained was more or less the Arab equivalent of John Smith. Mohammed was fifty, perhaps; his face was just beginning to wrinkle. He spoke surprisingly good English, pointing out things he thought we might find interesting. The ruins of small temples or shrines stood here and there, but not many. Farther away from shore we saw columns and obelisks now and then, the remains of what had been great temples. Mostly the old land had been supplanted by the new. In the far distance behind us we could see Giza and the pyramids, miles away yet still visible.

After a time Danilo put an arm around me, and I leaned against him. Almost at once I realized it might not be a wise thing to do. What would Mohammed make of it? I looked over my shoulder at him, and he winked at me. Nothing to worry about there.

The Egyptian countryside was as lush and green as any place I'd ever seen. Better than Ebensburg, certainly—there were no strip mines. All around us was the most profuse growth. Mostly the land was cultivated. Egypt is a long, narrow, green strip along the banks of the river; beyond that is desert. Every available bit of land was farmed to feed the country's large population. Here and there we saw small villages, some no more than half a dozen mud-brick huts clustered together on the riverbank.

Men and boys worked the land, often wearing nothing but loincloths. Others worked in galabias. Some of them sang at their labors. Teams of oxen plowed. They walked slowly, sullenly in their wooden yokes. Danilo said it all looked much the way it had in his youth, millennia before. It would hardly have surprised me to see a royal barge pass us on the river. West Penn University seemed a lifetime away.

It was all so beautiful and so strange compared to the things I'd always known that I barely stopped to wonder where we were going. What were these "places where no train would stop"?

We dozed off and on; the movement was so gentle. I think Mohammed must have too, but I didn't want to be so rude as to look back and see. As we traveled, there was less and less conversation.

We came to the great oasis called the Fayum, a huge, miles-long fertile region. Date palms grew in abundance, and there were citrus groves, vineyards, even apple orchards. Without saying a word to us Mohammed pulled up to shore and tethered the boat to a big old palm tree. We went quickly ashore and filled our arms with apples, limes, and grapes, then dashed back to the riverbank and set sail again.

I bit into a particularly large, particularly green lime. "I feel like Saint Augustine, stealing those apples he repented for for the rest of his life."

Danilo grinned. "His guilt over the apples was nothing compared to he guilt he felt for loving another boy when he was young."

I looked at him, wondering what Mohammed might make of our exchange. "You're not going to tell me he was one of us, are you?"

"Good Christ, no."

On the distant horizon, just at the limit of my vision, I thought I could see pyramids. I remembered that this region was the seat of the pharaohs of the Middle Kingdom. I had seen their statues, or photos of them, done in a surprisingly realistic style for ancient Egypt. They looked sad, or tired.

Suddenly, quite abruptly, Danilo leaned close and kissed me. I looked back to Mohammed in alarm, but he was smiling a benevolent smile.

The great oasis receded behind us, and there was more of the familiar farmland, more of the small villages. It was noticeably warmer. We had left the European winter far behind us. Mohammed stripped off his galabia and wore nothing but a loincloth. His body was lean, muscular, pleasingly dark.

A massive square tower of stone rose up on the western bank. I recognized it: the Meidum Pyramid. It had collapsed during construction, killing thousands of men. All that remained was a central core, a great stone block whose sides sloped gently inward. Around its base was the rubble from the collapse and under it the unexcavated bodies of all those workers. No archaeologist had ever dug there, even though the pyramid was one of the most fascinating monuments in the country.

Everywhere death existed side by side with vibrant life.

Just before sunset Mohammed pulled to shore again. The jolt of the *Cleopatra* touching land woke Danilo, who had been sleeping in my arms. Groggily he looked around, then turned to ask where we were. Mohammed said one word, "Ibada." Some yards inland I could see another small village, a few dozen mud-brick houses. There were a few children playing in the streets; no one else was visible.

Ibada. I had never heard of it; it meant not a thing. But I was still a far way from being an expert on Egypt. "Why are we stopping, Danilo? What's here?"

"Come on. This is one of the places I especially want you to see."

The setting sun made everything seem to glow with a wonderful red-orange life, and the long dark shadows made a vivid contrast. We jumped ashore and headed not to the village but to a low rise just beyond it.

It was a vast open field. At first glance there was nothing. Literally nothing, no vegetation, for the first time along the river, just dirt. Then I began to realize that it must be the remains of a city. I could see, I thought, where streets would have been. And here and there columns stood, most of them broken; I could see what must have been their capitals lying on the earth. The place was much larger than I'd realized at first.

Danilo took a few steps, and I followed him. He bent down and ran his fingers through the dry soil. "Look at what time and humanity have done to love."

I was lost. "Is this Amarna?"

"No." He looked at me, then pressed his hand to the earth again. "We'll be there soon enough."

He was in no mood to be communicative. I didn't quite understand why. But I left him to himself and wandered off among the ruins, what there were of them.

It must have been a magnificent place. The streets were wider than most in Pittsburgh. There was a crumbling ghost of an amphitheater; I guessed it must have held a thousand people or more. I traced the foundation of what would have been a temple, I thought. Nearly sixty feet by sixty. This had been no provincial town. Then a fragment of stone caught my eye. On it was inscribed the name of the god Eros in Greek and Latin. This had been a Greek city, or a Greco-Roman one, not Egyptian.

The sun set and the sky began to darken. On the eastern horizon a white glow shone; the waning moon would rise soon. I saw Danilo walking among the shadowed ruins, much as I was doing myself; but he seemed preoccupied, as if he knew it all and was grieving for what had been here. Off at the edge of the city Mohammed stood, quiet, watching us.

I crossed the open space to Danilo. "Please tell me, where are we?"

He looked up into the sky, then at me. "The temple you found was his. The temple of the beautiful young god."

"Eros." I said it confidently.

"No. Eros was honored here, as was his mother Aphrodite. But this city was built to honor the young god who had died here. He drowned in the Nile not far from where Mohammed moored our boat."

It finally dawned on me. When I said his name it came out almost a whisper. "Antinous."

"Yes." His voice was low too. "I walked at Hadrian's side when he laid out the city, much as Alexander had done four centuries earlier at Alexandria. This was the greatest monument to love ever built."

Antinous had been a boy in his late teens—my age, I realized—when he came here with his lover, the emperor Hadrian. Somehow the boy had drowned in the river. And the emperor's grief encompassed the whole of his empire.

"You should have seen them together, Jamie. I have never seen two human beings more obviously mad with love for each other. They were two halves of one soul." He kissed me. "Like us."

Still again I found myself looking cautiously to Mohammed, but there was no sign he found our love in any way objectionable.

"It rocked the empire. The death of the beautiful boy athlete shook the world, Jamie. Hadrian made him a god. Temples were erected all across Europe and Asia. For centuries after Hadrian's death people worshiped in temples devoted to his young lover. Not till the Christians took power and began to stamp out what they called 'pagans' did his cult die out."

"A fit god for us, Danilo."

"A fit god for the world, if the world would only see." His voice turned bitter. "Certainly he's more deserving of worship than the tripartite man-god."

The moon was above the horizon now. Everything took on its spectral white glow. Amid the ruins of Hadrian's love we kissed again. And made love.

It seemed there was nothing in the world but Danilo's touch. A spark of pure pleasure shot through me; for that moment nothing else existed. The touch of the divine. Around us the ruins seemed even more vast than I had realized. The city seemed to stretch on forever.

As we had so many times, we rested in each other's arms. There was no pillow; we rested our heads on a broken capital. I thought I saw two men there with us, making love too: Antinous and Hadrian. But it was only a fleeting dream.

When finally we got to our feet we brushed dust and bits of rubble off each other. Danilo dressed. I stayed naked. When we got to the Nile again I did what I knew I had to. I stretched my body and dove in. The water was cool and dark.

"Jamie, no! This is where he drowned." He tried to catch hold of my foot but I swam away from him and splashed him playfully. "Jamie, come back!"

But I kept swimming. It was the first time I'd been in the water for weeks. It felt wonderful. I was aware that my fingers felt fine, no pain.

When I finally swam back to shore Danilo grabbed me angrily. "Antinous drowned here. You might have too."

"No. We're the new history, Danilo, you and I. What happened to them will not happen to us."

"Don't be a fool, Jamie."

"I'm not. I'm alive. No water in my lungs, see?"

"Don't do this again."

I smiled. He had never tried to give me an order before. "Now take me to your father's city."

Mohammed had watched it all impassively. For a moment I wondered what he made of us. Then I decided it didn't matter.

The moon climbed higher in the sky, and there were thousands of stars. They all seemed to grow brighter with each passing minute. The boat glided on the surface of the Nile like a ghost hovering over the face of the waters.

In little more than two hours we were there: Amarna.

Like the City of Antinous, it was a city no more. A vast open plain stretched off from the river. It was possible to see where streets had been, at least the larger ones. But of the buildings that had stood there, not one remained. Outlines of their foundations could be seen in the brilliant moonlight. Here and there a few stones were still piled together. And at the far ends of the place I could see the ancient boundary markers that a team of French archaeologists had found and set up again, back in the nineteenth century. You could almost feel the presence of the inhabitants' ghosts.

There was the faintest breeze, the only indication we were still part of a living world. From under his seat in the *Cleopatra* Mohammed produced three torches. Danilo lit them, and we headed off through the ruins to the low cliffs beyond. I could see entrances, black doorways gaping there.

As we walked Danilo mostly stayed silent. But now and then he would point something out. "This was the Temple of the Sun. My sisters and I used to play in the courtyard."

"And Tut?"

"He was never well."

He gestured to our left. "The Street of the Fish Merchants. I've never tasted such delicious things."

"Not even in Alexandria?"

"An upstart city."

Alexandria was 2,400 years old, by Danilo's standard an upstart. What must he think of me?

It took us more than an hour to make our way to the cliffs. The entranceways yawned more and more noticeably. It was where the people of Amarna had cut their tombs—into the living rock.

"There," he pointed, "was the tomb prepared for my father. And my mother's is just beside it. My two little sisters who died were buried in it." He hesitated for a moment, then kept walking. "I still remember the ceremonies. The first burial rites I had ever seen. Mourners filling the city with their cries. Priests in leopard skins looking fierce and lethal. It was all rather terrible."

I think he was talking for himself more than for me. Family memories, still vibrant in his mind after three millennia.

The tomb entrances were carved with hieroglyphs and images of the gods, and of their occupants. We did not stop to examine them. There wasn't time. It had already been a long night, and there was more to do.

Finally we came to the last of the tombs, farthest to the south along the cliff. The doorway was perhaps eight feet high. Inside was perfect blackness. Danilo held up his torch so I could see the inscription over the lintel. I mouthed the words: PER-NEFER-SET-HOTEP. It did not sound right, too long for a name, not complete enough to be an expression of anything else. I looked at him, a bit puzzled, and for the first time all night he smiled.

He turned to Mohammed. "You will wait here for us."

Mohammed nodded, and we stepped inside.

Our torches seemed blindingly bright in the surrounding blackness. It took my eyes a moment to adjust. There was a flurry of activity. Something rushed over our heads. I ducked. Danilo told me, "Bats. There isn't a tomb in Egypt that isn't occupied, sometimes by worse things than them."

"Will they bite?"

"No, they're far too timid. But if your reflexes make you look up at them, keep your moth closed. When they launch into the air, they urinate."

"So much for the romance of Egypt."

I had been expecting a tomb to open before us. Instead there were two more doors, side by side. Over one was carved PER-NEFER-SET; over the other, SET-HOTEP. My Egyptian was still halting, but I thought the first one meant something like, "Beautiful is the house of Set" and the other "Set is complete." I kept my translations to myself, though. No sense emphasizing my ignorance, not then, not there.

Danilo seemed to know what I was thinking. "Look inside them."

I walked first to one door, then to the other. Now that my eyes had gotten used to the level of light, I was surprised at how much I could see. They were huge tombs, typical of what I knew of Egyptian tombs from that age. And they were mirror images of one another. Every last detail, the inscriptions, the images of the gods, all of it was mirrored from one tomb to the other. I had never heard of anything like it, and I looked to Danilo, quite baffled.

"They were lovers." He smiled faintly. "Two of my father's most trusted courtiers. The high priests of Set."

It made sense. They had had their names joined in their joint tomb. Per-nefer-Set-hotep: joined for eternity.

"At the rear of the tomb, in the room where you would expect to find one sarcophagus, you will find a common room with two, side by side."

We walked there. The tombs were larger than I'd thought at first. Now and then a bat or two, undisturbed by our first entrance, would suddenly stir and fly off and out. A parade of gods and goddesses processed along the walls. And there were images of the royal family. I looked from Danilo to his likeness in the stone. Allowing for the conventions of their art, the likeness was unmistakable.

As he said, the separate tombs joined again at the burial chamber, which held two sarcophagi, side by side, so close you couldn't have gotten a sheet of paper between them. On the wall behind them was carved the great god Set, seated in divine majesty. The two lovers stood before him, holding hands. I took Danilo's, and for a time we stood there in silence, contemplating love that strong and that ancient.

I knew that there was also a tomb that had been cut and prepared for Akhenaten himself, and another for Nefertiti. They were never used. The fate of their bodies was quite unknown. But I asked Danilo if we could see them. They would have more images of his family, and I wanted to see them.

His response surprised me completely. "We are standing in my father's tomb." He walked to the wall and traced his mother's features with a finger. "He wasn't a fool, despite what the old priests all claimed. And he wasn't mad. When the end was coming, he arranged with Per-nefer-Set and Set-hotep to be buried here, where the traditionalist priests could not find him."

He stepped to the rear wall and uttered a few words in ancient Egyptian—it sounded like a prayer—then pressed hard on the face of Set. The wall opened. Before us was the burial chamber of Akhenaten.

The sarcophagus was gold. The carvings one the walls were also layered in gold leaf. In our torchlight the room seemed to blaze.

Danilo walked to his father's coffin and pushed at the lid. Slowly it began to shift. I helped him. It slid aside. There was the mummy of the heretic pharaoh, arms crossed like all the mummies I had ever seen. There was no burial mask, as with his son Tutankhamen. This must have been a hasty burial. But the mummy was wrapped in fine white linen; time had hardly yellowed it. The cloth was layered evenly, almost geometrically.

Danilo kissed me. "It is time for you to meet him. And to join us."

He began to pray. I could hardly follow the words. It was a chant, almost hypnotic. I caught the name of Set repeated again and again; there was not much else I understood.

After a few moments my attention drifted to the golden images on the tomb walls. As Danilo chanted his hymn my eyes strayed from Osiris to Isis to Horus to Anubis…Ptah was there, the god of intellect, and Khnum, the potter god who fashioned humankind on his wheel. I saw Bes, the deformed dwarf god who oversaw childbirth, and Sobek, the crocodile god. The gods of Egypt marched in procession, making obeisance to the great god at their head. And it was Set, of course, seated in grandeur at the head of all the rest.

Suddenly Danilo fell silent. I moved to his side. He was gazing at his father's face. And suddenly the long-dead pharaoh began to move.

The eyelids opened, revealing empty sockets. Eyeless, the head turned and stared at us. Slowly the arms unfolded. I took Danilo's hand.

Akhenaten sat up in his coffin. Slowly, painfully it seemed, he grasped its sides and began to stand.

Finally I found my voice. "Danilo, what's happening? This can't be."

"Shh."

The mummy stood. Slowly, achingly it stepped down from the sarcophagus and stood before us. Tall and thin, like all his representations. He swayed unsteadily. Danilo bowed; uncertainly, I did the same.

Danilo stepped close to him. They embraced. They kissed. After three millennia the Kissing Kings were kissing again.

The mummy spoke. Its voice was no more than a rasp, a grating whisper. Danilo answered. The only word I understood in what he said was "love." The mummy looked to me. Not knowing what to do, I bowed again, lower than before.

When I looked up Danilo was holding his golden knife. "Jamie, this is a holy place. Do you understand that?"

I did.

"And the gift I have given you…you must accept it finally here or not at all."

"I thought I had already—"

"No, It must be sealed in the presence of the god."

I touched his face. He stood quite still. I kissed him. There was nothing in the world I could possibly want more than Danilo, my love.

He took the knife and held it to his throat. And cut.

Blood flowed. More than I expected, more than I thought possible. I knew what I had to do. I kissed him again and drank. My body was overwhelmed with sexual pleasure, with the surge of life itself. I felt like I might explode.

When I finished I looked to Akhenaten. From his throat too, blood was flowing, or something like it. From the dried, withered body, impossibly, fresh blood flowed. I looked to Danilo and he nodded slightly. I went to his father, kissed him, and drank. And the wave of pleasure in my flesh surged even more intensely.

I felt Danilo behind me. We made love, my two fathers and I. Time after time, one flood of sheer divine pleasure after another. Finally it became too much and I slept, or maybe I passed out, I don't know which.

When I woke the torches were out. There was faint light coming from the entrance. The sarcophagus cover was back in place, the great pharaoh asleep again. Soon it would be dawn.

The night's experience had drained me, left me weak, like the wildest sex I'd ever had but even more so. I had to hold on to Danilo as we made our way back to the boat. Once or twice Mohammed had to help him. I was aware of nothing in the world but Danilo's arms around me and the coming sunrise.

In the boat I slept again, in Danilo's arms. I felt his lips pressed against my face. The morning sun warmed us, the Nile carried us, the breeze filled our sail. Once when I awoke a royal falcon had landed on the prow; I had the impression Danilo was talking to it. Then it lifted into the air and flew into the sun's face. Dreams. I know there were more, but I don't remember any of the others. But I felt a part of the universe in a way I never had before.

We reached Luxor in late morning. It had been Thebes in ancient times, the greatest city in the world. Homer called it "Hundred-gated Thebes." I saw why at once.

We sailed past the Temple of Karnak on the east bank. Danilo pointed out one feature after another, the famous Avenue of Sphinxes, the line of great pylons or gates, the columns erected by this pharaoh or that. The sun of centuries had bleached away the color, but he told me it had all been painted riotously in its day. "This the largest religious complex ever built. Larger even than the Vatican."

"Larger than Branson, Missouri?"

He snorted. "There are a few more spells I should have said over you."

Not long after, we came to the town of Luxor itself. Bahr Street stretched along the shore; there was a small museum, quite new, quite lovely in the way of modern Islamic architecture. Then came the Temple of Luxor, much smaller than Karnak but quite perfect in its lines. Just past the temple came a small park and then the famous Winter Palace Hotel. The great and the near great had stayed there. I recognized it from *Death on the Nile*. Danilo ignored my film buff's enthusiasm.

There was a dock in front of the hotel. Mohammed moored there, helped us get out things into the hotel, and said goodbye. In a short time he had shared so much with us, or rather he had seen us share so much. I wondered if he knew, or guessed, what had happened in the twin tombs at Amarna.

The desk clerk gave us a suite of rooms on the top floor, over-looking the Nile. From that viewpoint I could see a bit of the west bank. There were ruined temples, colossal statues or the remains of them. In the far distance I could see the range of low hills where the Valley of the Kings was located.

We settled in, had some lunch, then crossed the river in a ferry. On the west bank Danilo hired a horse and carriage. The driver looked me up and down. "A young American."

How on earth could they tell? It was beginning to annoy me. Danilo said it was obvious to anyone but an American.

"What's that supposed to mean? Not all of them can tell."

"Not all of them have said so. Tourism is an important indus-try. And they want their baksheesh."

"I don't understand."

He smiled. "Americans don't like to realize they're so obvious."

I was annoyed and I let it show.

"Why, Jamie, you can dish it out but you can't take it."

The driver took us to the Ramesseum, the famous temple where Shelley had written "Ozymandias." Colossi, or parts of them, still littered the earth. Impulsively I recited the line: "Look on my works, ye mighty, and despair."

There were other temples to see, and the Colossi of Memnon, gargantuan statues of Amenhotep II. "The northern one used to sing each morning," Danilo told me, "to greet the sunrise."

I had read about it in a few books on archaeology or I'd have thought he was pulling my leg. All the ancient travelers had heard it. One of the Roman emperors, alarmed by the sighing of its song, had the openings in it covered with cement.

The Valley of the Kings. I had heard about it so many times, not just in movies. It was huge, desolate, and full of tourists. As we pulled up to the entrance the driver pointed to a modern building, a combination tourist center and restaurant. He pointed to a particular group of visitors. "More Americans."

He had to be wrong. I wanted him to be wrong. I approached them. They were from New Jersey.

Avoiding the knots of tourists as much as possible, we saw the tombs, at least the famous ones. Most of the others were closed to visitors, though Danilo said he could take me into them if I really wanted him to. Seti I—or as I thought of him, Cedric Hardwick— Thurmose III, the great warrior-king, Amenhotep III, Danilo's grandfather. There was no nostalgia. "I never knew him," Danilo said. "He died before I was born."

There were also a great many empty tombs. Barren stone, unadorned, unused. One was labeled TOMB NO. 55. A sign explained, in Arabic, French, and English, that one unidentified body had been found there. Archaeologists believed it to be that of Smenkhare, the son of the heretic pharaoh. It made Danilo fall silent. I wanted to ask him about the cousin whose body had been in the tomb, but his mood warned me off.

Finally we went to the tomb of his brother. It was the smallest one in the Valley, at least of the tombs actually used by kings. But it was magnificent, the colors on the walls still alive and vibrant. In the final chamber lay the king's sarcophagus, bright blinding gold. His remains were inside, resting were they had been laid three millennia before. The one pharaoh whose mummy was left to repose where it was intended to. Danilo spoke not one word.

When we emerged from the tomb the sun was beginning to set. He told me he was going to stay the night there. "You go back to the hotel alone. Give the driver ten pounds. He'll be quite happy."

"Are you sure you'll be all right here?"

"The guards will leave me alone."

"That's not what a meant."

"I know, Jamie." He hugged me. "Go ahead. I'll see you in the morning."

I lost sight of him as the carriage headed back toward the Nile. I did not know if I wanted to be with him there. I had seen so much already—experienced so much already. I wasn't at all sure I wanted more.

Night fell quickly. I had a quiet dinner in the hotel, delicious fish. Then, feeling restless, I went out for a walk. The Luxor Temple was lit brightly by floodlights. I crossed the street into that little park. Paved pathways led among trees and flowering shrubs; the air was quite full of their scent.

There were other men there, walking singly or in pairs. It became apparent even to this sheltered boy from Ebensburg that they were cruising each other—quite furtively, but it was unmistakable. Two of them would meet then disappear in the shrubbery or simply leave together.

A young man approached me. My age, maybe younger. He had thick black hair and deep brown skin. He smiled. "You are an American."

I was irritated but didn't let it show. "Yes."

"From New York?"

"No, from Pittsburgh."

"Ah, Pittsburgh, Pennsylvania. The Steel City."

"You know America."

"How can we not? So much depends on it." He did not make this sound favorable. He looked around. "You must be careful. There are police. Men are arrested here all the time."

It did not surprise me.

Suddenly, abruptly, the floodlights on the temple went out. Luxor was officially closing down for the night. The park became dark. The young man took my hand. "Can we be friends?"

I hadn't expected anything like this. "Uh…I guess so."

"Good. Come with me. We will walk." Leading me by the hand he took me out into Bahr Street. There were antique street lamps made to look Victorian; I wondered if they really were, or of it was for the tourists. He looked at me and smiled an enormous smile. "My name is Mageet."

"I'm Jamie. Nice to meet you."

"Jamie." He seemed to like the sound of it.

There was no moon yet; it would rise late. The Nile was dark; only the lights from the town lit it, flickering on the surface. There were other people out walking, enjoying the warm night. A few of them, the tourists, looked startled at the sight of us hand in hand. Most of the Egyptians paid no notice.

"My brother is in America. He was arrested."

I wasn't at all sure how to react. "I'm sorry."

"We don't know when we'll see him again."

"Is he—?" I groped for something intelligent to say.

"A student."

We passed the museum. Lovely little building. Mageet asked me if I had been inside. "They have a small but choice collection. Most of the good things were taken by the French and the British. And by your Metropolitan Museum."

"That was a long time ago."

He shrugged. "A hundred years." Ahead of us loomed the Temple of Karnak. Columns towered, obelisks soared into the night sky. "Not so long, really. We will get them back." He grew silent; we walked that way for a while.

The temple complex was huge, much larger than it had seemed from the river. It took us several minutes to reach the main entrance. Mageet stopped walking. He looked away from me awkwardly. "Would you like to take me to your hotel room?"

This I had expected. "No, I'm afraid not. I'm with someone."

"The older gentleman."

"You've been watching us."

"You are beautiful. You have the body of a swimmer. Like Antinous." He hesitated. "How could I not watch?"

"Well, I am quite in love with the older gentleman."

"He is not here." He reached up to touch my face, but I recoiled. "We would not be arrested. I have a cousin in the police."

"Really, Mageet, thank you. But it isn't possible." I didn't have a knife.

Plainly disappointed he turned and left. As he was going I pressed a five-pound note into his hand. He gave to back to me. "I did not want your money. I only thought we might…never mind. Good night. It was nice to meet you, Jamie."

He walked away without saying anything else. I stared after him for a while, wondering if he'd look back. He didn't.

Karnak. I had to see it. The guard at the entrance tried to stop me. It was time for me to flex my new power, if I really had it. I stared into his eyes. "You will let me in. Then you will forget about me."

Compliantly he unlocked the gate, and I went inside.

Night: Everything was in shadow. There was only starlight. Titanic columns surrounded me. Ancient sphinxes littered the ground. Obelisks touched the sky; Danilo told me they had been plated with gold. I wandered for what seemed hours. At one place I came upon a statue of Tutankhamen; the features were unmistakable, even in the night. It was the one trace of him that remained after the priests had done their work. The statue was renamed for Ramses II, but the beautiful face was Tut's; there was no mistaking it.

Off in the Valley of the Kings I knew Danilo was with him. I had to force myself not to wonder what they might be doing. That I did not want to know.

Eventually the moon rose and bathed the vast complex in cold white light. A monstrously large scarab beetle, carved in granite, blocked my way. It was chilling, it was beautiful. I could have stayed there forever. Then I happened across a snack bar, shuttered for the night. The sign read: THE TEMPLE OF COCA-COLA. So much for my mood.

There was something I had to try. Something I remembered from the apocrypha Millie used to read. A story about Jesus Christ when his family hid in Egypt. There was something he had done, or so the story said, that I had to try myself.

I left the temple complex and walked to the edge of the Nile. The water lapped gently. Moonlight gleamed on its surface. From farther downriver, away from the town, I could hear faintly the croaking of frogs.

I got down on one knee and pressed my fingers into the earth. There was a thin layer of mud. Under it was clay. Firm, workable. The clay the ancients had built with. I took handfuls of it and fashioned it into little animals. A cat, a dog, a lion, a giraffe…I made a dozen or more. The last one was the Set animal.

At the very lip of the river I lined them up, bent down close to them and breathed. I breathed life into them. Slowly, one by one, they stirred. Clay eyes opened, clay mouths gaped. They bent their heads up to look into my face, then they bowed to me.

At my command they marched in a row. I made them rear up on their hind legs and balance. I made them bow again. When I whistled, very softly, the C-minor nocturne, they danced for me. My little creatures danced to the sad, distant music of Chopin.

I held my hand to the earth and the Set animal climbed into it.

When I lifted it close to my face it nuzzled me. The little cat rubbed itself against my shoe, exactly like Bubastis.

Bubastis. I had been away from home so very long, it seemed. It was time to go back. I was hardly the same man. The menagerie in living clay told me that, if nothing else did. I picked up my little clay cat and it licked the tip of my nose.

I glanced at the moon. It was the Eye of Thoth, scribe of the gods. I sent my little animals scampering to their freedom. The cat and the Set animal lingered near me the longest, but after a few moments even they ran off and vanished into the shadows of Luxor. I wondered how they would live, or how long. When the sun baked them dry, would they lose life and movement? Or would they remain creatures of the night and live forever?

I had the blood of kings in my veins, I knew it now beyond any doubt. But I had not begun to understand what it meant.

CHAPTER 10

Pittsburgh. Winter. Snow and ice in the streets, bitter wind. There was a storm the night Danilo and I got home, a severe one. We had flown home; Danilo had to teach in the new semester and time was short. But there were delays in both New York and Pittsburgh. The cab took nearly four hours to get us home from the airport.

When we finally reached our house it was late night and lights were burning. Our neighbor was there, playing with Bubastis and keeping the place warm. He had lit a fire for us. We gave him the souvenir we'd brought for him, an Old Kingdom vase, very rare, very valuable. He looked at it and registered disappointment. Real Egyptian artifacts tend to be unimpressive; tourists like the flashier imitations that are made by the hundreds and sold as "authentic Egyptian," which in a way they are. When Danilo told him what it was worth, his frown turned to a smile very quickly.

Bubastis was all over us. She had grown still more. Having her greet us so enthusiastically made the house feel more like a real home. I played with her and cuddled her for a long time.

I had decided to skip the spring semester to focus on my pianism and my swimming.

A week or so later Danilo dropped a bombshell on me. I was at the piano, trying my hand at the Schubert D-major sonata, when he came in and put his hands on my shoulders. He couldn't have been more obviously agitated. "Jamie, I want you to get your own place."

I had been so happy living with him. And I had done my best not to be a nuisance in any way. I went numb. "But Danilo, I…I…"

"It is only for show. A precaution. You need to have your own residence. You were only supposed to be living with me as a temporary measure, remember?"

"No one will ask about us. You always say so."

"Someone is asking. My colleague Feld is prying. I think he may even have been sniffing around the fourth subbasement."

"But can't you simply—can't you compel him to stop? I've seen you do it with other people."

"I can make him stop, yes. But I think he may already have told other people, and I have no way of knowing who. The administration, maybe even the police, if he really was down there."

"Ask him. Make him tell you."

"The damage has already been done." He sounded as sad as I felt. "This is only for show. Understand that. You can still sleep here, eat here, live here, really. But I want you to have your own place, on the record, in case untoward questions are being asked."

It all came out of nowhere. I hardly had time to think how I felt. "Danilo, you've always warned me against denying my nature."

"I am not asking you to deny who and what you are, Jamie. There is nothing I would want less than that. But your connection to me. You need to be more circumspect about it."

"Other faculty members have affairs with students. I've seen them. Everyone has."

"It is not a matter of our affair. The legal authorities may become involved. I don't know what Feld may have seen in the sublevel. Or what he may have guessed."

This was as troubling as the rest of our talk. I had to ask it. "What could he have seen?"

"In time, Jamie."

"I can't deny my nature. You've taught me that. My nature is to love you." I added, weakly, "And yours is to love me."

"And I do. That is why I don't want you vulnerable to the authorities. Love me any way you want to. I am yours. Part of my love must be protection. You must understand that."

I was not at all sure I did. Not that kind of protection.

Fortunately there was an empty apartment in a house just across the street from Danilo's. The police let me into my old place and we moved my furniture there.

The landlord was a retired steelworker named Dougherty. He was unfriendly; he kept making comments about what a mistake it was to rent to a student. I kept telling him what a quiet life I lead, no parties, no carousing, but it didn't make much difference. Even Danilo's vouching for me didn't help.

The house was old and drafty. There were stained-glass windows, a lot like the ones at Danilo's house, but they were faded and cracked. Bubastis didn't seem to like the place. Neither did I. Danilo found a spinet for me. Some workmen moved it in the day after I moved the rest of my things.

After a few days the landlord confronted me and asked why I never seemed to be at home, even at night. I looked him firmly in the eye and instructed him not to ask again and not to mention it to anyone else. He didn't.

Except in the narrowest, most technical sense, I was still living with Danilo. I regretted the necessity. I knew, or suspected, that it meant something awful was going to happen to us.

My hands felt fine. The blood of the pharaohs had healed them. I spent hours at the grand, playing Chopin, Schubert, Poulenc…Roland was amazed at what I could do. When I asked him to let me play in the spring recital he was obviously a bit reluctant. But I played the Chopin second for him and got it note-perfect.

He took my hands in his and felt my fingers. "Michael Columbus said it would be a year or more before they healed properly. If they did at all."

"He was wrong."

"So I see." He couldn't keep his puzzlement from showing. I wished he'd express a bit of pleasure or at least satisfaction. "I guess you'll be playing this spring, then. Some Schubert, maybe?"

"No, the Chopin second. I have to show everyone I can do it."

He looked me up and down. "Is everything all right, Jamie?"

I played dumb, told him I didn't know what he meant.

"Are you sure you're feeling all right? Over all the…unpleasantness?"

"Is that what you call it when somebody dies, Roland? Unpleasantness?"

"Don't be disagreeable, Jamie. I know you understand why I'm concerned."

I did. And I knew it was foolish to spar with him. "I'm fine, Roland. Thanks."

Danilo had a heavy teaching load in the new semester. The university had asked him to take a freshman Western Civilization class to cover for a teacher on sabbatical. He did it without much enthusiasm but told me, "At least I'll be able to teach them a thing or two about history they never heard in high school."

He spent a lot of time at the department. One afternoon I stopped in to see him and ran into Peter Borzage. He was carrying a Roman bust in marble, some emperor or other. He smiled, put it down and hugged me like a long lost brother. "It's so good to see you, Jamie."

"You too." I hoped I sounded sincere.

"You have a bit of a tan."

"Egypt changes a person, I guess." I made myself smile. I wanted to say, "You're still pink," but I held my tongue.

"Can we have lunch? I want to hear all about it."

"Another time, okay? I'm meeting Danilo."

"Oh." His disappointment was plain to see. "How about tomorrow, then?"

I had tried to discourage him every way I could think of short of actual rudeness. Fortunately Professor Feld came around the corner just then. "Peter, don't leave things lying around like that."

Peter looked down at the bust. "It's not 'lying around.' It's—"

"Don't argue with me. Get that upstairs now. And be careful with it."

Peter blushed, picked it up and rushed off. I never thought the day would come when I'd be happy to see Feld.

He turned on me. "Aren't you on a leave of absence, Dunn?"

I smiled and nodded. "Mm-hmm."

"Then what are you doing here?"

"A leave of absence isn't a quarantine, professor."

"I'd watch that attitude."

I decided to toy with him. "This is just a guess, but your wife nags you a lot, doesn't she?"

He glared at me and stomped off.

Danilo wasn't in his office. I thought he might be downstairs. But as I descended the steps to the subbasements I heard something odd. Piano music. A Chopin waltz. I recognized it—it was me playing. He must have recorded some of my practices without my realizing it. Not that I cared, but I found it strange. It was coming, I realized, from the deepest basement. Something made me stop and wait on the stairs. What could Danilo be doing there, with me to serenade him?

I heard someone behind me. It was Feld. He was looking past me, down to the subbasement, looking unhappy as usual. "What is going on down there?"

I made my face blank. "It sounds like music, doesn't it?"

He took a step downward, then seemed to think better of it. "Professor Semenkaru has the oddest habits."

"You can't imagine."

"That music is echoing up the staircase. You can hear it all over the building. I have some restoration work to begin on that bust of Nerva, and all I can hear is that."

"It's not that loud."

"I say it is. I'm going to go down there and—"

"I wouldn't." I said it as firmly as I could.

"Are you attempting to give me an order?"

"No, I'm attempting to keep you from doing something you'll regret." I had been flippant with him before, but I had never talked to him with such authority. Egypt had changed me, all right.

He looked at me, obviously not knowing how to react. Slowly he turned and went back up, looking over his shoulder at me from time to time.

The D-minor waltz came from below. I didn't remember playing it at home, but I must have since Danilo had managed to record it. For a moment I listened. It was full of young enthusiasm, but I was playing too fast and my technique was suffering for it.

Not at all sure what to make of it, and not at all sure I wanted to know just then, I turned and went back upstairs. Me, my music, in that dark, awful place.

Peter was in one of the Greco-Roman galleries standing before a sculpture of a discus thrower. It was quite beautiful; I'd noticed it myself often enough. He obviously thought he was alone. He reached up and touched it, caressed its foot. Then he leaned forward and kissed it. His fingers traced the line of the stone sandal.

I cleared my throat as tactfully as I could.

He turned, saw me, and blushed the most brilliant red. "Jamie! I—I—"

"It's all right, Peter." I smiled at him.

"I know what this must look like."

"Yep."

"It's not that."

"Oh." I pretended to be disappointed. "Well, I'll just leave you to whatever it is, then."

"No, wait!"

I paused.

"Jamie, I'd really like to get together with you sometime."

He was single-minded if nothing else. I forced myself not to sigh. "Danilo has a professional conference this weekend," I said. "Would you like to go out dancing?"

"Dancing?"

I nodded. "I'm not much on a dance floor, but—"

"You mean to a—a—"

"Yes, I guess I do. To a—a—" Why couldn't I resist goading him?

"Someplace public?" He said the word as if it was the most distasteful one in the language.

"Well, yeah. It's kind of hard to dance in a phone booth."

"I was hoping we could just spend some time together. You know what I mean…get to know each other."

I knew exactly what he meant, and I wanted no part of it. "I'll have to let you know."

"Oh." His disappointment showed. "Well, then, could we maybe—"

"Look, Peter, I really have to get moving. Errands to run. You know."

I left as quickly as I could. Absurd young man. There was really nothing I could say to him. Besides, he was attractive. Talking to him was making me hungry.

It wasn't just my musicianship that was repaired, it was my swimming. I spent time in the pool every day, and my body responded to the workouts better than it ever had, it seemed. The other jocks seemed not to know what to make of me. Though the specific words had never actually been mentioned in the news or anywhere else, it must have been fairly obvious to them all that Justin and I were, or had been…well, not the right kind for a sports program. Greg too, of course.

They weren't exactly unfriendly, but no one seemed very glad to see me. And I usually found myself alone in the locker room. There were queers in sports. People knew. Good lord, how will the department ever recover its reputation? Sports builds character.

But after a week of twice-daily workouts, I unofficially broke the school record for the backstroke. Again, they seemed not to know what to make of it. They couldn't have looked more puzzled if I'd sprouted fins and scales. But Coach Zielinski caught up with me in the locker room and told me it was time for me to start swimming meets again.

I toweled my hair. "I don't know if I want to."

He smiled a smile that looked rather forced, I thought. "Look, we all know what you've been through. That awful stuff with Wilton, the murders and all. But the team needs you. You're almost good enough for the Olympics."

I pulled on my Calvins. "Almost? Then why bother?"

His frustration showed. "You could win the state title."

"I'm not sure I want it."

It was a kind of blasphemy. I could see it in his face. "The team needs you, Dunn."

I pointed out that I hadn't heard a damn thing from any of them since the "unpleasantness" started. When he protested how busy everyone was, I told him I'd think about it. He shrugged, turned his back on me, and walked away. I could just hear him telling this staff and the other swimmers about it. The fagboy thinks he's special or something. Maybe everything he's been through has made his mind crack. How could anyone not want a state title?

Swimming had become a way of self-expression for me, like music. Maybe it always had been, but I don't think I quite realized it till then. I had swum in the Nile, I had swum where Antinous drowned. What was a state title?

The atmosphere turned even less cordial at the sports building after that. I was not one of them. Worse, I didn't want to be one on them. Ultimate betrayal. Once, late at night, I found myself remembering my encounter with Greg there. And wondering how many more of them were like him, or could be.

Greg. About a month later his lawyers exhausted all their appeals and he was extradited to Pittsburgh. It made me a bit nervous. He had escaped from the Pittsburgh holding facility once before.

One of his lawyers left a voice-mail message for me. Greg wanted me to visit him. I went a bit numb.

I was to meet Danilo for lunch that day. He was in his office, reading and smiling. The journal with his piece on our archaic relief of the Kissing Kings had just been published. He handed it to me. My name was on it, under his, in slightly smaller type. He stood up and stretched. "Now we belong to the ages."

I thumbed through the pages. "I'll read it later."

"There should be a copy in today's mail for you at home."

"What do you say about us?"

"Jamie, it's a scholarly article, not a love letter."

"Really? I thought it was both." He smacked me on the butt with the magazine. "Why don't you ever listen to my music up here?"

This seemed to catch him off guard. "You mean…?"

"I've heard it coming up from the basement, Danilo. Everyone has. Feld bitches about it nonstop. But I think he's afraid of you."

"Good."

I hesitated. "Take me down there."

He looked away from me. "Are you sure you're ready?"

"Greg Wilton wants me to visit him in the county jail. If I can face him, I can face anything."

Danilo turned thoughtful. Quietly he said, "You know you're a great deal stronger now. You break records. Greg can't hurt you."

"He's behind bars. It'll be like a scene in a Big House movie."

"I'd prefer you not to go."

"I think I have to." I smiled, then stopped. "I'm aching to see what he thinks might happen between us."

"Let's get some lunch. I'll take you downstairs later in the week." He smiled. "All right?"

I could have gone down on my own, of course. My curiosity was strong. But that was not the way Danilo wanted it, so I waited.

The county lockup. Cops, most of them overweight; civil servants in bad clothes and worse haircuts. There was an unpleasant smell in the air, I couldn't quite decide what. Some combination of disinfectant, urine and…what? Fear? Despair? Lust?

The building was old, Victorian. Massive stone walls, heavy steel everywhere. The electric lights were harsh. Sounds echoed. The kind of penal facility they don't build anymore.

The visitors room was exactly what I'd expected. A row of little cubicles, chain-link fence separating prisoners from their company. I had told the D.A.'s office I was going. They tried to talk me out of it, but I had made up my mind. They told me to be careful what I said. If Greg's lawyer was there, leave at once. I agreed to that. A guard pointed to a cubicle and told me to sit and wait. I sat and waited.

Greg was in slate-gray overalls. I was expecting handcuffs but there were none. He walked breezily up to his side of the barrier and sat down, one leg propped over the back of his chair. "Little Jamie." He said it with a sneer.

I smiled. "Little free Jamie."

"You look good. Travel agrees with you."

"How do you know about that?"

"You know lawyers. They like to gossip. Are you still fucking that old man?"

"Let me understand this. You asked me here so you could bore me to death?"

"I have a job to finish." He grinned.

I got up to leave. "I'll just be going then."

"Stop."

I looked at him through the wire. "A jailbird trying to give a free man orders. That's good."

"Don't you want to know why I asked you to come down here?"

"I'm quivering with curiosity."

He leaned forward and put his fingers through the chain-link. "I want to know what you are. You and your professor 'friend.'"

I sat down again, spread my arms, and looked puzzled. "As you see."

He lowered his voice. "I killed you. I stabbed you in the throat, like that other little cocksucker."

"Would you repeat that a little louder? The police officers didn't hear."

He hissed, "You should be dead. Or dying. Instead you went off on a world tour."

"And you're behind bars. Isn't life funny?"

"Why isn't there a scar, at least? I cut your goddamn throat." He pushed at the barrier. "I want to know what you are."

"What were the words you used that night? Pansy. Fagboy. That's me."

Suddenly he jumped to his feet and pounded on the wire

screen. It held. But I sprang up and backed away. A cop came and slammed the barrier with his nightstick. Greg sat down and became quiet. I looked to the cop.

He yawned. "Maybe you ought to leave. You're upsetting him."

"I'm upsetting him?" I couldn't believe I was hearing it.

"You should have seen him on the court. He was one of the best."

"Yeah, and sports builds character."

He smiled. I understood. "Right."

From the other side of the screen Greg said softly, "Look, Dunn, please, we need to talk. I'm sorry about that."

I told the cop it would be okay, and he went back to his post. Warily I sat down. And glared at Greg. "All right, what? And make it good."

"What are you going to say at the trial?"

"Why, Greg, it's not till next fall. I haven't given it a bit of thought." It was fun teasing him, it really was.

"Are you going to tell them…are you going to tell them about Justin and me? There's been talk, but nobody knows for sure. Except you."

I dumbed myself down. "What on earth do you mean? What is there to tell?"

He was getting pissed again. "So help me, I should have killed you, you goddamn little queer. I don't know why you're not dead."

"All right, let me get this straight. You're a cold-blooded killer. You slaughtered the guy you said you loved. And it's okay for people to know that you killed him, but not that you loved him."

He jumped up and tore at the barrier again. Again it held.

I recoiled a bit, then recovered my composure. "Well, that answers that. I think I'll be going now, Greg."

"No, I'm not through with you."

I got to my feet. "Have a nice day." And I ambled off to the entrance. The cop scowled at me in what I thought was an especially unfriendly way.

✳

Nighttime. Danilo and I walked about the campus, sometimes holding hands, sometimes not. There was snow in the air, large drifting flakes. It was not heavy, not yet, but it promised to turn into a storm. Academic Tower, floodlit as it always was at night, soared into the sky and vanished in the snowy night.

Danilo was preoccupied. I let him lead the talk. "Have you ever read e.e. cummings?"

I told him I hadn't. "Was he…?"

"No, but he was a good poet. He wrote that summer is a lie."

"Wise man." I wasn't quite sure if I meant cummings or Danilo.

"Dead man. Winter and night are permanent for him."

It was a disturbing thought. "Danilo, what are you saying?"

"Only that I envy him. I don't suppose you've read Sappho either?"

I shook my head.

"She said that the gods considered death the greatest evil, but that was only because they don't die themselves."

His mood and his talk were upsetting me more and more. It was only too clear what he had on his mind.

We walked for a while more, across the bridge that spanned the hollow, to the park where Tim and I had gone together my first day on campus. There was a stand of young trees, all quite barren of course, black branches scraping the air. A layer of snow was beginning to cover the ground; it scattered enough light for the night not to be dark. Danilo caught hold of a tree and swung himself around it like a schoolboy, or a lover in an old movie.

"I know what you're thinking, Jamie. You're thinking this scene could have been directed by George Cukor or Edmund Goulding."

I laughed. "Women's directors. You know me too well."

"They had their truth as we have ours. And they all intersect, don't they?"

I asked what he meant.

"If anything should happen to me…" He left the sentence unfinished but reached into his pocket. He pulled out a small brass key on a silver chain and handed it to me. "To my private storage vault. The address is on the key tag. They have your name there. You will have access."

I looked at the key as if it were the most unpleasant object in the world. "Danilo, what could happen to you? You've survived so much. You've survived everything in the world."

"Feld has definitely been sniffing around the subbasements. I think he's been telling people what he found there."

"Stop him."

"I think it is too late. He might have told anyone."

"Then move whatever is there."

"He had a camera."

"Oh." A wave of numbness was coming over me. Or of fear. I wasn't sure I knew the difference.

"Once they connect me to the killings, they'll release Wilton."

"No!"

"Be on your guard."

The snow was coming down much more heavily. "Danilo, you can't leave me."

"For a time. Only for a time, Jamie."

"There's too much I don't understand yet. About you. About myself."

"You will learn."

He kissed me, the most passionate kiss ever. I realized I was crying.

"Come with me now, Jamie." He took my hand and we began to walk, across the bridge and back to the campus.

"Where are we going?"

"To the museum. I still have time to teach you more."

We walked. I pressed myself close against him, so there was no place for him to put his arm except around me. A snowflake stuck to my eyelash and I brushed it aside. There was no more talk as we walked.

The building was dark. Danilo unlocked the main door, heavy bronze, and let us in. He switched on all the lights. The museum blazed.

"Shouldn't we be more careful?"

Instead of answering he took my hand and led me to the descending staircase. "Come along."

At the first level we stopped. He turned on the lights there and went directly to the vault. The combination lock seemed to fly under his fingers. The heavy steel door swung open. Danilo reached in and took out a small parcel wrapped in cloth. He placed it firmly in my hand. "Open it."

I looked at him, then at the package in my hand. "What is it?"

"Open it." He smiled gently. "I had envisioned this moment happening somewhere beautiful, outdoors, perhaps in a glorious sunset, not on a winter night in the basement of a deserted building by artificial light. But the moment has come."

It was a small painted box. I knew the style; it was from New Kingdom Egypt. Slowly, carefully I removed the lid. Inside were two gold rings. Each had a flat bezel covered with hieroglyphs in cartouches. I squinted and could barely decipher the names: Akhenaten and Smenkhare.

Danilo took my hand. "These were my father's last gift to me."

My head was spinning. If I were a heroine in an old movie I'd have batted my eyes and said something like, "But this is so unexpected." Instead I felt my jaw drop open. I stammered like a fool. "D-danilo."

Wordlessly he took the Smenkhare ring from the box and placed it on my finger. I looked at him and realized I was shaking. In all my dreams I had never thought… I kissed him then took the other ring and slid it onto his finger. He said something softly in the language of the ancient world. I knew enough to understand the words: "With this ring I marry you."

We held each other for a long time without moving. Outside the storm was picking up and we could hear the howling wind.

"Now, Jamie, come downstairs with me."

Again I realized I was trembling. I had had time enough to think what must be down there. But I had to see.

Down. Memories of that other time down there began to take hold of me.

Second subbasement. I was shaking.

Third. Danilo put an arm around me. "You are master now. Don't be afraid."

And then we were there.

The lights were dim. We followed the corridor to the place where the walls widened. And I saw them.

Stacked up in corners, propped against walls. The missing men, more than a dozen of them. They were all naked, every one of them, and they were pale. I could see just how pale even in the half-light. Corpses, piled everywhere. I had expected it; nonetheless I was a bit shocked.

"Danilo, you...you...this..." I didn't quite know what I wanted to say.

He clapped his hands. Abruptly they opened their eyes. Blinking, they turned their heads to us. Among them I recognized Josh Mariatta, who had been missing since I first came to school.

"Why are they here, Danilo?"

"Proof against hunger and thirst." He laughed a bit. "My own private organ bank, if you like."

He clapped again and they got unsteadily to their feet.

I crossed to Josh and planted myself in front of him. He blinked. Something made me touch him. I held up a hand and pressed a fingertip to his cheek. The pressure seemed too much for him; he staggered backward into the wall. But he looked at me and his lips formed my name. "Jamie." The others repeated it, a chorus of rasping echoes.

I turned to Danilo.

He moved behind me and put his arms around me. "This is only a fragment of the power you may wield."

"They're dead."

"No. They possess death, but it is in life. Or they are alive in death. As you prefer. I chose them because they were used to this condition, in their way. You—we—may compel them to do anything."

He held me more tightly.

"And the ones who turned up dead after being missing?"

"I had used them up."

From somewhere in the air around us music began. Piano music, the Chopin funeral march. It was me playing. I turned and looked into Danilo's eyes.

"Yes, Jamie, this is you. It is part of me. I can summon it whenever I need to. I can fill the air with it."

He pulled me back against a wall. The living-dead-men moved. Each of them took another in his arms and they began to dance. Slowly, intimately they danced. After a few measures they kissed.

The music turned into an agitated waltz. They began to fondle each other, there in front of us. The kissed deeply. Athletes, artists, students—their bodies were beautiful, and they touched in the most sensuous way. They danced and made love to the music.

"Look at them, Jamie. I have given them the freedom they never had the courage to take for themselves."

I watched as one by one they reached climax in one another. Slowly the music died. They looked to Danilo and me.

"Go back to your sleep now."

They did. Yawning, stretching, they went back to the places where they had been before, some alone, some on top of others. And they were still again.

Danilo led me back upstairs. "They are yours now. My wedding gift. Do with them what you will."

"Anything I want?"

"Anything. Free them, slaughter them, copulate with him, drink their blood. But survive. Compel them to do your will. With men like them it hardly matters. There are certainly enough of them. You may always master more of them."

I hesitated. "Let's go home now. I want to go home." I kissed him.

Suddenly Peter Borzage was there, staring at us, or rather glaring. "I knew it. I knew you two were…" The word lovers seemed to stick in his throat.

"Yes," I said firmly. "We are."

"You and this old man. Professor Feld said he thought so."

"Older than you think. And Feld is a fool, Peter." I took a step toward him. "Besides, he doesn't do a thing to me that you don't want to."

"No! I'm not like that!"

"You are, Peter. Admit it."

"I'll report you to the administration. We will. There are rules, guidelines."

"Not for us." A step closer. "We survive, and we will prevail any way we can."

He was beginning to look a bit frightened. "What you're doing is a sin."

"Peter, you don't know the half of it." I reached out and caught him by the throat. There was no knife I could use. I bit into his carotid artery, tearing it. He died quickly enough. And he was delicious. Soaked in his blood, covered with bits of his flesh, Danilo and I made love there on the museum floor.

I wanted to clean up what was left of Peter, but Danilo insisted we leave him where he was.

The ending was ironic. And perfect. Feld had shown the police photos of the bodies. Feld was now the suspect in the disappearances, which, the police decided, must be separate crimes from the killings. Peter Borzage had been his assistant. Feld must have been trying to divert suspicion from himself. He was indicted and released on bail. It gave us both a lot of enjoyment.

*

Several nights had passed. It was clear and cold, snow covered the ground, and there was a bright crescent moon, its face pale with earthlight. Danilo was standing at the front window watching it.

His mood had grown steadily darker for days. The thought of losing him, of being alone in the world again, had me almost frantic. But I didn't know what to do.

He was looking old. So was I. He suggested we go out for a walk. I knew the real purpose.

"Not here, Danilo. Not in town. We can't. They'll know."

But he insisted.

And it was plain how hungry we both were.

The night was frigid, arctic. Our breath was heavy smoke. The air stung. Danilo took my gloved hand in his. We didn't talk much. I only had one thing on my mind—him, how much I wanted him. What was there I could say? Inside my glove I felt the golden ring on my finger.

The campus was lit brightly, as always. Academic Tower soared into the night sky, floodlit. There were couples and groups of students, faculty, crowding the streets, talking and laughing. Traffic was heavy. I wondered briefly why they weren't all at home, sheltering from the cold. One more reason to feel apart from them all.

The museum was dark. We walked in a circle around it. In an alley at the rear we stopped to kiss.

Farther up the alley someone stirred. Whoever it was was in shadow. Danilo called, "Who is there?"

"Who are you?" It was a young man's voice.

We walked a few steps into the alley. He was under a sheet of cardboard, lying on an exhaust vent, trying to keep warm. A slight bit of moonlight showed us he was in rags. A street kid. He stood up, looking vaguely afraid. Danilo asked him what he was doing there.

"Sleeping. What's it look like?"

"You shouldn't be here. This is private property. The guards will be around."

"I didn't know."

I got close enough to get a look at him. He was young, maybe sixteen, not much more. "You should be at a shelter."

"No. They won't take kids like me." He shoved his hands into his pockets. The cold was making him shake. "You want a blow job?"

I suppose I should have expected that, but it caught me off guard. "What?"

"Twenty." He looked from one of us to the other. "Each."

"No, thanks." I thought if he had better clothes and a haircut he'd be attractive.

"So you're…?" Danilo made a twisted gesture.

"No. I'm no fag."

"Oh." Danilo looked at me from a corner of his eye and smiled.

I wasn't at all sure I wanted it to happen. I got between them. "What's your name?"

"Jonas."

"Jonas what?"

"We doin' business, or are you gonna fuck off?"

Danilo stepped up to him and put a hand on his shoulder. "Business."

"Forty. Up front."

"You're cute." Danilo smiled gently as he said it. "Jonas."

The kid seemed to relax a bit. I saw the knife come out from Danilo's pocket. He should not have been doing it there, not in town. The police would—

The kid saw the knife and screamed. Suddenly there were lights everywhere around us. Three cops appeared, I couldn't tell from where. They had their guns drawn, and they began firing.

Danilo was hit. Then again, and again. I saw him stagger back a step, then straighten up. He cried "Stop!" His shout was loud, almost deafening. It startled even me.

It seemed to hit the cops and the kid like a battering ram. They froze, standing in place.

He turned to me. "You see, Jamie. I can't stay here. They'll watch everything I do. There are too many of them."

"Danilo, no, don't!"

I saw him bend down, as if he was curling himself into a ball. When he straightened up again he had changed. He was the creature

I had seen at the Great Pyramid, a falcon-headed man, eight feet tall. I could almost feel the power in his muscles, in his wings.

"Jamie, I love you. And I will be back."

He spread his arms, and his wings were twenty feet across. With a terrifying cry he rose into the air and flew off into the night. By moonlight I saw him circle Academic Tower. He crossed the face of the moon. Then he was gone.

It had happened too quickly for me to know how to react. Gone, he was gone. I pulled off my glove and pressed my lips to his ring. Then, not much caring about the others, who were still standing rigidly where he had left them, I turned and went slowly home. To my apartment, not his.

The next morning, the news was filled with stories about three city policemen and a boy who was working as a decoy for them found frozen alive in the alley behind the museum. I suppose I could have brought them out of Danilo's trance. I suppose I should have. But I didn't much care.

A few days later there was still no sign of him. I lived in my own little apartment and stared at his place across the street, feeling the way Moses must have when he saw the Promised Land, knowing he'd never live to reach it.

I found myself revisiting places we had been together, the park, even the Z. Alone. The cold didn't bother me much.

I went to the museum. A prominently posted notice announced that Professor Semenkaru's classes had been canceled due to his unexplained disappearance. The exhibits all seemed strange to me, though I'd seen them a hundred times. Mummies, sculptures, papyri…Danilo had touched them all.

There were other students walking about, making notes for their classes. I needed to be alone. Impulsively I went down to the subbasements. The floor where Danilo and I had worked that first day was quite empty, deserted. The walls were cold.

Then at the fourth sublevel I felt warmth, just a bit. Traces of Danilo still in the air? I decided to stay there a while and followed the corridor to the place where it widened. My footsteps echoed loudly on the flagstones. Nothing there could hurt me now.

It dawned on me, belatedly, that the lights were already on. When I reached the end of the corridor, Feld was sitting there on the stone floor, in a corner, hands covering his face. He looked up at me. The place was otherwise empty. There were no corpses.

"Where are they?"

I waved my hand in a little mock salute. "Professor Feld."

"They were here. I gave photos to the police."

I put on the least sincere grin I could manage. "I don't have any idea what you're talking about."

"Semenkaru. He was the villain. I always knew it. Are you so stupid you didn't?"

"Professor Semenkaru. Let's show a little respect."

"He was an evil thing. He would have seduced you into it too sooner or later."

I crossed the open space to him and stood at his feet. "Yes, he would have taught me a great deal, if you hadn't interfered. He'd still be here."

"You knew what he was?" He looked up at me.

"He was warm and handsome."

"He was filthy with sin."

I'd had enough of this. "And now the police suspect you of his crimes. What did you do to Peter Borzage?" I decided to tease him.

"Nothing, I—"

"He was your assistant."

"I—"

"If I had planned it, I couldn't have imagined a nicer repayment."

This seemed to strike him unexpectedly. "You mean you were—"

Slowly I nodded. My smile became even wider. "You drove away the man I loved."

For the first time he began to look a bit concerned. His eyes widened and he tried to get to his feet. "I knew he was like that.

I thought you might be." I kicked him firmly and he got down again. "But I never thought you were actually…there are rules about that."

"We broke them. Shattered them."

"Then you—"

Something like genuine fear was creeping into his face. I confess it gave me a little buzz. "Yes." I mimicked him. "Then I—"

He tried to get up again, and again I kicked him. He stumbled and fell into a corner. I crossed to him and kicked him still again, as hard as I could. He cried out. Slowly, softly, the sound of the Chopin C-minor nocturne began to fill the air. He looked around frantically, trying to see where it was coming from.

I squatted down beside him. "What's wrong, professor? Don't you like classical?"

"Let me out of here."

"You were a lot more interesting when you used to try and give me orders. Begging doesn't become you."

"W-what are you going to do to me?"

I kicked him again, in the side of his head. "Goddamned self-righteous interfering bastard! You drove away the man I love. You meddled in my relationship instead of staying decently out of it. You tell me—what should I do to you?"

"The police…"

"The police suspect you now. Even in Danilo's disappearance. The news this morning said so."

"I know." He was whimpering. "I thought he might be down here."

"He's gone."

He seemed to brace himself for another kick. But I took a few steps back away from him. He looked around anxiously, gauging the chance he might get away. But there was no way that could happen.

"Do you know the history of this building, professor?"

"What?" My question couldn't have been more unexpected. "I—I—"

"Did you know it used to be part of the Underground Railroad?"

He seemed to go numb. At any rate he didn't answer me.

"There are all kinds of nooks and recesses and hidey-holes."

Nothing, no response. Did he know what was coming?

I let out a loud shout, like the one Danilo had shouted just before he left. From their places of concealment came the dead-alive. Feld's face was, to my enormous pleasure, filled with the most pathetic fear. They fell on him and began tearing. And eating. In a few minutes there was nothing left but his bones. In a few minutes more even they were gone.

EPILOGUE

It has been more than three and a half months since Danilo left.

I look for him constantly and everywhere. Everything that might be him, a shadow, the rush of a bird's wing, makes me stop and remember what I had, or rather what we had. He is nowhere.

I wonder again and again where he might be. Could those police bullets have hurt him? Is he wounded and desperate somewhere? Could I heal him as he healed me?

There is no answer.

None.

The dead-alive men are still concealed in the museum basement. They keep me alive.

The police and the district attorney have decided that Greg Wilton committed Justin's murder but that Feld was responsible for the other killings and the disappearances. No one had any idea why. His own disappearance, just after his assistant vanished, was taken as evidence of his guilt, for some reason. The university cut off his widow's pension. Case closed, at least until Greg's trial.

So far I have not sacrificed anyone else. But I look in the mirror and know that I will have to, and soon.

I went to the private bank in downtown Pittsburgh and opened Danilo's vault.

Gold, it was filled with gold. My own Fort Knox. I would not have to rely on my trust fund anymore.

There was a thick leather portfolio. In it I found drawings signed by Leonardo and Michelangelo, bold sketches of the young men they loved. There was a small gold statue, a foot and a half tall, of a male angel; I thought it must be by Cellini. Manuscripts signed by Chopin and Schubert; a longhand copy of *Moby Dick* in Melville's own hand. A lost keyboard sonata by Handel. And a great deal more. I have not begun to catalog it all.

At the spring recital, and despite some misgivings on Roland's part, I played the Chopin second.

Perfectly.

I was a minor celebrity on campus, so the auditorium was full; people were standing at the sides and back. A young woman played Beethoven; a piano trio played Tchaikovsky. Then it was my turn.

Don't get me wrong, I knew enough about human nature to know why they were there. They wanted me to make a mistake; at least the other students and the faculty did. Who did this boy, this swimmer, this jock, think he was, tackling such a challenging piece? They were waiting. Jamie would blow it this time as he did before.

From the wings I could see people checking their programs. "Frederic Chopin (1810–1849). Sonata No. 2, Op. 35, in B-flat Minor." There was a bit of buzz, at least among people who had heard me play it that first time. Then I walked on stage, and there were gasps. I was wearing leather—a black leather suit and a floor-length trench coat. Unheard of. I heard someone ask, in hushed tones, "What would Chopin think?"

Trying not to smile at that, I sat down at the keyboard. There was scattered, uncertain applause. No one seemed to know what to expect. I paused, to let a bit of suspense build.

Then I began the solemn first movement. And a hush fell over the audience. I swear there wasn't even a cough. I had them.

Second movement, the scherzo. I was master of the music, I played it perfectly and with brilliant feeling. Again the audience was mine. From the corner of my eye I looked to see what they were doing. And they were listening, quite in my grip. No one was thumbing through the program or checking the time or doing any of the hundred things people in an audience do. They were listening. They were mine.

Third movement: the funeral march. I played it for Danilo, for my lost love. I played it for Tim and for Justin. And even, just a bit, for Greg who could hardly understand the richness and terror of my life or the awful depth of my loss or the sweet things I had gained. The audience was still mine. I looked, more than once.

They were perfectly still. They might have been wax or marble.

At the end of the movement I waited. Let them think I was unsure. Then I attacked the finale like a passionate lover.

Perfectly, I played it perfectly, not missing a note, not having the least trouble with the manic fingering. And I poured even more feeling into it than I had into the funeral march.

Almost literally at the moment I struck the last chord they rose to their feet, cheering. I might have been a rock star, not a classical pianist. Students flocked to the stage; the faculty was more reserved. I saw Roland standing at the side of the hall, looking troubled.

The cheering went on and on. I stood and I bowed, again and again. People climbed onto the stage. The tried to kiss me. The boys I let do it. There was one, in particular, who I found so attractive. I told him I'd meet him later.

In that moment the blood of a thousand generations of kings, artists, philosophers surged in my veins. Even though Danilo was gone he was there with me.

And I was only beginning to try my wings.

Author's Note

As must be obvious, I've taken considerable liberties with Akhenaten's religion. There is some evidence that a Set cult survived for many centuries in ancient Egypt, more or less underground, but very little is known about it, and connecting it with Akhenaten and his sons is pure invention.

On the other hand, the images of the so-called Kissing Kings are quite real. And there's also the tantalizing fact that Akhenaten bestowed names on Smenkhare that he had formerly given to his wife. Images of two pharaohs kissing, a father and son—just try and imagine two of our own leaders allowing themselves to be shown that way. The Bushes, for instance?

The dual tombs of the priests of Set, which I place at Amarna, are based on a pair of real tombs in the necropolis at Sakkara, just outside Cairo. The owners were Ni-ankh-Khnum and Khnum-hotep. Their names are joined in the tomb inscriptions, in exactly the way I describe. Lovers together for all time.

These facts tend to make a lot of traditional-minded Egyptologists, er, edgy. There were thirty dynasties of pharaohs, scores of rulers over some 3,000 years of history. It's fairly well known that they routinely married their sisters and at times even their daughters. Smenkhare married his sister Meritaten, for instance. But institutionalized incest is one thing. Don't dare hint that even one of the pharaohs might have been a fag—good heavens, no!

Egyptologists are hardly alone in their nervousness, of course. The last decade has seen studies of Alexander Hamilton, Abraham Lincoln, T.E. Lawrence, Chopin, Schubert, Emily Dickinson, Joe McCarthy, Roy Cohn(!), and scores of others—all of which either ignore evidence their subjects were queer, deny that such evidence even exists, or try to bluff it out of existence. Thanks to writers like Louis Crompton, John Boswell, and a great many specialists in specific periods, these attempts to bleach queerness out of the historical record are looking more and more desperate.

But it's a slow, uphill fight. Homosexuality may not frighten the horses anymore, but it makes a lot of academics really skittish.

—John Michael Curlovich